GHOST GIRL

THE 3RD FREAK HOUSE TRILOGY, BOOK #1

C.J. ARCHER

CHAPTER 1

Hertfordshire, Spring 1889

The ghosts crowded around to get a better look at my corpse. Hands skimmed over my face like feathery kisses from cold lips. A little blonde spirit girl brushed her fingers through my hair, hypnotized by the dark curls that sprang free. A fat gentleman with florid cheeks peered into my eyes, the skin on his heavy brow crumpling with concern, and a gray-haired woman wearing only a nightgown knelt at my side. She fussed over me, inspecting me for wounds. She turned to lift my skirt and I gasped in horror. One side of her face was red and puckered, the skin resembling half-cooked meat. She'd been burned to death.

"No obvious wounds," she said, apparently unconcerned by my ill-mannered reaction. I ought to have been more prepared—I'd had a lot of experience with the dead, after all —but I was out of sorts. It seemed death could muddle one's thoughts.

1

"You shouldn't be here," the man said. Did he mean me? "Do you hear me?" he shouted.

I winced and the girl jumped in alarm.

"Of course she can hear you," the woman said, her voice as brittle as a dried leaf. "She's dead, not deaf."

"She should be in the Waiting Area."

"Are you sure?" the little girl asked.

"About what?"

"That she's dead. She seems so...alive." She was still studying my hair, letting it cascade through her fingers, her big eyes intent on the strands. She suddenly stopped and sniffed it. "She doesn't smell dead."

Please don't let me be dead.

I opened my mouth to say something, but no words came out. The ghosts were checking me over once again for signs of injury or illness. Surely they should be able to see that I'd been sick? The fever ought to be evident in my eyes and the color of my cheeks. I'd seen the ghosts of people who'd died from fevers before. Their faces were perpetually damp and hot, the skin beneath their eyes bruised.

The woman was lifting my skirt again, and the gentleman joined her to look. I struggled to sit up and push my skirt down, but I couldn't even seem to manage that.

"Leave her." The commanding voice sent the ghosts scattering to the corners of the bedroom.

I turned my head on the pillow and a breath escaped my lips in a wheeze. It rattled in my chest, but it was definitely a breath. Perhaps I wasn't dead. Please, God, I don't want to die.

I would have prayed harder, but I was distracted by the bare-chested man in my bedroom. The last man I'd seen in a similar state of undress had been in spirit form. He'd died in a mine collapse. His body had been nothing like that of the fellow who stood by the door, however. This man's arms crossed over a magnificently muscular chest, just above a stomach ridged with yet more muscle. Did his arms bulge like that because of the pose or were they honed to masculine perfection from physical use? My sister-in-law, Celia, would suffer an attack of hysteria if she knew I was gazing upon a man's bare skin. In my defense, I couldn't very well not look. He was, after all, standing right there.

Ordinarily ghosts were a little smudged at the edges, as if they were disappearing into a mist, but the large half-naked man was as fully realized as I was. Yet I didn't think he was human, either. What kind of fellow walked around in nothing but a pair of tight leather pants with a sword strapped to his hip? Certainly no Englishman would be so indecent.

I dragged my gaze from his chest, up his broad shoulders to his face. Another wheezing gasp escaped from my heavy chest. I must be dead. Surely this was some sort of angel come to take me away? No mere human could be that handsome. Dark hair framed smooth skin, stretched over bold cheekbones and chiseled jaw. His face was saved from being too angular by the ends of his hair curling at his ears and nape, and the curve of his mouth. His lips were set firmly together as he studied me through a pair of eyes the same shade of blue-green as the ocean I'd crossed mere months before.

Could the afterlife really be filled with half-naked, handsome men like him? Celia would not be happy to learn that. I giggled. Then suddenly the man and the ghosts were gone, and I was once more back in the guest bedroom of Frakingham House with Sylvia Langley at my bedside. Her huge blue eyes were filled with tears and her nose was about to drip. She pressed a blessedly cool, damp cloth against my forehead.

"Oh, Cara." The tears wobbled on the edge of her eyelids, but didn't spill. "I thought I'd lost you that time."

I tore my gaze away from her face to search the room for my angel. It wasn't easy. My eyeballs felt like they were on fire, much like the rest of me, and my neck ached. A crack of light between the edges of the drawn curtains told me it was daytime, yet candles burned on the mantel and a low fire glowed all shades of orange in the grate. The smoke didn't hide the pungent scent of illness.

"Here, try some soup." She held out a bowl and spoon, her expression one of hope and urgency.

"I'm not hungry." I could barely manage a whisper.

"You have to eat. Dr. Gowan said so."

"The doctor was here?" I didn't recall being poked and prodded.

"Yesterday morning. He'll return today." She held up the spoon. A drop of thick white soup splashed back into the bowl. "Cara, I'm going to send a telegram to Emily if the doctor tells me there's been no improvement. And believe me, I don't see any improvement. If you don't eat…"

Sweet, demure Sylvia had quite a backbone when she set her mind to it. I sipped the soup. It wasn't hot and had little taste, but it stayed down, unlike the piece of toast I'd nibbled last time. "How long have I been lying here?"

"Four days."

Four! Good lord. I must have been unconscious most of that time. I remembered little. "Am I the only ill one in the house?"

She nodded and I closed my eyes in relief. It would seem I wasn't contagious. "Samuel and Charity have returned to London permanently, and Bollard came home two days ago." Her features relaxed upon mentioning her uncle's friend, servant and laboratory assistant. Bollard the mute had been banished from Frakingham by August Langley, but it would seem their disagreement had been resolved and he'd been welcomed home again.

I consumed more soup but could not finish the bowl, and she set it aside. "I would still like to contact Emily," she said.

"Please wait. She'll only worry and I seem to be improving." I pushed myself up into a sitting position to prove it. My head swam and my limbs complained, but I managed it. My niece, Emily Beaufort, was seven years older than me and had her own family to care for. I didn't want to burden her unless absolutely necessary. "What does Dr. Gowan think is wrong with me?"

Sylvia fluffed up the pillows at my back, her blonde curls bouncing at her temples in time with her movement. "He says it's a fever."

"Brought on by what?"

She shrugged. "He doesn't know. He asked me if there was something in particular you were doing when you first became ill, but I couldn't think of anything. Can you?"

I frowned down at my hands in my lap. They were unusually pale, or as pale as my hands could ever be. My complexion was what polite people called exotic and the not-so-polite labeled dirty. My father was a Frenchman of African descent, and it was through him that I'd inherited both my coloring and my ability to see spirits. Emily too, since he was her grandfather. We were genuine mediums in a country overrun by fakes, but no longer advertised that fact.

"I was down at the ruins when I first felt ill," I said, referring to the Frakingham Abbey ruins situated on the edge of the lake, just visible from my bedroom window. "It was the day we uncovered the bones of Garrett and Owens, and I saw Garrett's spirit."

"I remember," Sylvia said with a shudder. "But no one else fell ill and I was there, as were Charity and Mr. Myer."

I'd been trying to converse with the spirit of Mr. Garrett

but it had been nearly impossible to get any sense out of him, mad as he was. He'd been angry with Myer and shouted at him. He'd spoken ancient words in verse form, as if he were cursing him.

No. Oh no.

Had he cursed me instead? Was I under some sort of supernatural illness and not a physical one? If so, Dr. Gowan couldn't cure me.

"It's impossible to say what caused this," I said lightly in an attempt to remove the frown lines from Sylvia's pretty face. "But I seem to be improving." There was no point in letting her think I was worsening. I was, after all, awake. That had to be a good thing, despite the dull ache pulsing through my body and the pain in my chest.

She smiled. "Indeed you are looking a little like your old self again. Now, I'm going to take these down to the kitchen and bring back fresh water."

I returned her smile and sank down beneath the covers again with a sigh of relief. Holding myself upright was exhausting. I watched her leave then closed my eyelids. They felt heavy. Everything inside me felt heavy, and cold. I shivered and tried to snuggle deeper into the blankets, but it wasn't enough. A chill settled under my skin and seeped into my bones. The click clack of my chattering teeth was the only sound in the room.

And then it wasn't. The ghosts were back and their whispers seemed to surround me.

"...shouldn't be here," the man was saying.

"Go back," the woman said, shooing me with her gnarled hand, crippled from the fire.

The little girl suddenly appeared at my side, bending over me. She kissed my lips. Her mouth was cool and damp like mist. "Poor you. Cursed for all eternity."

"Cursed?" I murmured. My heart sounded a single, thundering beat in my chest. "What do you mean?"

"Leave her." That low, masculine voice had me turning toward it again. My angel stood in the same position, arms still crossed over his chest, as if he hadn't moved since my last…visit.

"Am I dead?" I whispered.

"Not quite." He had an accent, but I couldn't place it. It was similar to my father's French one, yet different too. A little harsher, perhaps. I would need to hear him say more to place it.

"The ghosts said I'm cursed."

He nodded and lowered his arms. His right hung close to his side, but his left had to contend with the sword at his hip. It was the most enormous sword I'd ever seen, the tip almost reaching to the floor, and the man was very tall. If it were mounted on the wall, it would likely pull off the plaster, it was so heavy looking. He approached the bed. He didn't so much walk across the floor as prowl.

I should have felt afraid to have a big, armed, half-naked man in my bedroom; but I wasn't. I felt safe with him there, as if he were protecting me from something.

"Are you my guardian angel?" I asked, tilting my head to follow him as he drew close to the bed.

One corner of his mouth lifted in amusement. "I am a warrior."

Warrior. I frowned, trying to recall why that term seemed so familiar. Through the fog of fever I could just remember the spirit of an old monk telling me that a supernatural warrior had once been summoned at the abbey ruins when a group of demons escaped in the sixteenth century. He hadn't been seen since. If this were he, then he was older than he looked. And fiercer. Demons were strong creatures and the warrior had battled many of them to send them back to their realm.

"What are you doing in my bedroom?" I asked.

His blue-green gaze flicked over my face, twice, the second time slower. It lingered on my mouth and finally returned to my eyes. They focused with an intensity that had my already warm cheeks flaming.

"It is not your time," he said. "This curse was not meant for you." I did like the way his harsher tones blended with the lilting French ones, yet it sounded odd too. A slightly maniacal laugh bubbled out of me. "You find it amusing to be cursed?"

"No!" My voice squeaked. I cleared my throat. "No, of course not. I want to know more. Tell me how to break it. Do I need to speak a counter-curse?"

He nodded. "There is an ancient book. You will find the words in there."

"I know the one. It's been quite the topic of conversation around here lately." The spirit of the monk had mentioned it and Myer desperately wanted it. "No one knows where the book is now. We have a page torn from it, though, with three spells on it."

"Which ones?"

"The incantation to open the portal down at the abbey, another to close it, and one that summons you, the warrior. You were last here over three hundred years ago." It seemed absurd to be talking to a supernatural creature as if he were a house guest. I was used to conversing with ghosts, but he was something else entirely. "At least, I assume it was you."

"It was. I sent back the beasts." He said it matter-of-factly, as if he battled packs of demons all the time. Perhaps he did.

"Is it a problem that we don't have the book?" I asked.

He gave a single, curt nod. "You cannot survive without speaking the counter-curse within its pages."

My heart sank. My blood trickled icily through my veins. I closed my eyes and concentrated on my rough breathing. It was time for Sylvia to contact Emily. It was time for me to tell her goodbye and have her pass on my love to my brother and Celia, all the way across the ocean in Melbourne. That book was gone. People had been searching for it for a long time. My family and friends could spend a lifetime looking for it and never find it. And I didn't have a lifetime. I had, perhaps, hours.

"We must search for it."

I opened my eyes and was struck once again by the beauty and strength in his face. If he were present in the afterlife, it might not be too difficult to endure. "What do you mean? For one thing, I'm too ill to search for anything and, for another, you're…wherever you are."

"I'm in spirit form, but this is not my natural state…or home." His hesitation wasn't lost on me. It would seem he didn't think of his place of residence as his home. "You can only see me because you're a medium, but you're not dead. Yet."

"That's a relief."

"You have the words to summon me," he said. "Speak them and I will come to you in your realm."

"You can't come if I don't?"

"No."

"Where is your home?"

"In between."

"So it's another realm?"

His nostrils flared and the fingers of his sword hand curled into a ball. "It's in between. When we're together in your realm, you'll be strong again."

I shook my head. "I don't understand."

"I am the warrior," he said with gentle patience I hadn't expected from such a formidable looking man. "I battle demons here, and I can also lend you my strength. But I must be by your side, always, or you'll become ill again."

"Do you mean I will be able to walk around and feel entirely well if I summon you?"

"Aye. As long as we are together, my strength is your strength. You will feel well."

"Oh. That sounds marvelous." Being near this magnificent man and being well again seemed too good to be true. "We can search for the book together."

He nodded. "Summon me, Cara, and I will come." He said my name in the French way with an emphasis on the last vowel and a purring of the R. I liked it very much. "I can only come if you call me."

I smiled up at him but he was suddenly gone. The ghosts too. Sylvia, however, was once more by my side. She was in tears, but they stopped upon seeing me.

"You're awake! I thought…oh, Cara, I thought…"

"That I was dead?"

Her bottom lip trembled. "I came back and you were asleep again, but so terribly hot. Hotter than last time. You were muttering something too. Something about a book. Do you want me to read to you?"

"No." I licked dry lips and she helped me take a sip of water. "The parchment, Sylvia. Fetch it."

She blinked slowly. "The one with the spells?"

I nodded, but even that act exhausted me. I closed my eyes and concentrated on my breathing. It hurt to fill my lungs but I knew I had to do it. The air squeezed into my chest and rattled like a ball in a cage. "Please," I whispered.

Clearly Sylvia had been exposed to a great many supernatural events recently because she didn't argue. If someone had asked me to retrieve a page of supernatural spells that had strangely come into my possession I would have fired off a hundred questions first.

She hurried out of the room and I waited. She seemed to be back in an instant and I wondered if I'd drifted into unconsciousness during her absence. There wasn't much time left. Every breath took enormous effort, as if someone was pressing down on my chest, stopping the air from getting in. My mouth was dry, my tongue thick and gluey.

"You're so hot." She pressed a cool cloth to my forehead and blinked watery eyes back at me. There was real fear in them.

"The spell?" I whispered.

She unrolled the parchment and held it up for me to see. "Cara, I don't understand. Opening the portal is terribly dangerous."

"No portal. Summon…warrior."

"Oh! I see. But are you sure there's nothing to fear? I mean, we know nothing about such a creature. What if he's as dangerous as the demons?"

"He's not." I didn't have the energy to reassure her more than that. The blood in my veins slowed to a sluggish crawl and I felt so terribly cold. There wasn't much time left. I shivered and she settled another blanket over me, tucking it tightly around me.

She began to read the words on the parchment.

"No. I must…"

She held the page up so I could see it and I began to read. The words were old fashioned and the text written in a curling script, making it a difficult task. But at least it was a form of English. Still, I struggled to say the words aloud. Every syllable cost me a breath I could ill afford to expend. I only hoped the pauses between each one didn't hinder the spell.

As soon as I uttered the last word, I felt the air in the room shift, although all windows and doors were closed. I looked to the spot where I'd seen the warrior in my unconscious state and smiled at the figure standing there, arms crossed over bare chest, handsome face pinched with worry and his intense blue-green gaze on me. The moment I saw him I felt better, healthier. The pressure on my chest eased and I drew in a deep, quiet, breath. The fog in my head dissipated and my skin no longer burned while the blood froze in my veins. I sat up and my smile broadened.

He nodded with satisfaction, his jaw softening with relief. "I am here," he announced.

Sylvia screamed and collapsed on the bed in a dead faint.

CHAPTER 2

I helped Sylvia to sit up and sip some water. How rapidly our roles had reversed. I felt perfectly normal, although in desperate need of a bath to wash away the lingering effects of the fever. She blinked first at me, then at the warrior. Another sound escaped her lips, this one quieter and more like a gurgle, but no less shocked.

"Cara...he's...he's naked!"

The warrior moved slightly, somehow enhancing his musculature more. His face changed too. I got the distinct impression he was trying not to laugh, although his lips were still set in a firm line and his jaw was rigid. His eyes, however, shone.

"Only half-naked," I murmured, tearing my gaze away from his face to his body. "It's perfectly all right for us to see him like that."

"Are you quite sure? Because I don't feel all right. I feel a little light-headed." She touched her temple as if to fortify her mind.

"It's only skin. We all have it."

"Yes, but it does seem wrong to look at him in that state. The sight may corrupt our moral fiber."

"If you think so then avert your eyes. I would hate for your moral fiber to be in any danger," I mocked.

"Oh, I will. Soon. Quite, quite soon. After I've learned every little thing there is to learn from such a specimen. He *is* quite the specimen," she said, tilting her head to the side as if the different angle could teach her more.

"You're interested in science?" I asked idly.

"I am now. Aren't you?"

"Indeed."

"So *he's* the warrior."

I nodded.

"How intriguing. I can see how he'd be very good at destroying demons and the like. I imagine all those muscles would prove useful."

"I imagine they do." I smiled at him and he arched his brows at me, waiting. He seemed unmoved by our whispered discussion and open observation, although the slight lift of one corner of his mouth and the sparkling eyes implied otherwise.

"What do we do with him?" Sylvia asked.

"He's going to help me find the book of spells that the parchment was torn from." I nodded at the page that had slipped to the floor when she fainted. "The book has a counter-curse in it that will cure me."

She whipped around to face me. "You're not cured? But you seem so much better."

"I feel better. Mr. Garrett's spirit cursed me, and we must read the counter-curse aloud to break it. It's in the book that Mr. Myer wants so much, the one that Brother Francis's spirit mentioned but is now lost."

"Why would Garrett curse *you*?"

"I don't think he meant to. He was looking at Myer at the

14

time, and it's my guess he was trying to curse *him*. Since Garrett was in spirit form and I was the only one who could see and hear him, I suppose it affected me instead."

"That's rather unlucky."

"So now all we have to do is find the book."

"And the warrior is going to help you?"

"I am," he said, speaking for the first time.

Sylvia jumped. "He understands us!"

"Of course," I said.

"I had thought…oh, never mind. How are you going to help us?" she asked him.

He shrugged boulder-like shoulders. "That is for you to decide. I must stay near Cara, however, or she will sicken and die."

Sylvia's gulp was audible. "So you're protecting her from the illness? Er, curse?"

"Yes. Where she is, I must be."

She stood, just as a light knock sounded on the door. "Sylvia? It's me," came Tommy the footman's voice. "How is she?"

"Much better," she called back. "Come and see for yourself."

"Wait!" I shouted. But it was too late. Tommy had the door open and was stepping into the bedroom before I could stop him.

"Bloody hell!" He gawped at the warrior. Although Tommy was tall, the warrior was taller and broader. He turned to the newcomer and rested his hand on the hilt of his sword, giving me rather a nice view of the muscles rippling across his shoulders and down his back. Two long white scars striped the middle of his back and another smaller one puckered the skin on his arm.

Tommy's eyes widened and he put up his fists, settling into a pugilist's stance.

"You can't fight him!" I cried, racing to Tommy and laying my hand on his arm. "He's the warrior. You know, the otherworldly being who fought the demons in the fifteen hundreds. I summoned him to keep the curse at bay."

Tommy lowered his fists, but didn't relax. "What curse?"

I explained everything we'd learned so far and the reason for the warrior's presence. It did not seem to ease Tommy's concern, however. He eyed the newcomer up and down and was sized up in return.

"Sylvia!" he snapped. "Look away. He's naked."

I sighed and Tommy took the liberty of covering my eyes for me, but then he dropped his hand and marched past the warrior to Sylvia and covered hers. She stepped aside and glared at him, hands on hips.

"Stop fussing, Tommy. I'm not going to faint at the sight of a little manly flesh." She scoffed, and I bit back a smile. She wasn't going to faint *again*.

"I don't like this," Tommy said, studying the warrior once more. "I'm sure Mr. Langley won't want his niece exposed to such a sight. Or her friend."

"I don't see that we have a choice," I said. "The warrior must remain to keep me well."

"Can't he at least put on decent clothing?"

The warrior arched a brow at Tommy and took in his footman's livery of black jacket and trousers with crisp white shirt, tie and gleaming shoes. "I cannot swing a sword in *that*."

"This is England, 1889," Tommy said with a thrust of his chin. "We don't use swords, we have guns."

"Guns do not kill demons."

"Neither do swords."

"Mine does."

We all looked at the blade strapped to his hip. It must have been forged in the demon realm to be effective on the creatures. We knew of only one other weapon—Jack Langley's knife.

"We probably should find him some clothes," I said. "Perhaps an old shirt of Jack's will do."

Tommy and Sylvia shook their heads. "None will be big enough," Tommy said. "Bollard's will fit in length, but not across the shoulders. We'll have to get something made up."

"I'll measure him," Sylvia said quickly. "Then we'll have the measurements sent to Mr. Irwin, the village tailor, and ask him to make us two shirts as quickly as possible, and a full suit too."

"*You* are not measuring him," Tommy announced. "No females will touch the warrior."

I turned away from their bickering to the man in question, only to find that he'd been watching me again, his brow creased, his eyes hooded.

"I apologize for bringing trouble to your home, Cara," he said.

"No trouble," I said breezily, waving off the other two as they stopped arguing, giving each other the silent treatment instead. "Now, first things first. What are we to call you? Do you have a name?"

"Quintin St. Clair."

"Quintin? You don't look like a Quintin." Not that I knew what a Quintin looked like; but the name didn't suit the strapping fellow filling the bedroom with his significant presence.

"It was the name my father gave me," he said, sounding a little offended.

"You have a father?"

"Everybody has a father. Mine is long dead."

"Oh. Yes, of course, I just thought that since you were some sort of supernatural creature that you were made rather than born."

"I am human, like you, but much older."

"How old?"

"I was born many years ago. That is all you need to know."

"I see. Well, since you don't look like a Quintin to me, may I call you Quin?"

He considered it then gave a single nod. "Quin will suffice."

"It's from the Latin, isn't it? Quintus, meaning fifth?"

"And St. Clair sounds French," Sylvia said with triumph. She'd been trying hard to improve her languages, although she'd yet to master much beyond the basics.

He nodded. "I was the fifth son, and the last."

"Tell us about yourself," I said.

"No. We must find the book so I can return."

"Return to where? You haven't really explained where you're from."

"In between."

"Yes, but what does that mean? In between what?"

His gaze shifted away from me. "Where was the book last seen?" It would seem the topic of his origins was off-limits for now. I would try again later.

"Down at the abbey ruins."

"Take me there."

Tommy held up his hands. "Slow down. This is a lot more complicated than simply heading outside and digging a few holes near the ruins. Myer has been searching for the book for an age. Added to which, it's growing late. Dinner will be ready soon. And might I remind you that Cara has been ill? She needs rest and food. Tomorrow we'll think about finding the book. Tonight, you will have to…" He shrugged, apparently at a loss as to what supernatural warriors did when they weren't fighting demons.

"Eat," Quin said, swallowing heavily. "I would like to eat."

"You're hungry?" I asked.

He blinked and a small line connected his brows. "Aye."

"You seem surprised. Are you hungrier than usual?"

"I don't ordinarily need food or drink."

"Good lord." Sylvia's eyes widened. "Do you mean to say you haven't eaten in hundreds of years? You must be starving! Tommy, have Cook prepare dinner early. We'll be right down after we introduce Mr. St. Clair to Uncle August."

"You introduce him," I said to her. "I need to take a bath first." Frakingham House was fortunate in that it had one bathing room, located in a part of the house that had been very recently renovated. Water reached it through pipes hidden behind the walls without the servants needing to carry buckets upstairs. I bathed often.

Sylvia marched to the door, all brisk determination. Tommy didn't move. "I'm not leaving you two alone with him," he declared.

She clicked her tongue. "Don't be a ninny. He's perfectly harmless."

"We don't know that."

"He could have hurt us before you entered, but he didn't. He behaved as a gentleman should. Except for the issue of his clothing, that is, and that could not be helped."

Tommy hesitated and I opened my mouth to reassure him, but Quin spoke first. "They are safe with me. I'm here to protect Cara, and won't harm anyone she does not wish harmed. This is a decree that I must obey."

"A decree from whom?" I asked, seizing the opportunity to find out more about him.

Quin didn't answer. Tommy, apparently reassured, backed out of the bedroom and left, but not without pinning Quin with a sharp glare first. Quin didn't seem to notice. He was watching me. His undivided attention was unnerving and I felt my face heat with a blush. The warmth reminded me that I needed to wash away the remnants of the fever.

"You can take Quin to meet your uncle," I told Sylvia. "I'm going to have a bath."

"I must remain with you," Quin said.

"It's all right. Mr. Langley is only upstairs."

He shook his head. "That's too far. I must be in the same room as you, Cara."

"The same room!" Sylvia flapped her hands at her reddening cheeks. "No. No, no, no. That will not do. Cara cannot have a bath with you present, or do the many other things a lady must do in private." Her face was a picture of horror. Poor Sylvia. Even mentioning the word bath in the presence of a man went against her—and most of society's—sense of decency. "It's quite impossible," she said again. "I forbid it."

Quin ignored her and watched me. He seemed to have a remarkable ability to block out those he didn't want to hear.

I sighed. "I think he's in earnest, Syl. He must remain close."

"But it's indecent!" she spluttered. "Immoral! Disgusting!"

Quin's face lifted in amusement, proving he had been listening. "I will turn my back. Does that suffice?"

"Hardly."

"I'll place the bathing screen around the bath," I assured her. "And you can remain if you wish."

She pursed her lips and finally nodded. "Very well. If you absolutely must bathe."

"I must." Best to get the experience over with. I knew I'd be quite safe, yet it would still be odd having a man nearby.

"Then so be it."

We headed to the bathing room and I turned on the taps to fill the copper bath. Quin passed his hand through the running water. "What magic is this?"

"Indoor plumbing," I said. "It's quite a recent invention."

He nodded his approval and flicked the water off his hand

into the bath. "I like indoor plumbing very much, although I don't see the need for you to bathe. You don't appear dirty to me."

"Perhaps not, but I need one to feel human again."

His eyes flared as he studied my length. "You are quite human, Cara. Being a spirit medium doesn't make you any less so."

I smiled. "Thank you. I know. It was merely an expression."

Sylvia busied herself with the screen then directed Quin to stand on one side. He did and looked into the toilet bowl then up at its cistern above. "What is this for?"

Sylvia's face colored. "I, er... That is, I'd rather not say." She fussed with a towel, unfolding and refolding it, over and over.

I laughed. "What Sylvia is too embarrassed to tell you is that it's used for private bodily functions. It flushes everything away with water stored up there." I pointed to the cistern. "Pipes feed into it and you pull this chain to send the water down into the bowl."

His gaze followed the exposed pipes. "A curious invention, but I see how ladies would like it." He stood on the seat of the toilet to peer into the cistern.

Satisfied that he was occupied with the magic of modern plumbing, I stepped behind the screen and undressed. A moment later, I sank into the warm water and hurriedly washed myself with lavender soap. Before I climbed out, Quin had flushed the privy three times. Each one brought a smile to my face, imagining his childlike wonder as he watched the water swirl down the bowl and disappear through the hidden pipes.

Sylvia handed me the towel as I stepped out then helped me dress in a clean sleeveless chemise, drawers, corset and petti-coats. I wore my mauve satin evening gown with the cream lace *tablier* down the front of the skirt and small bustle behind. It was quite formal, but we did have a dinner guest in our midst so I thought it appropriate. Sylvia tried to train my hair into something worthy of the gown, but gave up with a sigh.

"Leave it," I told her. "It's hopeless."

"We'll have time tomorrow to fix it into something more suitable," she assured me with a nod that sent her own beautifully sleek, well behaved curls dancing around her face.

We rounded the screen to see Quin leaning back against the sink, his arms and ankles crossed in a laconic pose. His warm gaze was anything but lazy, however. It flew straight to my bare shoulders, and grew even warmer. I swallowed heavily.

Fortunately Sylvia hadn't noticed his scrutiny or she would have made a fuss. "I must leave you two to prepare myself for dinner. Cara, are you able to introduce Mr. St. Clair to Uncle August and Bollard?"

"Of course. We'll see you shortly in the dining room. Come with me, Quin."

"You ought to call him Mr. St. Clair. And he ought to address you as Miss Moreau."

"If he is to accompany me to the bathing room, I think we can be on a first name basis."

"I suppose you're right." She sighed. "Standards are slipping these days. I don't like it."

I led Quin through the house to where Mr. August Langley lived and worked. It wasn't far, being in the same wing as the bathing room. Quin took great interest in every object, piece of artwork and sconce we passed, touching or picking them up to study them further.

"It's probably quite different to the houses you're used to." I didn't know how old he was, but he had been alive and in warrior form before the dissolution of the monasteries in the fifteen-thirties. That made him at least three hundred and fifty years old.

"It's as large as a castle," he said, pausing to look through an open door that led to yet another bedroom.

"Have you seen many castles?"

"Two."

"Really? Which ones?"

"Windsor and Edinburgh. What is this used for?" He inspected a lamp that had been left on a side table.

"Light. It's a gas lamp that can be carried at night." I picked it up by the handle and held it aloft.

He tapped the glass cage. "Show me."

"I have nothing to light it with at the moment. Perhaps later, when it grows darker." It was still daylight although the sun had already sunk low. We would be dining earlier than usual.

"Windsor and Edinburgh," I prompted him. "Which monarchs were on the throne at the time of your visits?"

"You ask too many questions for a lady, Cara."

"I'm curious about you."

"So I see," he said wryly. Yet he gave me no further explanations or answers.

"Is there a reason you're not telling me anything about yourself?"

"I tell you only what you need to know."

"I think I need to know more about the person keeping me alive than his name."

"I disagree."

I blew out a breath. The man was exasperating. I tried a different tactic. "What were the castles of Windsor and Edinburgh like when you visited them?" I had limited historical knowledge of either castle, although I suspected they'd been altered over the centuries. His description of them might help me glean something. I would grasp at anything at the moment.

"Nothing like this castle. What is it called?"

So much for that. "Frakingham House, although some label it Freak House. It's not a castle."

"Freak?"

"It's a person that is not ordinary." *Like me.*

"Then why not name it Extraordinary House?" He looked to the paneled walls and up to the decorative ceiling rose, hands on hips. "*C'est très extraordinaire.*"

Clearly I wasn't going to get any more from him than that. "You speak French."

"Of course."

"Any other languages?"

"Latin, some Occitan, and a little Arabic."

Occitan was an old language associated with the troubadours who roamed southern France in the middle ages. As to Arabic, it wasn't at all common for an Englishman to know.

"Come," he said. "Show me to your master."

"Mr. Langley is not my master. He's my friend's uncle."

"You are not his ward?"

"No. I'm visiting from London where I live with my niece and her husband at present. Before that I lived in Melbourne for some years, but I originated from London. I was born there, in fact." In a filthy lane, perhaps, or the crowded room of a tenement. I didn't know. My mother had died when I was young and my father was quite mad and hadn't been aware of my birth until my mother dumped me on him.

"Melbourne? I have not heard of it."

"It's in the colony of Victoria, on the other side of the world. It wasn't discovered in your time."

His eyes widened in alarm. "How did you not fall off if it's on the other side?"

I smiled. "A little thing called gravity."

24

"Another invention? What does gravity look like?"

My smile broadened. "It's not an invention, it just is. It's a complicated concept to explain, but suffice it to say, I did not fall off when I lived in Melbourne. Have you been to London, Quin?"

He hesitated, but must have decided that answering wouldn't give away too much. "Twice."

"What business did you have there?"

"My business."

"Where were you born?"

"Not in London."

"France, perhaps?"

He looked offended. "I'm an Englishman."

"From which county?"

He didn't answer and I sighed. "Very well, be mysterious. I do think it unfair that I know nothing about you when you know a little about me now."

"You know what you need to know. Come, show me to Langley's chambers. Then we eat."

Quin walked beside me along the hallway, shortening his strides to keep in time with mine. His presence was more powerful than anything I'd ever felt from another human. Perhaps because he wasn't quite human, no matter that he had been born one. Or perhaps it was because he was semi-naked and the evidence of his strength was obvious.

Langley's laboratory inhabited an entire wing of the second floor in the U-shaped house. Bollard opened the door upon my knock. His jaw fell open and if he'd been able to talk, I'm sure he would have been rendered speechless. He was, however, a mute.

"Bollard, this is Quintin St. Clair, the otherworldly warrior who has saved my life. Quin, this is Bollard, assistant and valet to Mr. Langley."

"Pleased to make your acquaintance," Quin said with a

small bow. When Bollard continued to stare, Quin looked to me, one eyebrow arched.

"Bollard," I said with as much authority as I dared muster. He wasn't a man I knew well, and I found him a little unnerving with his silent manner and hulking form. "It's good to see you back at Frakingham again."

That seemed to get his attention. He looked me up and down as if inspecting me for signs of illness and, seeing none, smiled. It softened his appearance and instantly made him more likeable.

"I'm sorry I wasn't well enough to welcome you home," I told him. "But I am glad that you're back, as is Sylvia. Now, do you think we may see Mr. Langley? We are in something of a hurry. Quin is hungry."

Bollard stepped aside and we entered the laboratory. Langley watched us from his wheelchair, positioned at the nearest bench where he conducted his tests. Despite the presence of a number of test tubes, microscopes and other modern scientific equipment, it was the wheelchair that piqued Quin's interest. He bent down to study the wheels and then the blanket covering Langley's crippled legs. He must have realized why the chair was mobile and nodded his approval.

"A useful device," he said.

"Miss Moreau?" Langley said without taking his shrewd gray gaze off Quin. "Who is this and why is he unclothed?"

"Quintin St. Clair, at your service, sir." Quin bowed. "I apologize for my attire, or lack of it. I altered my clothing some time ago, after discovering the sword is easier to wield when I'm not hindered by cloth. I had my hair cut for the same reasons. It used to get in my eyes."

This was more information than he'd given me, and I was somewhat irked to have been refused answers that he'd freely given to Langley. Was it because I was a woman?

I briefly explained to Langley that Quin was the warrior and he had come to keep me alive while we searched for the book of spells. Both Langley and Bollard listened, enraptured.

When I finished, Langley shook his head sadly. "And what if the book cannot be found?"

"It will be," Quin said with conviction that bolstered me. It was an option that I hadn't wanted to entertain, but had set up root in the back of my mind nevertheless.

"It has to be," I agreed. "If not…" If not, I would die.

Bollard gave me a grim yet encouraging smile, as if he had complete faith that we would find it.

Langley was less optimistic but I knew from experience that it was his nature to be cautious. "I hope you're right, Cara. I am glad to see you looking like yourself again. You had us all worried. Sylvia has been beside herself."

"I know. I'm sorry to have put you through that."

"It's nothing you need apologize for. At least we know what caused it and how to cure you." He linked his fingers over his paunch. His hands seemed ethereally white against the crimson smoking jacket embroidered with gold dragons. "Will you begin the search at the ruins?"

"I think so. Mr. Myer seemed to think the book is either located there, or clues to its whereabouts are buried at the site. We'll begin in the morning."

He unlinked his fingers and placed them on the chair's wheels. He pushed himself closer to me until Bollard grabbed the chair's handles and took over the arduous task. "You must have word sent to Samuel and Charity. They left with your health under a cloud and were quite concerned."

"Yes, of course."

"When you say that Mr. St. Clair must reside close to you, how close?"

"As near as possible."

"Very near," Quin added. "Or she dies."

I swallowed down my rising panic, but it didn't stop the back of my neck prickling.

Langley nodded. "Then I suspect you will be sleeping in her bedroom. Cara, since you are under my roof, this poses a problem."

"I understand, Mr. Langley." Any hint of impropriety would compromise me, and having a strange man in my room would be a most indecent, scandalous thing. My reputation would never recover and a young lady couldn't afford to lose her reputation. If she did, she could not marry well. While I didn't have marriage at the forefront of my mind, it was something I knew I must consider in the near future. The kinswoman of the future Viscountess Preston was expected to marry a gentleman of the highest quality. What was expected, however, and what I wanted, were two entirely different things. I had become used to the roughened gentlemen of the Antipodes. England's foppish ones were not to my taste at all.

"We'll be sure Tommy is the only servant made aware of the circumstances," I told him. "To everyone else, Quin will be a distant family friend occupying a guest bedroom."

"And how will you explain his presence here? How did he arrive? Nobody would have seen him."

"We'll think of something over dinner."

"I suggest you do, and quickly. Servants talk." He nodded at the door, dismissing us, but called to Quin before he exited. "If I learn that your motives are not honorable, Mr. St. Clair, I will find a way to have you sent straight to hell."

I wasn't sure how he could manage that, but Quin didn't question him. "Cara will come to no harm from me, nor will any of her friends."

Bollard rested his hand on Langley's shoulder, and I

sensed that the small gesture communicated something between them but I didn't know what.

Quin and I left and made our way downstairs just as the dinner gong sounded. Tommy served Quin, Sylvia and myself in the dining room. Langley and Bollard would dine together upstairs tonight. After all the recent visitors to Frakingham House, it was a quiet affair. Until Quin began to eat.

He eyed his fork with suspicion then avoided it altogether. He stabbed a whole slice of beef with the point of his knife and proceeded to eat it without cutting it first. I watched with curiosity, but Sylvia and Tommy eyed him with growing expressions of horror. After he stuffed the entire piece into his mouth, he pulled over the plate of roasted chicken and tore off a leg with his hands. He then ate it with the enthusiasm of a half-starved man. Juices ran down his chin and onto his bare chest. I picked up his serviette and dabbed it off. Ordinarily such behavior would have Sylvia protesting, but she and Tommy were much too concerned with watching Quin consume everything edible within reach.

"I've dined with some folks with poor habits before," Tommy muttered, "but his manners are something else entirely."

"Dining forks are a relatively recent invention," I told him. "If Quin hasn't eaten in this realm since his—" Since his what? Death? "If Quin hasn't eaten for many years, he wouldn't have used them before."

"Mr. St. Clair," Sylvia said loudly, as if speaking to a deaf man. "Watch me, if you please. This is how a gentleman eats." She took great pains to eat like a queen, only slicing off tiny portions then chewing with her mouth closed.

"It would take me a long time to eat my fill if I ate like that," Quin observed. Nevertheless, he picked up his fork and copied Sylvia, sitting opposite him. He couldn't get the rhythm right and looked awkward, although he managed to cut into the chicken with sheer brute force.

"Your fork should go in your left hand," I told him. He watched me, sitting beside him, and made a better show of it.

The rest of the meal went by pleasantly enough, although he couldn't take his eyes off the jelly for a full five minutes after Maud the maid brought it in. He poked it, licked it, wobbled it, and finally thrust his hand into it as if scooping up a mud pile. Sylvia almost had a fit, but I couldn't stop giggling. Quin ate the entire thing.

After dinner, we adjourned to the drawing room, including Tommy who insisted on remaining with us while Quin was present. We'd already decided to tell the other servants and the Harborough villagers that Quin was a relative of mine visiting from Melbourne. The exotic nature of that distant land would help explain his odd behavior and attire. We also discussed the sleeping arrangements. Sylvia and I would sleep in my bed, and Tommy and Quin would sleep on truckles pushed in after the other servants retired for the night. A screen would separate us. Quin seemed disinterested in our plans and took no part in the arrangements. All he did was stare at me with a curious expression on his face. I expected him to ask me questions, and more than once he seemed about to say something but stopped himself. Had he been going to ask me something personal? Why hadn't he?

His hesitations did not stop me from asking him questions, however. "Tell us about your realm," I said.

"I cannot."

"Cannot or will not?"

He didn't answer.

"Very well. Tell me how you knew I was ill. I assume you don't attempt to save everyone dying from a curse."

"You are special, Cara."

I scooted forward on my chair. "I am? In what way?"

"You are a medium and the curse was not intended for you."

It didn't quite sound like a compelling enough reason for a complete stranger—a warrior, no less—to bring me back to health, but I let the matter slide. Clearly Quin didn't want to tell me much. Very well. I would let him have his secrets.

For now.

CHAPTER 3

I'd never slept in the same room as a man before. It was an odd experience. Tommy's snoring and Sylvia's tossing kept me awake. Every time she moved, she kicked me in the shin. However, my lack of sleep had a lot to do with Quin on the other side of the screen positioned at the foot of my bed. He didn't make a sound and I began to wonder if he even needed to sleep at all.

Curiosity eventually got the better of me, and I climbed out of bed. Usually it was completely dark in my room at night, but Tommy had insisted on keeping a candle burning on the mantel in case he needed to get up and protect us. It provided just enough light for me to see Quin when I poked my head around the edge of the screen. He lay on his back without blankets covering him. He still wore his leather pants and no shirt. Tommy lay on the truckle beside him, sound asleep. So much for our protector.

I ventured around the screen to get a better look. Quin lay with his hands resting on his stomach, a pose that reminded me of the effigies of long-dead medieval kings carved into stone. He'd removed his sword, but placed it within reach at his side. He claimed to have cut his hair, but it was still longish and splayed on the pillow around his head like a dark aura. The flickering light from the single candle turned his skin golden and cast shadows beneath his cheekbones and eyes. He really was a remarkable specimen, as Sylvia liked to call him. No Englishman I'd met had such a compelling presence, or a face as masculine and handsome as Quin's. I couldn't take my eyes off it. Oh wait, I could, just long enough to admire his shoulders, chest and stomach. His body had probably been honed from fighting against otherworldly creatures, yet was that what he'd always done? He said he was human, yet he clearly wasn't. At least not anymore. So what *was* he?

His eyes suddenly opened, sending me reeling backward into the screen. I rescued it before it toppled and woke up the others. "You're awake," he whispered, sitting up.

I tried to appear sophisticated despite being dressed in nothing but my nightgown. "I, er...that is, yes. I couldn't sleep. A lot has happened today and I'm finding it hard to digest it all."

"Digest?"

"Comprehend. What about you? Why can't you sleep?"

He raised one knee and rested his arm on it. "I don't feel tired."

"You can't get tired?"

"I don't know."

I edged forward. "How can you not know? You've been to this realm before."

"I haven't stayed long here in the past. This is the longest time."

"Why?"

"My work usually takes mere moments to complete. I kill the demons then I return to my realm." He shrugged in a nonchalant way that reminded me of my father, a typical Frenchman's shrug.

"So you have never stayed overnight?"

"No."

It was interesting that he told me that much. The fact he had not stayed overnight convinced me that he had never kept anyone cursed with a supernatural illness alive before. I was his first.

"Perhaps you simply don't require sleep, not being from this realm."

"Perhaps."

"Yet you *were* from this realm, once, long ago."

He gave me that quirk of a smile again. "You're asking questions of me without posing them as questions. That is—"

"Clever?"

"I was going to say devious."

I smiled. "We females must use all the wiles available to us."

His face darkened and closed up, as if shutting off his expressions to hide them from me. "Aye. Very devious."

His reaction made me think that a woman had featured in his life. A devious woman who'd caused him problems. A human woman, or some other creature?

"You are quite the mystery, Quin."

"My apologies, Cara."

"Don't apologize, just answer my questions."

He turned his face away.

"What happened to you? Why did you go from being human to being...an angel?"

"I told you," he whispered harshly, "I am no angel. I am a warrior. Warriors fight. We do not answer questions from devious maidens who do not know when to keep their mouths shut." He lay flat on his back and squeezed his eyes shut.

I sniffed. "Well. There's no need to be rude."

* * *

WE SPENT the entire morning searching for signs of the book's location down at the ruins, but without knowing what we were looking for, it was an impossible task. We studied patterns in the fallen stones, inspected them for inscriptions, and even dug some up. But there was a vast number of stones scattered across the site and much of the old abbey's foundations were still buried.

I was pleased to see that the ghosts of Garrett and Owens had disappeared, although I would have liked to have given Mr. Garret a piece of my mind. It was thanks to him that I was breaking my fingernails and getting my knees dirty, not to mention dying.

"This is hopeless," I said when my stomach growled in the early afternoon. Maud had delivered tea and cake mid-morning, but Quin had eaten all of it under her appalled gaze.

"You're right." Tommy sat against a low wall and tipped his head back to expose his face to the late spring sunshine. His hands were filthy and he'd smeared some dirt across his sweaty forehead. He'd done a marvelous job of digging alongside Quin, and seemed quite exhausted, poor fellow. "We could dig up the whole site and still find nothing. There must be a better way."

I sat back on my haunches and surveyed what we'd achieved in one morning. Piles of dirt and stones looked like small, pathetic blobs on a vast canvas. The abbey would have been huge in its time, only about half the length of the current house, but just as high. Its rubble seemed to go on and on.

"It *is* hopeless," I muttered, tears pricking my eyes. "We

can't possibly search it all, even if we knew what we were looking for." I swiped at a tear as it fell from my left eye.

Quin sat beside me, very close but not touching, and stretched out his longs legs. His presence lifted my spirits a little. "You must not give up hope, Cara. We'll find the book."

"But not this way."

"Then we'll find another way."

"There is no other way. If there were, Myer would have discovered it already and gone down that path instead of doing what we're doing."

"Who is this Myer?"

"A gentleman that nobody particularly likes."

"Including his wife," Tommy chimed in.

"He's very rich and is obsessed with the supernatural. He's actually the master of the Society for Supernatural Activity, a group of gentlemen and ladies with an interest in all things paranormal. Myer knows a lot, but it seems he wishes to know more."

"And he's prepared to get that knowledge through bribery, trickery, and lies," Sylvia added with a wrinkle of her pert nose.

"He sounds useful," Quin said.

I frowned at him. "What do you mean?"

"If he knows much, then he might help us find the book."

"He's been looking for some time," Sylvia said with a huff of exasperation. "To no avail."

I turned fully to Quin. He might be onto something. "You think he knows more than he's letting on?"

"Mayhap. Or mayhap he doesn't know the significance of what he knows."

Tommy brightened. "That's a good point."

"Are you suggesting we ask him to help us?" Sylvia shook her head and plopped down on a stone. "I don't think he will.

Or if he does think of something new, he won't tell us what it is. He's far too selfish to share."

"Then perhaps we can ask him for access to his books," I said. "The Society for Supernatural Activity does have a large library of rare volumes on paranormal topics. He has offered Emily and Jacob access to them on occasion. Perhaps it's time we took him up on his offer. We don't have to tell him that we're looking for the missing spell book."

"Don't you think he's already searched through them?" Tommy asked.

"Probably. But he doesn't have one distinct advantage that we have."

"What?"

"Quin."

We all looked at Quin. He squared his shoulders and met my gaze. The color of his eyes deepened, but there was no other sign that he felt overwhelmed by my faith in him or the task ahead. Indeed, I got the impression that having others rely on him was nothing new.

"Where does Myer live?" he asked.

"London."

"How far is London?"

"Several hours by train or a little over a day by coach."

"And by horse?"

I smiled. "Much the same as it is by coach."

"Then we travel by train. What is it? Another new invention?"

"You'll see soon enough."

He stood and extended his hand to me. "We'll depart now."

I took his hand and allowed him to assist me to my feet. His fingers gently squeezed mine and held them a little longer than necessary. A small jolt traveled the length of my arm, warming me. He must have felt it too because those intense eyes connected with mine, albeit far too briefly. He let me go and stepped away.

"Wait a moment," Sylvia said as Tommy assisted her to stand. "We cannot go right this moment. Mr. St. Clair has no proper clothes."

"Mr. Irwin assured me he would have the first shirt ready by late today," I said. "That will suffice for now. He can send the other garments on to London when they're ready."

"Where are we to stay in London?"

"Emily and Jacob's townhouse, of course."

"All of us?"

"You don't have to come if you don't want to, Sylvia."

"I most certainly do. Tommy too. We are not letting you both out of our sight. Isn't that right, Tommy?"

"Whatever you say, Miss Langley."

She scowled at him. The two of them had an interesting relationship. Not quite one of servant and mistress, but not friends either. It must be strange for them, since Tommy was a childhood friend to Sylvia's cousin, Jack. I'd thought they were sweet on one another, but there were moments of frostiness between them that threw that theory out the window. I couldn't imagine the two of them ever acting on their feelings, if they did indeed have feelings for one another. For one thing, Sylvia was a snob; for another, her uncle would never allow it.

"Emily and Jacob would love to have us all stay with them," I assured her. "They have more than enough room. Oh." I sighed. "I'm going to have to tell her about my illness after all, and Quin's role in making me better. She won't like that he has to sleep in my room with me."

"Yet it will be safer to do so in the privacy of their home rather than a hotel," Sylvia agreed. "At least we can control who knows, to some degree."

"Then it's settled," Tommy said. "I'll make arrangements to leave tomorrow."

* * *

"BY ALL THAT IS HOLY," Quin murmured, his eyes as big as saucers. "What manner of hellish beast is *that*?" He stepped in front of me and reached for the sword that was no longer strapped to his hip.

I touched his arm to reassure him. "It's a steam engine. It's quite harmless, and will take us to London."

We stood on the platform at Harborough Station as the hissing, snorting train rolled in. I could understand how someone who'd never seen such a sight before would think it a dangerous creature from another realm. It seemed to be alive as it puffed steam from all orifices.

"We travel in one of the carriages attached to it. See?" I nodded at the line of carriages behind, but did not let him go. I was afraid he'd jump in front of the engine and either try to stop it from attacking me, or inspect the new curiosity. "You must stay clear of the wheels or you'll be crushed to—" What would happen to him? "Quin, are you immortal?"

My question captured his full attention, despite the marvelous invention pulling to a noisy stop in a cloud of steam.

"I am mortal in this realm."

I bit my lip and, for the first time, worried about him. I'd been selfishly absorbed in my own health and had not given a moment's thought to his. "What can kill you here?"

"The same things that kill any human."

There were so many things that could cause injury or death, from falling under the wheels of a fast moving train to any number of illnesses. Why hadn't I thought to check before we decided on this venture? It seemed so obvious now that the rules of life and death in this realm would not apply to him in the "in between" one but did when he was here.

"Quin, listen to me." I gripped both his forearms and turned him to face me. I felt his muscles flex instinctively beneath his crisp new shirt, then relax as he registered that I wasn't a threat. "You must be very careful. If you died because of me, I would never forgive myself."

He smiled gently. "Do not fear, Cara. I'm very strong."

"Yes. I can see that." I let go of his muscles—er, arms. "But you have no idea of the diseases and other hazards in this time."

"Are there more diseases now?"

"Actually, there are probably less, but—"

"Then do not fear for me. Let *me* worry about *you*."

"Oh." His conviction left me quite speechless. Many people had promised to care for me, ever since Emily and Celia had taken me in eight years ago, but none quite so thrillingly enigmatic as the warrior. "Thank you, Quin. I don't think I've had a chance to tell you how grateful I am that you're keeping me alive. It's a generous and selfless task, whether you've been ordered to do it or not." I cleared my throat. "Were you ordered? Or are you doing this of your own free will? And if it were an order—"

"Enough, Cara. You can thank me by not asking so many questions."

He marched off toward a frantic Sylvia, who was trying to attract our attention from the open door of the first class carriage. I sighed and followed, ignoring the curious stares of other passengers. I couldn't blame them for ogling. Quin did look odd, dressed in his leather pants and new white shirt with neither vest nor jacket. He held his hat in his hand, having almost left it behind in the Langley coach that had driven us to the station. We had convinced him to pack his sword in a valise, but not been able to get him to wear the hat.

The four of us settled into a booth and Tommy stowed our luggage then shut the door for privacy. Sylvia had insisted the footman join us, and not travel in second class, so that we could form plans together. It would be easier not to relay it all again later. I had the sneaking suspicion she simply wanted him beside her, however. The rough, jerky ride would make touching inevitable.

"I've been thinking," I said, as the train jolted forward. "We may not have to rely completely on Myer and the society's library. There is somebody else with just as many books and I'd wager his knowledge is as vast as Myer's."

"Mr. Culvert?" Sylvia asked. "Yes, of course. Why didn't I think of him before?"

"George is also far nicer and will help us willingly once we explain the problem."

"Surely he would have already helped us if he could," Tommy said.

"Not in finding the book. As far as I know, nobody has mentioned it to him. Have you? Or Samuel?"

He shook his head. "I doubt Samuel or Charity would do so. It would lead to all sorts of questions we couldn't answer."

We had all agreed to keep quiet about the parchment torn from the book, now in the possession of the residents of Freak House. With the likes of Myer after it, it was safer to keep it hidden. Discussing it with George Culvert now couldn't be helped. He was an expert demonologist who also happened to be Jacob's brother-in-law. We could trust him.

"Where was the book last seen?" Quin asked. "And when?" He looked cramped on the seat beside me, the small cabin not built for men of his size with such long legs. Between he and Tommy, the cabin felt crowded.

The door slid open and the conductor leaned up against

the doorframe to steady himself against the rocking carriage. Quin shot to his feet, sending his hat tumbling to the floor. He closed his fists at his sides and bared his teeth at the trembling conductor.

"Quin!" Tommy, Sylvia and I shouted.

"Sit down," I said, taking his hand and tugging, hard. He did not sit and continued to glare at the poor conductor, who looked as if he was caught between wanting to flee and calling for help. "He just wants to check our tickets."

"You must forgive him," Sylvia said to the conductor with a nervous laugh. "He's foreign."

The conductor muttered something about foreigners under his breath as he straightened his tie, and I hoped Quin didn't understand the insult.

Tommy handed him our tickets and the conductor punched holes in them before handing them back. "Mind he stays in here and doesn't frighten the other passengers," he barked. "Shouldn't have foreigners roaming about first class, if you ask me."

"Nobody did ask you." I pulled on Quin's hand again.

He did not sit until the conductor was out of sight and the door closed again. "That man was ill mannered," he said. "He should knock before entering."

"You need to be more careful," I told him. "People don't go about threatening others in this realm. Not these days, anyway. We are no longer a war-like society."

"You don't have wars?"

"Well, yes, occasionally."

"But we are not barbarians," Sylvia said. "We're far more civilized than we were in the sixteenth century."

"And earlier," I said without taking my gaze off Quin's. "Quin is older than the sixteenth century."

"Or is he ageless?" Tommy muttered, arching his brow at

Quin. "Perhaps he doesn't belong to any particular historical period."

Quin said nothing.

"I don't think he's ageless," I ventured. "If that were the case, he wouldn't have small lines at the corners of his eyes. Have you noticed how they don't quite disappear, even after he has stopped smiling?"

Sylvia and Tommy leaned forward. Quin leaned back. "You're right," Sylvia said. "He must be older than us if he has wrinkles."

"I do not have wrinkles."

"You do," I said. "Small ones. No gray hairs, however."

He ran his hand through his dark hair and frowned.

"Late twenties or early thirties is my guess," Tommy said cheerfully.

I felt a little horrid for teasing Quin, but he had asked for it by not answering our questions, and it was amusing to see him suddenly worry about aging, something which would probably continue now that he was back in our realm. I supposed the aging process had stopped in the realm he'd been living in for the last few centuries.

"Seven and twenty," Quin snapped. "I am seven and twenty."

"In what year were you born?"

"Cara." His voice was a low growl that invited no argument. "I have exercised patience with your impertinence, but no more. Tell me the last known whereabouts of the book. Since it is important to your survival, I expect you will *want* to help me find it instead of disobeying me yet again."

"Yes," I muttered, not quite able to bring myself to apologize, despite feeling like I'd offended a prince. "Of course. We must maintain our focus on the end prize." *My life.* I swallowed and studied my hands in my lap. Opposite, Tommy stretched out his legs.

Sylvia cleared her throat. "The last time we know the book was seen was during the dissolution of the monasteries. The abbot had it. He tore out a page and gave it to Brother Francis to speak the spell that summoned you, Quin."

"That's not quite right," I said, trying to recall the exact words of the priest's ghost. "The abbot did give the parchment to Brother Francis, but he may have torn it out some time previously. Indeed, he may not have torn it out himself, but an earlier custodian could have. Brother Francis never mentioned seeing the book at all, ever."

"Then we're even more in the dark than we thought."

I nodded. The task ahead of us was enormous. The book itself may not even exist anymore. I knew everyone was thinking it, even though no one said it. The weight of their unspoken words filled the cabin.

What would happen to me if we couldn't find it?

I turned to the window and watched the scenery whip past. My heart felt heavy in my chest, my energy sapped, although I knew that was because I'd slept poorly the last two nights rather than the illness.

"Cara," came Quin's soft voice after what must have been half an hour. I turned from the window to see Sylvia resting her head against Tommy's shoulder. They both had their eyes closed, although I couldn't be certain if they were asleep or not. It was possible they enjoyed the close proximity that sleep offered and were merely pretending.

I blinked wearily at Quin. He seemed troubled, and a little pale, his lips pinched. "What is it? Do you feel ill? Sometimes the motion of the train can upset one's stomach. Sitting nearer the window can help. Shall we swap seats?"

I rose, but he caught my hand. "Sit. Please."

I sat. "What is it? What's worrying you?"

"You're not angry with me?"

"No. Yes." I sighed and looked away. "I don't know. I'm not

used to being chastised, I suppose. I find it a bitter pill to swallow."

"Your father never managed you?"

"Managed me? No. He had little to do with my upbringing and even less involvement in teaching me the finer points of obedience. He allowed me to do whatever I wanted."

"An irresponsible man. All manner of ills could have befallen a girl in the streets of London."

They had, to an extent, although I had fared better than many children left to fend for themselves entirely, like Tommy, Charity and Jack. "My brother became my guardian in more recent years. He was strict, although he never admonished me for asking questions. He encouraged me to be curious, in fact."

"Then he created a rod for his own back, and that of your future husband."

I narrowed my gaze at him. "What do you mean?"

"A woman should not ask too many questions."

"Why not?"

"It creates problems."

"What sort of problems?"

He arched a brow at me and I bit my lip. I was asking too many questions again.

"I warn you, Quin, I will find it difficult *not* to ask you things. It's in my nature to be curious."

"Then you must forgive me when I command you to stop. It's in my nature not to speak of certain matters."

Make that *any* matters. I sighed. "I'm afraid we're destined to clash on occasion. I don't take kindly to being commanded. My future husband will have to respect that."

"Your father and brother failed in their duty as your guardians."

I bristled. "Not Louis. He was a very good guardian and

brother. He was there when I needed him and paid for a first-rate education, better than many boys received."

"Education?" He stared at me. "You can read?"

I smothered a smile. "Of course. I read the spell to summon you here, don't forget. I also speak and read French and Italian, have a good knowledge of history and botany, and achieved honors in mathematics."

"What is the use of all that knowledge to a woman?"

"Sometimes I ask myself the same question," I muttered. Despite being allowed to attend lectures at Oxford and Cambridge, women couldn't become full members of the universities. Even if we could, there was little practical application for all that learning afterward, aside from becoming governesses, an occupation that my family considered beneath me. I was as yet undecided about my future. While attending lectures held more appeal than sitting through endless rounds of social calls with vacuous young ladies, it was decidedly dull compared to the adventures I'd had so far at Freak House.

He grunted. "A little understanding of numbers can be of service to a lady running a household, I will admit, but as to the other things, I cannot see the point. How does history help her sew, embroider or heal the sick? And what is botany?"

I wasn't sure whether to laugh at him or argue. Perhaps it was a little too soon in his visit to hit him with my modern sensibilities. To be fair, not too many present-day men liked the idea that I was smarter than they were.

"Quin, you are positively medieval."

That earned me another grunt. "If we are to be always near one another, we should not argue," he said.

"Agreed. I'm sorry. I want you to know that I appreciate your being here. We both know what would happen if you weren't."

He looked away and his throat flushed. "Do not thank me."

"I must. I owe you my life."

"Enough," he said through gritted teeth. "Do not thank me again."

"Very well, if it embarrasses you."

"Embarrasses me?" He paused, blinked. "Aye, it does."

I frowned at the hard planes of his jaw, the heaviness of his brow as it crashed over his eyes. I got the feeling he wasn't at all embarrassed. He seemed like a brazen, unabashed man, as a matter of fact. So why would he not accept my thanks? What, exactly, was he hiding?

CHAPTER 4

*T*he platform at King's Cross Station pulsed with passengers coming and going. Some stopped to buy flowers or refreshments from one of the many stalls, while others lingered with loved ones as people surged around them. Porters carried luggage or pushed wheeled trolleys piled high with crates, and railway staff kept a watchful eye on scruffy unattended children—the pickpocketing industry thrived at stations. Steam hissed and spat from the engine, momentarily cloaking our little party. Through the clearing haze, I saw a face I hadn't seen in months. My heart lifted. How good to see him again!

"Mr. Faraday!" I waved, but he did not respond, despite looking directly at me with those slate gray eyes of his. How odd. Surely my appearance was familiar to him. We had become good friends on the long journey between Melbourne and England. At least, I thought we had.

"Mr. Faraday!" I called again. "Nathaniel!

He walked off, although I could still see his hat above the others in the crowd for several more seconds before he was finally swallowed up altogether.

"Handsome fellow," Sylvia said, following my gaze. We stood a little apart from Tommy and Quin as they divided the luggage between them. "Who is he?"

"A gentleman I would like to meet again. Come with me." I grabbed her hand and dragged her after me in the direction of Nathaniel Faraday. I wouldn't have bothered with most acquaintances, but Nathaniel was different. Before parting at the dock, he'd promised to write to me at Emily's and I had promised to respond. He had not kept up his end of the bargain, and that was the end of that.

Yet here he was in the flesh. It was the perfect opportunity to confront him. Perhaps a girl ought to take silence as a sign that a gentleman had no interest in her, but I didn't like to be slighted. It had happened more times that I cared to admit. Perhaps associating with a brown skinned woman at home in London wasn't acceptable, whereas striking up a friendship with one on board, where he knew no one, was. It was the sort of ill-mannered double standards that made my blood boil.

The more I pursued him along the crowded platform, however, the less I wanted to reconnect with him. Just the thought of it was tiring and made my head ache. My chest tightened too and I felt a little out of breath.

I slowed and watched Nathaniel disappear around a corner, my heart sinking at his disregard for me. I'd thought I was above caring about the opinions of others, but it would seem I wasn't.

I squeezed my stinging eyes shut, but a wave of dizziness had me reaching out my hand for the nearest solid object.

"Cara!" Sylvia caught my arm, steadying me. "Are you all right? You look rather ill and you were swaying, just now."

My skin prickled with heat and my vision blurred. I pressed my hand to my chest, but I couldn't suck in enough air to draw a full breath. "I think...I'm going to faint."

"Cara!"

As I fell against her, I had the fleeting thought that I'd done something very stupid. I'd left Quin's side. Did he know? Would he find me in time before the illness took hold?

I grappled with the questions in a bid to stay conscious. I tried to stand but couldn't, and Sylvia struggled with my weight.

"Tommy!" she cried. "Quin! Here!"

My heavy, burning eyelids closed. I could feel the bodies of concerned onlookers pressing all around us. Somebody called for a doctor, another suggested water, and a man with a thick northern accent thought loosening my corset would help.

Then suddenly they were gone and a pair of strong arms scooped me up. Quin. I recognized his scent and the crispness of his shirt beneath my cheek. I relaxed into him and drew in a strong, full breath.

I was alive and well, thanks to my warrior.

He carried me to a bench tucked into an alcove near the ticket office. A trail of passengers followed us, anxiety etched on their brows.

"She's all right now," Sylvia assured them. "Thank you for your concern."

I smiled and thanked them too and they departed, satisfied I was restored to good health. Quin set me gently down on the seat and knelt before me. His concerned gaze searched my face and he pressed the back of his hand to my cheek. Then his expression cleared, only to become darker, fiercer.

"Did you wish to test me?" he snarled through an unyielding jaw.

"No!"

He muttered something in French under his breath. "That was foolish, Cara. You cannot leave my side."

"I forgot."

He stood and peered down his nose at me; his hands balled into fists at his sides. At that moment, despite being dressed in a modern shirt and lacking a sword, he looked every bit the warrior about to charge into battle. If I were his enemy, I would quiver. As it was, I swallowed hard.

"Your studies have not made you smarter," he said.

I sat up straighter. "That is grossly unfair, not to mention uncalled for. I momentarily forgot about the curse in the excitement of seeing a friend I hadn't seen in some time."

Quin turned his back on me. The seams of his shirt stretched as he crossed his arms. I glared at him but he did not turn around. I sighed and rubbed my temples where the remnants of a headache lingered. I didn't feel like arguing with him. He was right and I had done something foolish by walking off. Not to mention I was feeling bruised after being snubbed by Nathaniel.

Sylvia's cool fingers clasped my hand. "Are you sure you're all right?"

I nodded.

"Who was that man?"

I was about to tell her all about Nathaniel Faraday and how much I'd enjoyed his company on the ship—and thought he had enjoyed mine—but suddenly lacked the energy. "Nobody important."

She looped her arm through mine and together we walked ahead of Tommy and Quin, who were carrying our luggage. My back smarted with the sharpness of Quin's glare drilling into it, but I refused to turn around. It was one thing for him to be right, it was quite another to call my intelligence into question.

I couldn't ignore him the entire way to Emily's house, squashed together as we were in the Beaufort coach—his broad shoulder butted against me every time we turned a corner—but we did not speak. Sylvia filled the silence with endless chatter, none of which I heard. Quin didn't seem to either, intent as he was on the streets of London outside the window.

"You've been here before?" Tommy asked him when we'd almost reached our destination.

Quin nodded.

"Is it very different?" I said.

"Aye. There are more people, and buildings too. I have never seen so many. The city is endless."

Sylvia laughed. "Of course it ends, silly."

"It was not this smoky last time, and the smell is different."

"It does have a distinctive odor," Tommy noted. "You get used to it. I used to live here. Cara too."

"And I am living here again," I said with a sigh. I was still unsure if I liked the idea of residing in London. As much as I wanted to be with Emily and her family again, there were too many unhappy childhood memories lurking around dark corners. And it was rather smelly with the thick smoky air and many horses depositing their excrement in the streets.

Quin didn't seem to hear me. His gaze was intent on a church passing by our window. It wasn't a particularly old church, so why did it hold so much interest? It wouldn't have existed in his lifetime. Some ten minutes later we passed another church and another—London suddenly seemed to be full of them. He stared at each much longer than any other building along the way.

Perhaps he missed the comfort churches offered and wished to pray. He must be Catholic, since the faith of the English didn't change until Henry VIII came to the throne and Quin was certainly gone from this realm by then. "Would you like to stop and go inside?" I asked him.

His lips tightened and he turned away from the window. "No."

"We're in no particular hurry."

"No."

Tommy, Sylvia and I exchanged glances. "We could find you a Catholic church," I suggested.

Sylvia pulled a face. "If we must."

He said nothing, and from the cold look on his face, he did not wish to discuss it further. I was about to change the topic and ask him if he wished to visit the older parts of the city for nostalgic reasons, but bit my tongue. He had made it very clear that he disliked my questions and I didn't want to upset him more than I already had. I was grateful to him for his presence and what it meant for my health. It was time I showed some respect for his privacy and kept my curiosity in check, no matter how difficult that would be.

We arrived at Emily and Jacob's house in Belgravia, over-looking Eaton Square. The street was lined with tall houses joined together to form an elegant sweep of exclusivity and wealth. My niece's husband was well-to-do, although, to be fair, he was very generous with his wealth. Their house was a picture of quiet, calm authority, but it was all a façade as smooth as that of the building itself. Inside, a riot of noise greeted us in the form of a crying toddler and two older siblings needling each other. Emily was in the middle of dispensing judgment when the butler opened the door to us. As if we'd waved a magic wand, everyone suddenly fell silent. Momentarily.

"Aunt Cara!" squealed the two elder Beaufort children.

I caught them in hugs and was almost toppled over by their enthusiasm. I kissed both on their cheeks and held them out to look at them. "I am quite sure you've both grown while I was away."

But they weren't interested in my assessment of their sizes. "What was it like at Freak House?" Gabe, the eldest, asked.

"Did you see many ghosts?" Lizzy's huge blue eyes blinked back at me, all innocence, as if it were a normal question.

"One or two," I said looking past her to Emily. My niece raised one eyebrow at me. I would wait until the children were busy elsewhere before I told her one of those spirits had cursed me.

She hoisted her youngest onto her hip and pecked me on the cheek. "I'm so glad you're back. The children have missed you. We've missed you." She greeted both Sylvia and Tommy, not caring in the least that our footman had entered through the front door like a regular visitor and not gone belowstairs, as he ought. Then she turned her attention to Quin. "This would be the fourth member of your party you mentioned in your telegram."

Quin bowed. "Quintin St. Clair, at your service, Mistress Beaufort."

"Call me Emily," she said with a smile that did not waver from his face. I suspect she was trying very hard not to lower her gaze, so as not to make him feel self-conscious about his attire.

Gabe had no such qualms. "Why are you undressed?"

Emily grasped Gabe's arm and her smile turned harder. "That's not a very polite question, Gabe. Perhaps he was hot."

Quin bent down to Gabe's level and winked at him. "I find modern gentleman's clothing restrictive."

"So do I!" Gabe declared. "Last time I threw a ball, I pulled a seam and Nanny grew cross. She made me sit in the corner."

Quin nodded solemnly. "You ought to try swinging a sword. Nigh impossible."

Gabe nodded, equally solemn. "I imagine so. Mama, may I have a sword?"

"No! Run along to the nursery, children, and ask Nanny to come and fetch Mathew."

"I don't want to go," Gabe whined.

But Lizzy was already off, her black hair and yellow ribbons streaming behind her. "I'm going to beat you."

The challenge was enough to set Gabe racing after her up the stairs and out of sight.

"Come into the drawing room," Emily said, handing Mathew to me. I bounced the toddler on my hip and he giggled, his earlier tears forgotten. Emily beckoned the hovering butler. "Have the bags taken up to the guest rooms, please, Watkins. The ladies wish to share and Mr. Dawson will be sleeping in one of the guest rooms this time."

None of our party commented on this irregularity, since having Tommy sleep in a guest room would make it easier for him to sneak into our room and play protector after the servants were all asleep.

Watkins signaled to the footmen and they each carried two valises upstairs, passing the nanny on her way down. She took Mathew from me, bobbed a curtsey, and left as silently as she had arrived.

Tommy cleared his throat. "Excuse me, Mrs. Beaufort. I'll make my way downstairs and see if I can be of service there."

"You will not," she retorted. "You are not a footman here."

"But I cannot possibly—"

"You can and you will."

"But Mr. Beaufort—"

"Jacob will not object. He'll be home shortly." Emily signaled for us to follow her into the adjoining drawing room. It wasn't the formal drawing room, but the cozier one she used for family gatherings. It was smaller and furnished with deep, solid armchairs rather than the spindly sofas of the one upstairs. "Sit, and tell me all about Mr. St. Clair. Is he a supernatural being?"

"Yes," I said. "How did you know?"

"A guess," she said without taking her gaze off him.

"I apologize for my attire," Quin said, standing by the unlit fireplace, one elbow on the mantel like the lord of the manor.

"There was time only to have the shirt made," Sylvia said, her face flushed with embarrassment. "It has been the most awkward journey from Harborough, let me tell you."

"You mean you've been parading about in nothing but those trousers until the shirt was ready?" She eyed Quin's leather pants. "And I use the term trousers loosely."

"You're quite right," I told her loftily. "Quin arrived wearing those and the boots only. Kindly do not make him feel awkward about it."

Emily flushed. "I am sorry, Mr. St. Clair."

"Quin," he said.

"Quin. Be sure that you do not mention your previous state of undress to my husband. Jacob is not quite as understanding as I am, and he is very protective of Cara."

"I will relinquish him of his duty. Cara is now my responsibility."

"My health is," I corrected him. "I am no one's responsibility."

Emily made a scoffing sound. "While you're here in England, you are mine and Jacob's. You may have been allowed your freedom when you were a child, and again in Melbourne, but you cannot run wild now that you're a young lady living in London. It's much too dangerous for one thing, and unseemly for another."

I sniffed. "You seem to have forgotten that Jacob once

wore only a shirt and trousers in your presence before you were wed."

"That's different. He couldn't help his attire and nobody else could see him anyway. Now," she said, turning away so that she didn't see me roll my eyes. "Tell me about Quin. Your telegram told me nothing."

"It was too much of a risk to say more."

She eyed him up and down. "Is he a demon?"

"No!" I cried. "Can you not see that he isn't?"

"Not all demons are mindless, ravaging beasts, Cara. Those that come here on purpose can appear quite normal and blend into society easily. Only those that are summoned or wrenched out of their realm, as it were, are feral creatures."

"Jack is half-demon," Sylvia chimed in. "And he's normal. Almost."

I knew about her cousin Jack Langley's background of course, but I occasionally forgot. His mother had been a demon sent to our realm by her own people to retrieve a rogue demon that had escaped here. Since she was a shape-shifting demon, she'd taken on the likeness of a human when she arrived and passed herself off as a regular person for years. She'd conceived her son to a human father before dying shortly after Jack was born.

"Point taken," I said. "But Quin is not a demon."

Jacob entered and stopped short when he spotted the stranger, dressed in nothing but leather pants and a shirt, standing near the fireplace. Quin straightened to his full height and took a step closer. The two men sized one another up the way wild animals do.

Emily jumped to her feet and placed her hand on her husband's arm. "Jacob, this is Quin St. Clair. He's a supernatural something-or-other and has come to London with Cara and her friends. She was just about to tell me why."

"Yes," I said quickly. "But not until you sit down. Both of you," I said pointedly to Quin.

Without taking his gaze off Jacob, Quin sat on the edge of a wingback chair. He looked as if he would leap into action at any moment. Jacob settled next to Emily who had not let go of his arm. Her knuckles were white as she held onto him.

"Welcome," Jacob said tightly. "What sort of supernatural being are you?"

"A warrior," Quin said before I could get a word in.

"Indeed? And what does a warrior do?"

"Fight."

"Perhaps I should explain," I said quickly. I sighed and appealed to Tommy and Sylvia, but neither looked interested in taking over. "I've been ill with a supernatural curse."

After Emily and Jacob's concerned exclamations subsided, I told them how I'd become cursed and how to break it, and Quin's role in my ongoing health. I told them everything and finished with the fact that we could not be parted.

This was met with stunned silence that filled the room. Emily stared at me, but Jacob's darkening gaze didn't leave Quin's. The two stared one another down once again.

Tommy cleared his throat. "If I may say something here? Both Miss Langley and myself have remained with Mr. St. Clair and Miss Moreau the entire time. They have not been left alone. Not even at night."

"There was a screen erected at the foot of the bed," Sylvia added. "The situation is not ideal, but there is nothing that can be done about it. Cara needs Quin near her for survival."

"Has this been proven?" Jacob sounded doubtful.

"Is my word not enough?" Quin snarled.

"No."

Quin shot to his feet.

"Sit down, Mr. St. Clair."

"It has been proven," Sylvia said quickly. "Just now at the station, they were separated and Cara fainted."

"It's true," Tommy said. "They can't be apart or her fever returns."

Jacob gave a single nod, but Quin still looked as if he wanted to call him out over the insult.

"Quin." I stood in front of him and, thankfully, gained his attention. "Think of this from Jacob's point of view. I'm sure you would be equally horrified if your female relation spent the night with a strange man."

He considered this then tilted his chin at Jacob. "If she were my kinswoman, I would insist the man wed her. But I cannot marry Cara," he said over the top of my head.

Sylvia giggled, but Emily gasped. I sat and exchanged an exasperated look with Tommy. This encounter was not going as I had planned.

"That is a relief," Jacob muttered, "since I have no plans to marry her off to a warrior or any other supernatural creature."

I decided it wasn't the right time to remind him that Louis had stipulated I be allowed to marry whomever I chose. Emily and Jacob had gone out of their way to ensure that the man I chose was someone respectable, from a good family. So far none of their choices had inspired me to pursue the connections further.

"What shall we tell the servants?" Emily asked.

"We can do what we did at Frakingham," Sylvia suggested. "We set up Quin in a guest bedroom. After the servants retired, he and Tommy crept into our room and slept on truckles on the other side of the screen. It was all very discreet and completely respectable. Well, as respectable as the situation allowed."

"Let me assure you, the ladies were quite safe," Tommy said.

Emily gave him a smile of thanks, but I wasn't sure Jacob was convinced. He had not taken his eyes off Quin, and Quin glared right back at him. They reminded me of lions. I'd attended a lecture by a hunter who'd studied them in the wilds of Africa. Prides were protected by one strong, alpha male who fended off attack from other males that tried to take over the coveted leadership position. I half expected Quin and Jacob to enter into battle at any moment.

"We'll employ the same technique tonight," Emily said. "You must switch back again before the servants are up in the morning. And we must find you something more appropriate to wear, Quin."

"A suit is on its way," I said. "There was no time to have it made before we left, but Mr. Irwin assured us it would be ready and sent here by tomorrow or the next day at the latest."

The entry of a footman carrying tea and cakes broke the tension. We waited until he left before speaking again.

"How will you find this book?" Emily asked. "Do you have any ideas as to its whereabouts?"

"We need to speak with George Culvert," I said.

"I'll invite he and Adelaide to dine with us tonight. What about Charity and Samuel?"

"Oh, yes please," Sylvia said. "I would love to ask how they're settling into their new lives in London again. I do miss Charity."

Emily rang for the butler and instructed him to invite the Culverts, and Samuel and Charity, for dinner. Once he was gone, she asked Sylvia about Jack and Hannah.

"They'll be back very soon," she said. "Indeed, I've decided to throw a ball in their honor upon their return."

"You have?" I asked. "At Frakingham?"

"Yes."

"Oh." Tommy spoke so quietly that Sylvia didn't hear him.

Or if she did, she chose to ignore it. He sounded unsure, but whether that was because, like me, he assumed no one would attend an event at Freak House, or because he disliked the idea of Sylvia associating with gentlemen of her own class, it was impossible to say.

"Marvelous," Emily said. "If you would like to discuss the guest list, I will see that the invitations are delivered." Which meant she would personally mention to each and every guest that *she* would be in attendance. Emily had considerable influence among a certain set, and whatever she did, others would follow.

The remainder of the afternoon dragged. I was acutely aware of Jacob and Quin continuing to glare at one another. Emily's name-dropping didn't help either. She'd already decided I had to meet three single gentlemen of her acquaintance, and Sylvia had agreed to invite them to the ball. Emily went on to describe them and I became increasingly bored. How could any man sound interesting while I sat beside Quin?

As much as I disagreed with his attitude toward women and education, I liked him on the whole. He was handsome and interesting, although it could be that he was made more interesting because he was such a mystery. Jacob seemed intent on uncovering as much as he could about him, which only ratcheted up the tension even more as Quin refused to answer.

"Why will you not tell us where you came from?" Jacob pressed.

"I have told you," Quin bit off. "I'm from a realm in between."

"What is it called?"

Quin said nothing.

"Who lives there?"

"I do."

"Who else?"

"Other warriors."

That was new. "There is more than one of you?" I asked.

His only response was to turn his flinty glare onto me.

"Anything else you can tell me about the place?" Jacob asked. "What does it look like? How many souls live there, for instance?"

Nothing.

"You say you were born here, as a human."

"Aye."

"So how did you get to be in this other realm as a warrior?"

"That is my affair."

"I think not." Jacob's tone was deceptively lazy, but no one in that room was deceived. "It is now my affair, and Emily's."

Again, Quin remained silent. It seemed to be his way of shutting down conversations. Only it wouldn't work with Jacob, just as it hadn't worked particularly well with me. We were both too curious to accept silence as an answer.

"Jacob," I warned. "Quin doesn't like talking about himself. He's much too modest."

He huffed out a humorless laugh. "Modesty be damned."

"Jacob!" Emily placed her hand over his rigid one. "I think we should heed Cara. If Quin doesn't want to talk about his home, we shouldn't force him."

"I'm not forcing him. Tell me how you came to be in this other realm, St. Clair." Jacob waited, but Quin gave no answer. Jacob blew out an exasperated breath and I half expected steam to rise from his ears in anger.

"Goodness, look at the time." Sylvia leapt up and pointed to the clock on the mantel. The distraction was a welcome relief. Only Jacob sat silently fuming. I had no doubt that Emily would speak to him after we were gone and calm him down. He always seemed to listen to her. "We must prepare for dinner. Come, Cara, Quin. Don't worry," she said to Emily and Jacob as they rose too, "we'll be sure the servants are scarce when we squirrel him into our bedroom. We're quite used to trickery now."

"There are more servants here," I reminded her.

"Frakingham will be acquiring others shortly," she assured me, completely misunderstanding my concern. "By the time of the ball, we shall have dozens."

We filed out of the room, but Emily took my hand as the others passed me. She waited until Quin was out of earshot before whispering, "Follow my lead at dinner. We shall smoke him out in less obvious ways."

I gawped at her and she gave me a wicked smile. I'd been mistaken. It wasn't Jacob I had to worry about. Emily was far more devious than her husband.

CHAPTER 5

"*F*ascinating creature," George Culvert muttered to nobody in particular. He sat opposite me at the long dining table and had not taken his eyes off Quin since meeting him. Nor had his wife, Adelaide, but instead of curiosity, her usually friendly gaze was filled with wariness. She did not trust the supernatural as easily as her husband. Then again, he had studied it his entire life and inherited his father's extensive demonology library too.

I quickly explained what Quin was doing in a state of *dishabille* and why. That had only increased George's interest and Adelaide's shock.

Charity and Samuel were a little more polite and didn't stare at Quin quite so much, but it was obvious from the moment they walked in that they were curious. Neither showed any concern, however. They knew what good the warrior had done in the past, dispensing with the demons. Like me, they trusted that he wouldn't harm humans.

"Is he tame?" I heard Adelaide whisper to Sylvia as they sat.

"Oh yes," Sylvia assured her. "So far, anyway."

I wanted to remind her that he was not a dog, but Quin would have heard. Indeed, he would have heard everything they said too. I felt awfully embarrassed and I hoped my glare at Sylvia would convey as much.

George continued to stare as Tommy served the first course. Since our conversations would require privacy, he had proposed that he serve us. Emily and Jacob had both protested, but Sylvia and Tommy insisted that it was necessary. I wasn't so sure that it was a good idea either. For one thing, it would put out the Beaufort servants, and for another, Emily wanted to treat him as a guest and not a footman. Then again, it would allow him to be present for our conversation when he felt too awkward to dine with us as a guest.

"You say your origins are human," George said to Quin before the first course was even served. I silently bit my lip and appealed to Emily. She merely shrugged.

"Aye," Quin said.

"But you've been gone for a very long time. You were last in this realm during the time of Henry VIII. Is that right?"

Quin watched Tommy ladle soup from the tureen into the bowls. He looked ravenous and not at all interested in answering George.

"Are you dead?"

Quin's gaze flickered briefly to George then back to Tommy. He waited until we each had a bowl and Jacob picked up his spoon. As soon as the head of the household tucked in, so did Quin.

George watched him with fascination and seemed to forget about his soup entirely. The others were a little more circumspect but they too seemed intrigued by everything the warrior did. He must feel like an exhibit in a freak show.

"I see you need sustenance," George noted.

"Aye."

"Is that the case in your realm too?"

"No."

"Really? Interesting. Why not, do you think?"

Quin concentrated on his soup.

But George would not give up. "Tell me about your realm."

"It is in between," Quin said.

"In between? What does that mean?"

Again, Quin remained silent.

George's brow slowly scrunched into a frown. "In between," he finally muttered. "*Humph*." He arched an eyebrow at me. "Do you know anything else about him, Cara?"

"He is as unresponsive to my questions as he is to yours, I'm afraid." I shot him a wan smile. "He doesn't like talking about himself."

George pushed his glasses up his nose. "Yes, but I thought perhaps you might have learned something about him from the spirit world. You have put questions to one or two ghosts, haven't you?"

It hadn't occurred to me to do so. I glanced at Quin. He stared back at me, his gaze searching my face as if trying to read my mind. I shook my head, but I wasn't sure who I was responding to.

"You ought not ask him too many questions," Emily said.

"It is rather impertinent," Adelaide told her husband.

"Yet necessary," Jacob added.

Samuel nodded. "Agreed. If only I could—"

Charity gasped. "Don't."

He held up his hands. "I wouldn't! You know I don't do that against anyone's wishes anymore."

"Unless absolutely necessary."

His eyes brightened. "So you agree that this is necessary?"

"No!"

It was obvious to all of us, except perhaps Quin, that they were discussing Samuel hypnotizing our guest. Charity, for reasons of her own, had an aversion to her fiancé using his power on the unsuspecting. Samuel bowed to her better judgment, thank goodness. No matter how much I wanted to know Quin's secrets, I didn't want to use hypnosis on him.

George seemed to have given up his interrogation. He concentrated on stirring his soup in thoughtful silence.

"My apologies, Mr. St. Clair," Adelaide said. "My husband is terribly curious about the supernatural. By not answering his questions, you only increase his curiosity. He's very clever and does love a challenge."

George seemed to swell beneath his wife's fond gaze. He was still as much in awe of her as he ever had been. I had to admit they were an odd pairing. He was studious while she was the beauty, but both were shy in their own way. I supposed it was that characteristic which connected them.

"Then let's engage his curiosity in another way," I said. "George, can you look through your library for any references to a book of spells?"

"It would be my pleasure."

"We wrote a copy of the torn out page and brought that," Sylvia said. She beckoned Tommy and he pulled a piece of paper from his pocket and handed it to her. She gave it to George and he inspected the spells. "Don't speak them aloud. One opens the portal."

"The spell will not work from here," Quin assured her.

"I'll see what I can find," George said, handing it back.

"Keep it," Tommy said. "We made that copy for you." The original was hidden away in Sylvia's luggage. We'd brought it with us in case it was needed for comparison.

George tucked the copy into the inside pocket of his jacket. "Excellent. I needed a new project. Things have been far too quiet around here."

"Thank goodness," Adelaide muttered.

"George is a scholar of demonology," Emily told Quin. "He reads accounts about them in his books. He has a lot of books. Some of them are very old, written by early scholars. What is that phrase? 'If I have seen farther it is by standing on the shoulders of giants.'"

Quin blinked rapidly at her. "You know Bernard of Chartres' work?"

"Oh? Is that *his* expression?" Emily asked innocently. Too innocently. She was up to something. Jacob knew it too. He was smirking. "I thought it belonged to Isaac Newton."

"Newton is quoting Bernard of Chartres, the philosopher," George said, oblivious to Emily's manipulations. "Newton's version has become more widely known."

"Yes, of course." Emily smiled at Quin. He stared back at her as if she'd grown two heads.

"I am not the only educated female in this family," I told him.

His surprised expression turned to a scowl. "So I see."

"And her husband doesn't object, do you, Jacob?"

Jacob shook his head, still smirking. "If you wish to get along in our time, St. Clair, you will have to get used to clever women. Otherwise you run the risk of becoming their victim."

Emily rolled her eyes. "I am not nearly as clever as Cara. She would go to university if they allowed women."

"She can attend lectures," George said.

"The University College here in London would admit her," Samuel added. "There were several female scholars when I studied there. It's quite a progressive institution."

"All this talk of philosophy and education has made me hungry," Sylvia chimed in. "Tommy, is it time for the next course?"

As we ate the roasted meats, vegetables and lobster salad,

the discussion switched to Myer. "I'm afraid we need to visit him," I announced. "As much as we don't wish to, he's just too knowledgeable to ignore."

"He did leave Frakingham on a sour note," Charity said. "Is it absolutely necessary to involve him now?"

Langley had banned Myer from visiting the estate and ruins again after it was discovered he had lied about knowing how his former colleagues, Garrett and Owens, died. His single-minded pursuit of the book of spells had led him to become unpredictable and deceitful. He simply couldn't be trusted at the site or with the page in our possession. He was not even aware that we had it.

"I'm afraid so," I told her. "The Society for Supernatural Activity's library must be even more extensive than George's."

"It is," he said with a note of envy. "I've seen it, though not recently. Not while this Myer has been the master of the society. Do you plan on telling him what you're looking for?"

"I don't see that we have a choice."

"You can't tell him." Samuel looked appalled, Charity too. "He cannot be trusted. Sylvia, have you told Cara what we know about Myer's connection to Percy Harrington's ghost?"

"Who is Percy Harrington?" I asked.

"The master," Sylvia said. She did not look at Charity when she said it, but Charity flinched as if she had.

Samuel covered his fiancée's hand with his own. She gave him a small smile of reassurance. I felt a little nauseous, as I did every time I thought about the master and what he'd done to her. Charity had been kept prisoner by the master when he was alive, and pursued by his spirit after his death. It was uplifting to see her so happy now, with Samuel, in true defiance of her traumatic past. Her strength of character never ceased to amaze me.

"We haven't had a chance to tell you, Cara," Sylvia said.

"While you were ill at Frakingham, Emily wrote to tell us she'd learned the master's name from the spirit himself."

"Harrington," I said, frowning. "The name sounds familiar."

"Percy Harrington inherited his father's entire fortune, one half of Hatfield and Harrington."

"The bank?"

Samuel nodded and took up the story. "Percy Harrington died without children, so his fortune went to his father's business partner's only child. It was an agreement struck up between the original Hatfield and Harrington years ago, apparently. Her name was Edith Hatfield, now Edith Myer, Everett Myer's wife."

"Good lord." George was so riveted to the tale that he forgot to push his glasses back up his nose. They perched on the end, dangerously close to slipping off. "The Myers must be extraordinarily rich if she was the sole beneficiary of both fortunes."

"They are. Myer continues to have the largest share of the bank too, giving him a lot of control."

"Harrington's spirit told you this, Emily?" George asked.

She nodded. "He haunted his place of death until his spirit was summoned into the body of another gentleman, a banker for a rival company, Clement and Co."

Adelaide shuddered. "Possession," she murmured, setting down her knife and fork as if she'd lost her appetite.

"While possessing the body of Mr. Clement, he made some poor business decisions which has put Clement and Co. on the brink of financial ruin. He also did other despicable things while possessing Clement's body," Samuel added without going into detail.

"How did Harrington's spirit take over Clement?" George looked to me then Emily. "That requires a medium's help, and you two are the only ones in the city."

"The only ones we know about," Jacob said. "There must be another."

Adelaide gasped. "You must find her and warn her of the dangers of possession!"

"I asked Percy Harrington's spirit who it was, but he wouldn't tell me," Emily said. "She did eventually convince him that it was time to cross-over, so we have that to be thankful for. He wouldn't listen to me. He finally left this realm just over a week ago."

"So you see," Samuel said, "Myer seems to be involved at every turn. I think it suspicious that his wife's fortune—and therefore his own—was increased after the death of a man whose spirit went on to possess a rival. He cannot be trusted."

"Harrington's ghost didn't say anything about Myer?" I asked Emily.

She shook her head.

"It could be a coincidence," Adelaide said, though from her tone I could tell that she didn't quite believe it.

"Myer is certainly an odd fellow," Jacob said.

"And surprisingly not very well known," Samuel told us. "He has acquaintances, not friends, and nobody remembers his family. The gentlemen at his club claim that Myer is an excellent fellow, charming and witty, but he knows nothing about financial matters."

"Clearly he's not the brains behind Hatfield and Harrington," Jacob said. "His position as major shareholder is not hands-on."

"I actually learned more about Edith Myer than her husband," Samuel went on.

"Such as?"

"I had luncheon with your parents yesterday, Beaufort. Lady Preston knew Edith Myer around the time of her coming out. She remembers Edith as being a terrible flirt, not particularly bright but a lot of fun. She was never a beauty, but gentlemen enjoyed her vivacious company."

"Vivacious!" I blinked at Samuel. "That doesn't sound like the woman I met that day at the Butterworths'." The Harborough mayor and his wife hosted the Myers when they came to the village. It had been the first time I'd met them and I'd not been particularly enamored of either. Mrs. Myer was a sour woman with no respect for her husband and he had hypnotized her right in front of us. It had been one of the most awkward encounters I'd ever experienced.

"It would seem marriage has changed her," Charity said.

Nobody said as much, but it was clear that we were all thinking the same thing—marriage to a man like Myer, who had no qualms about hypnotizing his wife, would dampen even the most lively spirit.

We ate the rest of our meal amid quiet chatter. Only Quin didn't join in. He'd been silent for some time and even appeared to be off his food, until the pudding arrived in glass bowls. His eyes widened at the sight of the accompanying dishes of jellies, sweet cakes and chocolates. They closed in ecstasy as he tasted each one. I couldn't help smiling when he came to the chocolates shaped as strawberries. I wondered if I had that enraptured look on my face when I ate them.

Once the meal was complete, Emily rose and we followed her lead. "We'll all adjourn to the drawing room, since Cara and Quin cannot be separated. The gentlemen will have to go without cigars this evening."

"Fine by me," Samuel said. "The company of females is always more enlightening anyway."

"It sounds like a pleasant way to see out the evening," George added. "And a most interesting evening it has been thus far."

"Indeed." Emily frowned, thoughtful. "What is that line by

Danté? 'Remember tonight…' How does it end? Quin, do you know?"

Quin's gaze narrowed. "I do not."

"'Remember tonight…for it is the beginning of always,'" George said.

"A fitting quote," Charity said. When everyone turned to her, she merely smiled shyly at me. "I suspect so, anyway, since this evening the search for the book begins in earnest."

I smiled back, but I wasn't really listening to her. My mind was on what Emily had just achieved. An educated man from Tudor times would have known the Danté Alighieri quote. He had lived in the late thirteenth century, while the earlier quote from Bernard of Chartres that Quin had known was from at least a century earlier, if memory served. That meant Quin had been alive after Bernard and before Danté.

We filed out of the dining room, but I lingered until Quin was just out of earshot. I pulled Emily aside. "I didn't know you knew so much about medieval philosophers and poets," I whispered.

"I don't," she whispered back. "I quickly studied some before we came down to dinner. Jacob's library has a book that lists well-known quotes from medieval texts. It came in very handy. We now know your Quin St. Clair was alive in this realm between the early twelfth century and the late thirteenth."

My heart sank. "That's almost a two hundred year span."

She shrugged. "It was the best I could do. It explains his accent, though. The upper classes spoke mostly French, with some Middle English in the early middle ages."

My gaze connected with Quin's. He waited by the door to the formal drawing room, Jacob beside him, the others having gone in. If he knew we were discussing him, he showed no sign. "Thank you, Em. At least I'm a little closer to knowing something about him."

She caught my arm. Where before her eyes sparkled with mischief, they were now clouded with concern. "Don't make the mistake of getting to know him too well, Cara. He doesn't belong here and you do."

"I know that," I snipped back. "And it's a little early in our acquaintance to fear that I'll develop feelings for him."

"I'm not so sure about that." Her gaze drifted to Jacob. "It's been known to happen suddenly."

"Not to me."

* * *

WHENEVER SYLVIA HAD MORE than two glasses of wine, her sleep became restless. She kicked me beneath the covers and her breathing alternated between resembling a trumpeter's fanfare and stopping altogether. I didn't known what was worse, the noise or waiting for it.

With a sigh, I finally climbed off the bed and rounded the screen. "Are you awake?" I whispered to Quin.

He sat up and I could just make out his bare chest in the poor light. Since visibility was so low, it didn't matter that he was semi-naked or that I wore only a nightgown. But just to be safe, I wouldn't tell anyone.

"How can I not be?" he whispered back. "The train was quieter."

I smiled and sat on the end of the truckle near his covered feet. Tommy lay fast asleep on the other low bed next to Quin's. "It's been quite a lot for you to take in today," I said. "Your first train journey, first time in Victorian London, and meeting some of my family. I am sorry for Jacob's hostility toward you. It's not personal."

"He thinks I am a danger to you."

"Not a danger, exactly. More like a bad influence."

He *humphed* under his breath. "He doesn't know you well,

74

then. I've been with you mere days and I understand that you're not easily influenced."

"Am I that obstinate?"

His white teeth bared in a smile. "I would say determined and brave."

"Brave? How do you figure that?"

"Emily told me you traveled from Melbourne to London accompanied only by an old family friend who was also traveling the same route. She said you took care of your chaperone rather than the other way."

"Mrs. Dartmoor suffered terrible seasickness, poor thing."

"Not too many young ladies would thrive under such circumstances, but Emily claims you did. Nor would they attend lectures or write to the authorities about allowing women into universities."

"Emily shouldn't boast so much. Anyway, it wasn't the authorities, it was a newspaper, and it was only one letter. They did publish it, however."

"And you still wish to visit this Myer gentleman, despite the dangers he poses?"

I drew my knees up under my night dress and circled my arms around them. "It's unfortunate but necessary. We need the society's library and he is master of the society."

"At least I know those things about Myer now before we visit him."

"Does it matter?"

"It matters. I'm supposed to protect you. I need to know everything there is to know in order to perform my duty."

"You are here to keep the curse at bay."

"Aye, and protect you in every way I can too. While I'm here in this realm, we're bound, Cara. I must take care of you."

"I don't need anyone to take care of me." The automatic response was out of my mouth before I could stop it. Despite my conviction, a wash of tingles skittered up my spine at his words. "Thank you. I think." It was, after all, his duty to protect me. He wasn't doing it because he wanted to. It was important to remember that.

He drew up one leg under the covers and rested his arm on it while the other remained stretched flat. His foot touched my thigh. He did not move away and I liked to think it was because he wanted to strengthen the connection between us, but it was most likely because he hadn't realized.

"Will you reconsider visiting Myer?" he asked.

"No. Besides, I'll have you there to protect me."

"I cannot stop him hypnotizing you if he hypnotizes me first."

"Samuel can. He's promised to accompany us."

"There is no swaying your mind, is there?" There was a smile in his voice if not on his lips.

I grinned. "No. I'm determined and brave, remember?"

"Obstinate." He laughed softly and lowered his leg. That foot too brushed against my thigh and came to settle beside his other one, touching me, albeit with the covers between us.

Still, I froze. Touching in such an intimate place was indecent and Jacob would throttle him if he knew, but I found the gesture thrilling. My nerves would not stop pulsing in anticipation of what might happen next.

His feet suddenly shifted, breaking the contact. "Go back to bed," he whispered. "We shouldn't talk when others aren't present." He slammed down onto his back and rolled to his side, leaving one big brawny shoulder exposed above the bedcovers.

I sighed and turned away from the enticing sight. What had gotten into him? "Goodnight, Quin."

* * *

THE MYERS LIVED in a Mayfair townhouse situated in a coveted street overlooking Berkeley Square. If I thought Emily and Jacob were wealthy, the Myers were something else entirely. The drawing room in which we waited may have been spartanly furnished, but everything was of high quality, from the black marble mantel to the heavy chaise and wingback chairs. The thick pile of the large Aubusson rug meant it was new or the room rarely used. If Mrs. Myer was such a recluse, as everyone claimed, then it was likely she had very few visitors.

Samuel and I sat on the sofa while Quin stood by the unlit fireplace, his alert gaze on the doorway. One finger tapped the marble absently while the other remained behind his back. They were the only signs that he was a little on edge. He'd told us on the way over to Mayfair that he disliked having to rely on others for our safety; in this case, Samuel.

"I won't let him hypnotize her," Samuel assured Quin.

Quin hadn't responded, nor did he seem placated. I resisted the urge to settle my hand over his to reassure him as I'd seen Samuel do with Charity, and Emily with Jacob, when tensions ran high.

I was surprised to see the Myers enter the drawing room together, considering they were the least united couple I'd ever met. What surprised me even more was the sandy haired gentleman with slate gray eyes trailing behind them.

My gasp echoed around the large, empty room, and had everyone turning to me before we could even make the introductions.

"Nathaniel!" I cried. "Good lord, this is a coincidence. What are you doing here? And why did you ignore me at King's Cross yesterday?"

CHAPTER 6

"You didn't tell us you knew Miss Moreau," Myer said to Nathaniel.

"I wasn't aware *you* knew her." Nathaniel bowed smoothly, and when he straightened, his eyes danced over my face and figure. His smile broadened. "My humblest apologies, Miss Moreau. It's a pleasure to see you again. How long has it been now?"

"A matter of months," I said. "We came over on the S.S. Bombay together," I told the others. "Since neither of us suffered from seasickness, we often went out strolling the decks."

"The fresh sea air was very healthful."

My initial shock at finding him with the Myers was replaced by irritation at his snubbing of me at the station. "Why didn't you stop when you saw me at King's Cross yesterday?"

He frowned. "I didn't see you there."

"You must have. You looked directly at me."

"I'm so very sorry. You know me. I can be a little vague when my mind is on other things, as it was yesterday. Again,

I am deeply sorry and didn't mean to cause offence." He bowed again and when he rose, his gray eyes were more silver than slate. He took my hand and pressed it between his own. "I hope you can forgive my poor manners. I shall have to make it up to you."

I couldn't help smiling at his effusive apology. "You're forgiven."

Quin stepped forward and glared at Nathaniel until he let go of my hand.

"It's good to see you again, Mr. Gladstone," Myer said to Samuel. "And who is your new friend?"

"Quintin St. Clair," Samuel said. "A friend of Cara's from Melbourne."

"From the other side of the world! I thought the colonies were hot places, yet you don't seem perturbed by our cooler climate, Mr. St. Clair." He indicated Quin's shirt with a flip of his hand.

"My luggage was lost on the voyage," Quin said, using the story we'd laid out on the journey to Mayfair.

"He has to make do until his new suit arrives," I said.

Quin extended his hand and Myer shook it. "I'm pleased to meet you, Mr. Myer. Cara has told me much about you." He said it exactly as we'd coached him, yet I could still detect a hint of distrust in his tone.

Myer, apparently, did not. He puffed out his chest and gave his wife a triumphant smile. "Has she now? I assure you, only the good bits are true." He laughed and rocked back on his heels.

"Good lord," Edith Myer muttered with a roll of her eyes. "If you're going to stay then you might as well sit. Adamson, bring refreshments," she ordered the butler.

"We won't stay long," I assured her. Indeed, I had hoped not to see her at all. She might look innocuous, with her drab clothing and severe hairstyle that only widened already broad features, but she made me anxious nevertheless. Where Myer had all the power with his hypnosis, her tongue was dipped in vitriol and she wasn't afraid to wield it. Fortunately, she reserved her verbal lashings for her husband and had never directed her harsh words at anyone else. "We've come to ask permission to look through the society's library," I said. "Mr. St. Clair has an interest in the paranormal and has heard of the society. When I told him we were acquainted with its grand master, he became keen to meet you."

Myer threw his arms wide as he sat. He was as tall as his wife, but half her girth, with a face that would have looked too thin if it weren't for the abundance of sideburns. "Well, here I am in the flesh. Ask me anything you want, Mr. St. Clair. It's always a pleasure to meet a fellow scholar of the paranormal. Don't you agree, Faraday?"

"Of course, but, forgive me, you don't look like a scholar," Nathaniel said to Quin.

Quin merely shrugged.

"What do scholars look like?" I joked. "Me?"

He laughed. "Very amusing. No, I was thinking Mr. St. Clair looked like a prize fighter."

It was a little too close to the truth for my liking, so I changed the subject. "You have an interest in the paranormal, Nathaniel? I thought you were a historian."

"I am, but I have a confession to make. I'm actually a paranormal historian. I must apologize for not telling you, Miss Moreau."

"Call me Cara, like you did on board the Bombay."

He smiled again, baring all of his perfect white teeth. He really was very handsome, especially when he employed the full force of his charms. "Some people aren't so understanding about the supernatural, so I tend not to mention it until I know a person very well."

I suppose that was fair, since I hadn't told him I was a medium. "I completely understand."

"You do?" He looked relieved. "I was hoping I hadn't offended you again. I seem to be making a habit of it."

"Miss Moreau is a spirit medium," Myer said before I could recover enough from Nathaniel's earnest smile to inform him myself.

Nathaniel's eyebrows almost shot off his forehead. "You are? How intriguing. I've never met one before. How is it that you became one?"

"Perhaps you can discuss it another time," Samuel cut in. "Mr. St. Clair is keen to see the library."

"Aye," Quin said darkly. "I found some paranormal anomalies in Melbourne and wish to investigate what they mean while I'm in London."

"Really?" Myer leaned forward. "How interesting. Didn't you spend time in Melbourne, Faraday? Did you see anything unusual there too?"

My stomach plunged. If Nathaniel questioned Quin in detail about the city, we'd be in trouble.

"No," Nathaniel said.

I blew out a breath. Beside me, Samuel seemed to relax too.

"Can you describe these anomalies, Mr. St. Clair?" Myer asked.

"Merely a shift in the pattern of the air at a particular spot," Quin said. "It was cooler when it should have been warmer. That sort of thing."

"It sounds like the portal at the ruins. Don't you think, Gladstone, Miss Moreau?"

Samuel and I both nodded. Clearly Quin was describing what he felt at Frakingham Abbey.

"I will be eager for you to learn more, Mr. St Clair. I hope the society's books can tell you something."

"Such as how to close the portal once and for all," Mrs. Myer added.

"No!" Myer exploded. His face turned red and the veins above his collar popped out in thick blue ridges. "That would be foolishness indeed!"

She sniffed. "The portal at Frakingham seems to have caused problems—"

"It requires careful management, that's all." To the rest of us, he said, "If you learn how to close or destroy the portals, I beg you not to do so. It would be catastrophic for the surrounding area. In the case of Frakingham, it might destroy the house itself. You will find that information in one of the books in the library. It was one of the few things I could find out about portals."

"We won't attempt anything like that," I assured him. Aside from potentially destroying the Langleys' home, it would also stop Quin from coming and going between realms. It was necessary to allow him access; if not to fight demons then at least to keep him connected to the human world. To be completely cut off would be unimaginable.

Quin did not respond to Myer's plea. He sat as rigid as a pole in his chair, his expression unreadable.

"Forgive me." Myer turned to Samuel with an apologetic shrug. "I understand why Mr. St. Clair and Miss Moreau are here—she is his friend, after all—but why are *you* here, Gladstone?"

Samuel gave him a flat smile. "Insurance."

It took a moment for that to register with Myer, and when it finally did, he colored. "Oh. There is no need. You can trust me."

Nobody agreed or disagreed with him, not even his wife. She merely watched him through narrowed eyes. I felt a rush of sympathy for her. It mustn't be an easy life living with a man she not only disliked, but who hypnotized her into doing what he wanted.

"The society's library..." I began in an effort to swing the conversation back to less awkward matters. "When can we view it?"

"You'll be joining Mr. St. Clair?" Myer asked.

"Yes."

"How fortunate that he has such an agreeable companion. It will make the endless hours of research go much faster."

"My husband doesn't particularly like research," Mrs. Myer said as Adamson returned with a tray laden with tea things. "It's why he employed Mr. Faraday to do it for him. What a happy coincidence. The three of you can visit the society's library together."

"I don't mind research," Myer said before his wife had completely finished speaking. "But I seem to have come to a dead end. I'm hoping someone with more expertise will turn up something new."

"What are you looking for?" I asked.

"Details about the book of spells, of course, and where to find it."

"You no longer think it's located at the abbey ruins?"

"I don't know, since I no longer have access," he said pointedly. "Unless Langley sees fit to reverse his position and allow me access in exchange for allowing Mr. St Clair to look through the society's books."

"Mr. Langley doesn't care if Quin does or does not view your library," I said. "I am sorry," I felt compelled to add. We did need his permission to view the society's books, after all. It paid to remain polite.

Myer gave me another one of his non-committal smiles, while his wife's was more genuine, if somewhat triumphant. She seemed pleased that her husband's on-site research had been thwarted.

"Can we see the library today?" I asked.

Myer eyed Quin's shirt. "Perhaps tomorrow, when Mr. St. Clair is more suitably attired. The library is often frequented by gentlemen from the society who would be less understanding about his missing luggage than I."

"They are politicians, bankers and barristers," Mrs. Myer said. "Powerful and important men who set certain standards, for good or ill."

I huffed out an exasperated sigh. I wanted to get started immediately. Hopefully Quin's suit would arrive later today. "Tomorrow, then."

Myer nodded. "Meet me in St Michael's Alley, off Cornhill."

We had not finished our tea, but it seemed an appropriate time to leave and I wasn't keen to stay longer than necessary. I thanked our hosts and rose. Quin did too, but Samuel did not. I got a bad feeling about what was to come next.

"There's something that's been troubling me," he said lightly, as if he were simply chatting to an old friend. I knew otherwise, however, and I suspected Myer did too by the anxious look on his face.

"What is that, Gladstone?" he asked.

"You remember the spirit of the master?"

"How could I forget? I helped you capture him. Or the body of Clement, I should say. Poor fellow. I hear he's trying to recover the ground his company lost in the time he was taken over by the master's spirit. What of him?"

"He has finally crossed over, but before he did so, he told Mrs. Beaufort some interesting facts about himself."

"Such as?"

"Such as his name. Percy Harrington."

Myer gasped and swung round to his wife. "Did you hear that? Harrington!"

"I have ears," she retorted. "Poor Percy." She cocked her

head to the side. "Do you mean to say *he* was the master who tormented—?"

"Yes," Samuel said, cutting her off before she could mention Charity by name. "While everyone is relieved that he's finally gone, the mystery remains. Who was the medium who helped him possess Clement?"

Myer shrugged. "Miss Moreau and Mrs. Beaufort are the only mediums I know of. If I learn of others, I will be sure to inform you. Now, if you don't mind, Faraday and I have work to do."

He stood, but Samuel did not. "Don't you think it odd that Harrington was associated with you, Myer?"

"An unhappy coincidence. I actually have very little to do with the bank. Harrington was an acquaintance only. I hardly cared whether he lived or died, frankly."

"Except that your wife inherited his fortune."

"Well *that* is a happy coincidence." He laughed.

Mrs. Myer shook her head in disgust at her husband's disregard for a life, albeit the life of a horrid man.

Samuel stepped up to him and grabbed Myer's waistcoat at his chest. He twisted it in his fist, lifting Myer onto his toes. "If I find out that you knew about Harrington's games, before or after his death, I'll gut you."

"I say!" Nathaniel cried. "That is uncalled for."

Samuel turned his head slowly and pinned Nathaniel with a glare so cold that *I* shivered.

"We should go," I said gently.

Quin rested a hand on Samuel's shoulder. Samuel let Myer go and stalked out the door. I hurried after him, tossing my thanks to the Myers as we left. Quin followed us both out and down the front steps.

"My apologies," Samuel said. He stopped at the waiting coach, his breaths coming hard and fast. The Beauforts' footman stood beside the open door, his gaze suitably vacant. "I shouldn't have let my anger get the better of me like that."

I took his hand. "It's all right. I understand your frustration and it was deserved."

"Do you think he spoke the truth about not knowing Harrington all that well?"

"It's possible," I said. "I do believe he spoke truthfully when he claimed not to care about banking matters. He does seem more interested in the paranormal than the company."

"I'm not sure it was always that way."

"Oh?"

He glanced past Quin at the sleek black door of the Myers' home. "Lady Preston told me that Myer had pursued Edith relentlessly, because of her fortune. He might not want to get involved in the running of the bank but he does want the comforts its wealth provides. I believe he was somehow involved with Harrington but I don't know how to prove it."

Neither did I. I glanced at Quin to see if he had any suggestions, but he was too busy observing everything around him. He watched the people opposite, strolling through Berkeley Square, then glanced up and down the street itself, taking in each of the buildings. I got the feeling he would like to experience the city rather than watch it pass by through the window of a coach.

"Shall we walk home, Quin? It's not far."

"Aye. It's a fine day."

"I'll go on without you," Samuel said. "I'm meeting Charity for luncheon to discuss wedding plans."

I kissed his cheek. "It *is* all over, Samuel," I said gently. "The master is gone and Charity is happy. That's all that matters."

He drew in a deep breath and let it out slowly. "I know. You're right. I have to let it go or she'll never be at peace."

I was glad that he realized it.

Quin and I walked off, side by side, as the coach drove away with Samuel. "You performed admirably in there," I told him. "Nobody would have known that you were not from this time."

"If Faraday had asked me questions about Melbourne, we could have encountered problems."

"Thankfully he didn't. Let's hope he continues to be disinterested when we see him again tomorrow. It seems we're stuck with his company in the library." I wasn't sure how I felt about that. On the one hand, I looked forward to getting to know Nathaniel again, but on the other, we didn't want anyone connected with Myer to learn of our true plan.

"He will not trouble us for long."

I frowned up at him. "What do you mean?"

He didn't respond. He was too busy watching the gentleman and lady strolling toward us. Behind them was another couple; he also studied them intently. Once they passed, he thrust his elbow toward me.

"Take it," he said when I simply blinked. "It's customary for the ladies to hold onto the gentleman's arm in this time."

I didn't tell him that those couples must be well known to one another. They were not unwed acquaintances of marriageable age, like us. If Emily could see us, she'd warn me against being so familiar. My sister-in-law, Celia, however, would lecture me for an entire week on the proper behavior for young females. Thank goodness she was on the other side of the world.

We turned the corner and strolled past more of Mayfair's finest residences. Quin studied each of them with wonder. "The buildings here are magnificent. I've seen castle towers stretch that high, but not entire rows of houses."

"You'd be surprised at what else has changed since your last visit."

"Aside from the introduction of forks, privies and trains?"

I grinned. "Let's see. We have the postal service to deliver letters and typewriters to type them on. There are sewing machines and ovens, safety matches, and steamships. I came over from Melbourne on one." I pointed to the lamp atop the nearest post. "Some of our streetlamps use electricity instead of gas."

"We didn't have gas in my time. We didn't have lamps in streets."

"You tasted chocolate last night, but there's another confection called ice cream which you might like."

"You eat ice?"

"It tastes better than ice. There's a confectioner on Piccadilly who sells delicious flavors. I'll buy you one."

"I don't want you to buy me anything."

"Put away your masculine pride and let me buy you an ice cream. I insist."

He said nothing, but I gathered from his stiff jaw that he didn't like the idea of a woman holding the purse strings. I led him into the confectioner's on Piccadilly and he didn't object when I bought him a bowl of ice cream.

"I will find a way to repay you," he said, accepting the glass bowl and spoon.

I watched as he enjoyed his first lick of the confection, piled high in the bowl. His eyes widened and he nodded his approval. The ice cream didn't last long after that.

"Your time is interesting, Cara," he said after we handed the bowls and spoons back and left the shop. Piccadilly was a busy street in the middle of a sunny day, and I wondered if it had even existed in his time. It would have looked quite different if it had.

"I'm sure yours would be interesting to me if I went there."

He shook his head. "I wouldn't like you to visit, even if it were possible. No lady who gets about in coaches and is allowed her own money would survive long. Besides, there's neither ice cream nor chocolate."

"Completely barbaric," I joked.

He didn't laugh. "Aye, it is."

I quickly changed the subject and played tourist guide, pointing out anything I thought might be interesting. He listened intently and asked several questions. Once or twice he wanted to stop or detour, and he seemed particularly interested in the pastime of strolling through Hyde Park. We didn't go into the park itself, but looked in from Hyde Park Corner.

"You mean they aren't going anywhere?" he said, watching the strolling couples.

"They're walking for the sake of walking."

He pointed at a gentleman riding his horse through the arch into the park. "Is he going in there to ride?"

"Yes."

"Not hunt?"

"No. It would be far too dangerous to hunt with so many people around."

"Aye, but…what is the point?"

"To be seen, of course."

He shook his head. "Your time is interesting, but sometimes odd."

"Wait until you see someone riding a bicycle."

We wound our way through the quieter streets of Belgravia, away from the park. I was about to cross the road, but Quin held me back.

"We'll continue on this side," he said.

"Why?"

He shook his head, avoiding answering again. But the reason had just come to me. A narrow church nestled opposite. It was the one Emily and her family attended on Sundays, and I with them when in London.

"You can't possibly recognize it," I said. "It's not from your time."

"I don't." He seemed to know what I was referring to, even though I'd not mentioned the church as we walked hurriedly past on the other side.

I tightened my grip on his arm. "Enough, Quin. You have to explain what it is about churches that bothers you."

"They do not bother me."

"Then why do you recoil from them? You wouldn't even walk on the same side of the street as that one. I'm not asking you to go in."

My question was greeted with stony silence.

He'd told me he was human and not an angel, so he wasn't a heavenly creature, or from hell either for that matter. So why avoid places of worship? "Will something happen to you if you enter a church? Something…unpleasant?"

He jerked his arm free of mine and rounded on me. His nostrils flared, his eyes flashed like hard jewels, and his features twisted in anger. I shrank away. He'd claimed he was there to protect me, but at that moment, fear crept like ice through my veins.

"Stop it!" he growled. "No more questions, wench." He walked off, his long strides quickly leaving me behind. I gathered up my skirts and raced after him, but my heeled shoes weren't made for running and the pavement was uneven. I tripped and fell, landing on my knees.

I looked up, only to see Quin hadn't noticed. He was still walking in the other direction. I felt the first tug of tiredness and the chill of fever when he was ten feet or so away. I shivered and battled to remain alert, focused, but darkness crowded close. I was going to faint.

Quin kept on walking. Surely he wouldn't abandon his promise to protect me, all because I dared question him?

But from the look of his rigid shoulders and long strides, that was exactly what he would do.

CHAPTER 7

"Quin!" It came out as a pathetic rasp, but he must have heard.

He glanced over his shoulder then sprinted back to my side. The fever subsided as quickly as it had taken hold. He cursed in French then helped me sit up. I swayed into him. He cradled me and I rested my cheek against his chest. His heart thumped out a strong, rapid rhythm.

To my horror, a tear escaped and slid down my cheek. It was foolish. He had returned again and I was well. But the flood of fear I'd felt at his outburst and then as I watched him walk away left me shaken and unsure.

"I wasn't leaving you, Cara," he murmured into my hair, as if he sensed my fear.

I swiped angrily at the tear. "I didn't know that."

His lips touched my forehead where a dull ache lingered. I closed my eyes and drew in a deep, calming breath. It felt good to be kissed like that, even if it were merely a chaste, apologetic one. Very good. Indeed, no man who was not my relation had ever kissed me, or held me, or touched me in the way Quin did. Yet I was still very aware that only moments before he'd been so angry with me that he'd forgotten his purpose for being here.

"I'm sorry I angered you," I said, my voice a little more wobbly than I would have liked.

"It was as much my fault. I'm afraid I'm still growing used to your modern sensibilities."

"You mean you're not used to having wenches constantly question you?"

He pulled away from me and I felt the loss of his solidness keenly. "I hope you can forgive me. But, please, do not ask any more questions. There are some things you're better off not knowing."

I swallowed and tried to catch his gaze with my own, but he looked away. "Come," he said, voice rumbling in his chest. "I'll take you home."

He helped me to stand even though I had fully recovered and didn't need assistance. He tucked my hand into the crook of his arm again and we walked off like an old married couple. We received some stares from passersby who'd perhaps witnessed my tumble—or were scandalized by Quin not wearing a full suit—but none spoke to us.

I didn't tell Sylvia, Emily and Jacob about the incident. They were too curious about our visit to the Myers' home. We relayed the conversation, including Myer's denial that he was in any way involved in Harrington's possession of Clement.

"We're going to the library tomorrow," I said. "Now that Quin's suit has arrived, we won't be stared at." The clothes had been delivered while we were out, but Quin had yet to change.

"I expect Myer will watch over you while you research," Jacob said.

"He claims that research bores him. His historian will be there, however."

"Who?"

"A paranormal historian by the name of Nathaniel Faraday."

Emily frowned. "That names sounds familiar."

Sylvia gave a little gasp, but at my warning glare, she shut her mouth.

Emily didn't notice. Her eyes lit up and she smiled at me.

"Yes, it's the same one," I said before she asked.

Jacob's gaze flicked between us. "Who is this Faraday?"

"I met him on the journey back to England. I didn't realize he was a *paranormal* historian. I thought he was just a regular one."

"Did you ask him why he never wrote after promising to?" Emily asked.

"He promised to write?" Jacob sat up straighter.

"He did," Emily told him. "But nothing came of it. A pity. You made him sound quite dashing, Cara. I would have liked to meet him and learn his connections."

"Just how friendly did you become?"

"We were merely acquaintances," I snapped at him. "Since nothing came of it, I don't know why we're having this discussion."

"Because you might be seeing more of him and Louis has trusted you to my care while you're in England."

Quin, standing by the large mantel in the cozy sitting room, crossed his arms. "I didn't like Faraday."

"You hardly know him!" I cried.

"He was too familiar with you. I didn't like the way he held your hand in both of his. It was unnecessary, and the length of time he held it was inappropriate."

"It was not."

Jacob, standing on the other side of the mantel in an

almost identical pose to Quin, pressed his lips together. "Is that so?"

"This is ridiculous." I stood and beckoned for Sylvia to join me. "I'm going upstairs." My knees still stung from falling over and I wanted to inspect them. Since I wasn't allowed in my bedroom alone with Quin, Sylvia needed to be present.

We met Tommy emerging from the hidden servants' doorway on the second floor landing, carrying a newly pressed shirt. "You're back," he said. "How did you fair with Myer?"

"Come with us and we'll tell you." We couldn't discuss our business out in the open where the servants could come across us. This house wasn't as private as Frakingham, with its large, empty rooms and handful of servants. "Is that for Quin?"

He held up the shirt. "Irwin sent it along with the rest of the suit. It's in his room. I'll bring it to you, sir, and help you dress if you like."

"I can dress myself," Quin said.

"Do you know how to tie a tie?"

"It doesn't look difficult."

Tommy gave him a smug smile then went to fetch the suit from the guest bedroom that had been assigned to Quin while we three headed to mine. We checked up and down the hallway before slipping inside.

I sank down on the bed with a sigh and began to lift my skirts. Quin frowned. "Are you injured?"

"My knees sting a little."

"Cara!" Sylvia snatched my skirts out of my hand and pulled the hem down to my ankles. "What do you think you're doing?"

I sighed. "Turn around please, Quin, or Sylvia will faint."

He ignored my request and crouched before me. "Show me."

"It's just some minor grazes."

He gently lifted my skirts, making Sylvia gasp with horror and me hold my breath.

"You ought not to do this," she warned him. "It's indecent."

"He's not doing me any harm," I told her. Although my heart was in great danger of punching a hole through my chest, it beat so hard.

"But he can see your ankles and legs!"

"I'm sure he's seen ankles and legs before."

She gave a little whimper but thankfully stopped protesting when she realized it would do no good. Quin's knuckles grazed the side of my calf as he pushed the skirt and petticoats to my knees. He muttered something under his breath at the sight of the bloody grazes.

"Your stockings are ruined," Sylvia said matter of factly. "What happened?"

"I tripped."

"And you didn't catch her, Quin?"

He shifted his weight and cupped my calves with his big hands. My nerves jumped and my heart leapt into my throat. I didn't dare look at Sylvia. She must be on the verge of apoplexy.

"Take these off," he said, gently, plucking my stockings.

"Only if you turn your back." Sylvia's best governess voice had him dutifully obeying just as a knock sounded.

"It's me," came Tommy's voice.

Quin opened the door and let him in. Tommy took one look at me with my skirts bunched up above my knees and blushed. He quickly turned to Quin and shoved the suit at him.

"Behind the screen," he ordered the bigger man.

Quin did as he was told.

"Tommy, fetch a bowl of water and a cloth, please," Sylvia said, inspecting the grazes. "They don't appear too bad. A little cleaning up will do the trick."

I removed my boots and stockings while we waited for Tommy to return. A rustling of fabric came from behind the screen and a shirt was tossed over the top. A grunt of frustration soon followed.

"Are you having difficulty?" I asked Quin.

"This jerkin is not comfortable."

"It's a waistcoat."

"Just wait until he puts on the jacket and tie," Sylvia muttered. "He's going to hate it."

I grinned. "Thank you for not telling Emily and Jacob that I saw Nathaniel at the station. They would only have asked questions I don't have answers to."

"Why do you think he snubbed you if you were such good friends? Did he explain himself today?"

"He said he was too intent on his thoughts and didn't see me."

"Do you believe him?"

I sighed. "I don't know. I want to."

A smile slowly spread over her face. "You like him, don't you?"

"I don't know," I said in all seriousness. "I thought I did on the ship, but after seeing him again today..." I shrugged, unable to express what I felt anymore. I was still a little bruised that he hadn't noticed me at the station, but it was more than that and I couldn't put my finger on the reasons for my doubts.

"Damnation," growled Quin from behind the screen. "Why does a society that invents machines to make some things simpler have such a complicated piece of clothing to make dressing more difficult?" A balled up tie shot out from behind the screen and smacked into the side of the dressing table.

I pressed my lips together to stop myself laughing.

"Would you like help?" Sylvia asked.

"Aye," he muttered, sounding utterly defeated.

"Then wait for Tommy."

"Come here, Quin," I said. "I'll help you."

"You will not!" Sylvia thrust her hands onto her hips. "You aren't wearing any stockings!"

"He can't see my legs once I'm standing." I stood to prove my point.

"Your toes are visible."

I ignored her and picked up Quin's tie. He emerged from behind the screen wearing the new suit minus the jacket. "You look very dashing," I told him. He did, although I preferred him in his leather pants and just the shirt. Or, even better, without it.

"I give up," Sylvia muttered, plopping down on the bed. "Clearly living in the colonies is not a place to raise young ladies."

I ignored her slight against my home and slipped the tie around Quin's neck. "I used to help my little nephew dress for church on Sundays." I concentrated on my task and not on the fact that my fingers were brushing Quin's throat. "He hated wearing them too."

He lifted his chin to give me better access. "It's barbaric to force children to wear something that resembles a noose."

I grinned. "I feel as if I must apologize on behalf of all modern society. You will get used to it."

"Never."

"There," I said, tucking the tie behind his waistcoat and straightening it. I placed my palm flat against his chest. His heart beat steadily through the layers of clothing. "You look very handsome."

He looked down at me through half-closed, smoky eyes. "Thank you, Cara."

Tommy re-entered without knocking, took one look at me and gasped. "Cara!"

"I tried to stop her," Sylvia said, throwing up her hands in surrender. "But she insisted. She's very willful."

I retrieved the bowl of water and cloth from Tommy and sat on the bed again. Both men turned their backs to give us privacy and I lifted my skirts. Sylvia cleaned my knees a little too roughly. When she pressed hard against the bruise that had formed on my left one, I sucked air between my teeth.

"It serves you right," she said with a tilt of her chin.

I wasn't sure what that meant and didn't ask. I suspected she would only bring up my immorality again.

"Tell me about your meeting with the Myers," Tommy said.

Once again I went through the events of the morning.

"Is Myer going to join you in the library?" he asked when we finished.

"He says not."

"Good. That saves Gladstone from having to join you. He and Charity need some peace and quiet after everything they've been through."

"They do," Sylvia agreed quietly. She finished cleaning my knees and handed me a fresh pair of stockings.

"What do you know about Myer's hypnosis, St. Clair?" Tommy asked. "We know that Gladstone's mother was exposed to the portal's power when she was with child. Do you think the same thing happened to Myer's mother?"

"It's possible," Quin said. "I was summoned to that portal in a time when she may have been present."

"Wait," I said. "You've been summoned since Tudor times? I thought that was your last visit to this realm."

"That was the last time I battled many demons at once

at Frakingham Abbey. The last time I came through that portal was perhaps not too long ago. Time means little to me, but the clothing of the people who summoned me was somewhat similar to yours. She may have been there."

"Good lord." I pulled on my stockings, careful not to put holes in the delicate silk. "That explains the mystery of Myer's hypnosis then. At least we now know."

Tommy nodded. "I wonder if he does."

* * *

SYLVIA DIDN'T SNORE or kick me that night, but I still couldn't fall asleep. One of the men tossed and turned on the other side of the screen, rustling the covers. I got up and peeked around the corner. Quin lay on his back, his hands behind his head, the blankets crumpled around his waist. He sat up upon seeing me.

"You can't sleep?" I whispered.

"No."

"Why not?"

He shrugged and I was momentarily distracted by the movement of his shoulders. I wished there was more light to see him by. I rather liked the way his muscles moved beneath his skin.

"Come on, out with it," I said. "Something must be bothering you. Is it the tie?"

He smiled. "I despise the tie, but the thought of wearing it again doesn't keep me awake at night."

I smiled too and sat on the end of his bed. My hip nudged his feet, but he didn't pull away. His swallow and my hitched breath sounded loud in the silent room.

"What does keep you awake?" I didn't dare think what his answer would be. Didn't dare hope that it might be me.

Because what should we do about it? There was nothing *to* do.

"The connection between Myer and Harrington."

I blinked slowly, stupidly. "Pardon?"

"We only have Myer's word that he was not involved in Harrington's possession of Clement. I don't think his word can be trusted."

"Oh. Of course." I shook my head. I was such a fool for thinking he could possibly be in turmoil over my presence. "I don't think he can be trusted either, but there's nothing we can do about that. We can't just go through his things in search of a more tangible link."

"*You* can't."

My mouth flopped open. "You cannot be thinking about sneaking into his house?"

"Why not?"

"It's illegal, for one thing. You would be thrown in prison if you were caught."

"Prison would not be so bad. In my time, a thief would have his hand cut off, or his head."

I grimaced. "The upshot is the same. If you went to prison, we would be separated." And I would succumb to the fever and die.

He nodded slowly, his mouth turned down. "If it were not for that, I would attempt it."

"Why? You're here to find the book and cure me, not chase after ghosts that have crossed over."

"The medium who summoned Harrington's spirit into Clement's body must be stopped before she does it again. If Myer knows who that medium is, we must force him to tell us. I can have her punished."

"Or we could just talk to her and explain the danger. She may have done it quite innocently."

"As you did, some years ago?"

My face heated. Thankfully it was too dark for him to see. "You know about that?"

"Aye. After you became ill and I decided to cure you, I checked on your moral character. That was the only black mark against your name, and your youth and ignorance were noted."

Black mark? Noted? "Quin, where did you get this information from?"

He paused before answering, "My realm."

"And does every human have this sort of ledger against their name in your realm?"

"It's not for me to say."

Good lord. How extraordinary, and worrying too. I felt utterly exposed; worse, even, than if I'd been standing before him naked. "What else do you know about me?"

"That's all, Cara, I promise."

I hugged my drawn up knees and rested my chin on them. I wasn't sure I liked him knowing what I'd done when I was ten. I may have been young, but it was a mistake that had almost cost lives. I still felt cold when I thought about it.

He shifted down the bed and rested his hand on my arm. It was warm through my nightgown and reassuring. "I shouldn't have told you. My apologies."

"It's all right. I just wish I knew as much about you as you do about me."

He let me go and shifted back.

"You're a mystery, Quin. You can be so kind and good, and yet you suggest something like breaking into Myer's house."

"I told you, you should not trust me entirely," he said with a bitter twist in his voice. "I haven't always been of good character."

"I can't believe that. Not only are you here saving the life of someone you've never met before, but you want to learn more about an evil spirit and the medium who helped him when the matter has nothing to do with you. That sounds like someone of very high moral fiber."

"Enough, Cara. I don't deserve your gratitude. I am no angel."

He didn't *deserve* it? What an odd thing to say. Of course he did.

I stood. "Come on. Let's go and see what we can find in Myer's house."

"No. You were right. It's too dangerous. Go back to bed."

"I'm far too restless to sleep."

I tiptoed around the room and gathered up my gown. I tried to put it on as quietly as possible over my head, but Sylvia stirred. She rolled onto her side, mumbled something, then fell silent again. I continued dressing.

"Cara, no," Quin whispered from his bed. "What if Myer discovers us? He'll notify the authorities."

"We'll just have to convince him not to."

"How?"

"By telling him we'll ask Langley to give him have access to the ruins again."

Quin looked to the ceiling. "*Dieu*. You are stubborn and maddening. The worst traits in a woman."

"In anyone," I agreed, doing up the buttons down the front of my gown. It was liberating not to put on a corset or worry about stockings. "But it can't be helped. I've made up my mind. Come on, what are you waiting for?"

"For you to turn your back."

"Why?"

"What do you think I wear to bed?"

It took a moment for his meaning to register. "Oh!" My face may have felt hot before, but now it was positively on fire. I turned around and listened to him quietly dressing. I resisted the urge to peek over my shoulder and see his naked form. Just.

"Ready?" he said after a few moments.

I turned to see him wearing his leather pants and a shirt, his boots in hand. I picked up my boots and coat, and together we crept out of the bedroom. Neither of us spoke until we were safely outside on the street. It was utterly quiet. Not even a breath of wind disturbed the thick smoky air. Overhead, the streetlights glowed like suspended orbs in the night sky. There was no knowing where the moon could be positioned behind London's haze.

I threw on my coat, glad that I'd remembered it. "Are you cold?" I asked Quin.

"No."

We set off, and when I stumbled in the dark, he took my hand. His fingers closed around mine, an anchor in an uncertain sea. It was strange to be walking through London at night. At first it felt otherworldly, with the dense silences, but once we hit Piccadilly, I heard the familiar rumble of coach wheels and laughter of rakes and their doxies as they were driven to the next gambling den or party. Quin's head jerked at every sound, his entire body tense and alert. We may have been in the most exclusive square mile of London, but that didn't mean thieves weren't lurking in dark corners, waiting for an easy target.

We should not have come out. I was about to tell Quin that we should return home when we rounded the corner into Berkeley Square. The twinge of anxiety in my chest grew to a hammer blow. What we were about to do was madness. My heart raced faster the closer we drew to Myer's house. We stopped at the front steps and looked up at its towering stuccoed edifice and imperial arched windows. The task ahead of us seemed as insurmountable as the Dover cliffs.

I took a breath to speak, but Quin's hand clamped over my mouth. "Quiet," he whispered in my ear.

Then I heard it too. Footsteps echoed in the dark, somewhere beyond the veil of fog. And they were coming our way.

I froze, but Quin did not. He swung me around, hiding me from view. "Put your arms around me," he whispered.

I did, and was just registering how wonderful the strips of muscle felt as they flexed beneath my hands when he kissed me.

CHAPTER 8

I never expected my first real kiss to be in the middle of the night in a foggy Mayfair street. Then again, I hadn't expected my first kiss to be with an otherworldly warrior. Nor could I have anticipated that it would turn my bones to jelly.

His mouth didn't move at first, as I suspected his mind was on the footsteps, but after a moment, something changed. His lips explored mine, gentle yet insistent. His arms tightened around me and I responded by digging my hands into his hair and holding his head in place. It was scandalous, but I didn't care. I just wanted him to keep kissing me. The thrill of it was like nothing I'd ever felt before. I was weightless in his arms, and not quite *there*, or anywhere. It was as if his presence, his kiss, filled me up and left no room for sensible thoughts. There was only his mouth, his arms, his body, and the excess of sensations swamping me, from the tingles sweeping along my skin to the feeling that nothing would ever compare to this.

Behind him, someone clicked their tongue. Quin went

still. His grip tightened and he broke the kiss, but did not look around.

"Do that in the park, not outside my house. Go on!" The voice belonged to Mrs. Myer.

I glanced up at Quin. His eyes glittered in his shadowed face. He flipped up the collar of my coat and tucked me against his body, shielding me from Mrs. Myer. Dipping his head, he marched me across the street and into the park.

I sagged against the rough bark of a plane tree and let out a breath. "That was close."

Quin positioned himself so that his body shielded me from the street. He peeped around the trunk. "She went inside." He leaned back against the bark next to me. "I should not have done that. My apologies, Cara. How do you say it?"

"Sorry," I mumbled.

"Aye. Sorry."

But I was not sorry. I was glad that he'd been the first man to kiss me. How could I not be when it made me feel so good? "There was no alternative. She would have seen us if we hadn't, er, taken action."

"I admit that it was the first idea that came to me."

I smiled. I rather liked hearing that. "We should go home. This was a foolish idea."

He took my hand again and we headed out of the park. I glanced back at the Myers' house before we turned the corner. "I wonder where she'd been at this time of night." For a recluse, she was out rather late. And on foot too—very odd.

Fortunately we were not accosted by cutthroats on the way home and did not lose our way in the fog. Once we reached the front steps of Emily's house, Quin let go of my hand. He looked up at the front door.

"We discussed what to say if Myer discovered us," he said, "but not how to explain ourselves if Beaufort did."

"Jacob will do whatever Emily tells him to do. You may

not think him pliable, but he is in her hands. And she is more spirited than she appears on the surface. Don't worry about them. I won't tell them you ravaged me in the streets of Mayfair." I nudged his arm to show him I was joking.

He grunted. "I do not need to ravage women."

"Oh? Come to you willingly, do they?"

"Aye."

He trotted down the service stairs and put the key in the lock. I trailed after him, somewhat speechless, and received a dazzling Quin St. Clair smile as he opened the door.

* * *

THE SOCIETY'S library was tucked into the back of a coffee house located in a complex warren of narrow alleys in the old part of the city. The windows were clean but I doubted they'd seen sunlight in years with higher buildings overshadowing either side and opposite. The wood of the bar and tables was worn smooth by centuries of use and it wasn't difficult to imagine bewigged gentlemen meeting there to discuss trade and money when the coffee house first opened. Little had changed. The gentleman no longer wore wigs but they pored over the day's newspapers, and the snippet of lively chatter that I heard as we entered was about the latest financial reports. All talk stopped dead when they spotted me, however. Considering I was a woman, and half the age of most of the patrons, it wasn't surprising that I was the focus of their attention. Quin blended in a little better in his new suit.

"It was one of the first coffee houses in England," Myer said, nodding at the attendant behind the bar. He and Nathaniel had met us outside.

The attendant nodded back. "Morning, Mr. Myer, sir."

"They sprang up all over the city after coffee was introduced to England, but most have vanished as progress or fire destroyed them."

He used a key as long as his palm to unlock a thick wooden door at the back of the coffee house. The rough metal hinges creaked in protest at the disturbance. It was too dark to make out anything in the room, but the musty scent of old books was a sure sign that we had reached the library.

Myer struck a match and lit the lantern hanging on a hook beside the door. He handed it to Nathaniel who lifted it high. I expelled a soft breath of wonder at the sight. The room wasn't large—it could barely fit the rectangular table and four armchairs—but it was packed with books. There were no windows, and each of the four walls housed a floor-to-ceiling bookshelf crammed with tomes of all sizes. The only gap between shelves was for the door.

"Good lord," I said on a breath. I stepped into the room and spun around slowly. I'd been in private and public libraries before, but never had I seen so many old books in one small space. There were leather-bound covers, of course, and plain board ones too, and some books appeared to be simply a stack of pages tied together with ribbons.

Quin inspected the ones nearest him and Nathaniel made straight for the stack of small drawers at one end of the table. It appeared to be some sort of cataloging system.

"Have you been here before?" I asked him.

"No. Why?"

"It's just that you seem so calm. I mean...*look* at them all. I'm not a paranormal historian and I feel as if I've walked into a bank vault filled with gold."

He looked around the room, nodding in wonder. "You're right. It is marvelous. I suppose I'm just eager to start."

Myer set another lantern down on the table's surface. Between the two, there was enough light for us to work by. "As Faraday has figured out, those drawers contain cards for every book in here. The books are arranged on the shelves by their main subject and the cards cross-reference each one to other books. These texts are general ones," he said, indicating the shelves to the left of the door where the thickest volumes stood.

"And which ones have you already searched through for information about the book?" I asked.

"These," he said, indicating the general texts, "and that group over there." He pointed at the shelf directly opposite the door. "Most of them discuss demonology and the use of incantations. Now, I must dash. I have appointments here in the city. I'll leave you three to your own devices. Be sure to lock the door on your way out, Faraday." He gave Nathaniel the key and exited with a cheerful smile.

"He seems to have no qualms leaving people he hardly knows in here," I said once he was gone.

"He wants the book badly," Nathaniel said without looking up from the catalog. "But he has neither the expertise nor the patience to do the necessary work to find it."

He sounded very much like Edith Myer. "Why aren't you a member of the society already when you have an interest in the paranormal?" I asked him.

"Not everyone who has an interest in the paranormal belongs."

I knew the truth of that statement. Neither George, Emily nor Jacob wanted anything to do with it.

"As a historian, I wasn't interested in becoming a member," he went on. "Now, I'm having second thoughts. It may be worthwhile simply to have regular access to this library."

"Do you know George Culvert?"

His fingers stilled. "The name isn't familiar." He continued to sift through the cards in the drawer. "Why?"

"He's a demonologist. I believe his library is well stocked, although I haven't seen it."

"Do you know him?"

"He's a relation through marriage." I pulled out a very old book that consisted of nothing more than pages sandwiched between two boards, stitched together with a thin leather strip. It smelled of earth and felt cool to touch.

"Would you introduce me to him?" he said.

I paused, suddenly wishing I hadn't brought it up. I was simply trying to establish where a paranormal historian fitted into the world of supernatural scholars. It seemed odd that he wasn't a member of the society and didn't know George. I wondered if George knew about him.

Quin had begun inspecting the books that Myer told us he'd already searched through. He didn't seem interested in our conversation, and had hardly spoken to either Myer or Nathaniel since arriving. Perhaps he was worried he'd give himself away if he started a conversation. It was difficult to hide his accented speech and if Nathaniel asked him about living in Melbourne, we'd be in trouble.

Nathaniel didn't ask, however. He switched his attention from the catalog to the shelves. "You're not going to look through the books Myer claims to have read?" I asked him as he scanned a different shelf.

"No. I trust that his search was thorough. He may not like research, but I believe he wants the book enough to have exhausted the subject of incantations. I'll see what I can find elsewhere first. Those might be of interest to you, however, St. Clair."

I returned my book and concentrated on the group Myer had already looked through. I wasn't convinced that he would have searched them all thoroughly. For one thing, there were many, and for another he didn't have the advantage that we had. We'd seen a page torn from the book. We knew the cadence of the language used in the spells and that the pages felt thick and rough to touch.

We worked silently together, leafing through books at the table, sometimes slowly, sometimes flipping the pages quickly. Nathaniel's fair head bent over his text, his shoulders hunched and his nose practically skimming the page. At first I thought he was sniffing it, then I noticed his eyes screwed up tight. He must have poor eyesight. I was about to ask him if he'd forgotten his spectacles, but then I thought perhaps he might be self-conscious. Not too many handsome men liked the way a pair of glasses marred their good looks.

His fair locks were in stark contrast to Quin's darker coloring. I'd tried to feign disinterest in Quin all morning, but had failed miserably and found myself peeking sideways at him whenever I could. Our kiss had unsettled my nerves in a way that both alarmed and thrilled me. I had hoped it had unsettled him too, but so far I'd seen no evidence of it. He was as cool and composed as ever. Clearly he'd not been joking when he'd claimed damsels came to him. I'd wager they kissed him willingly too.

As the morning wore on, I grew colder. The room had neither sunlight nor fire to warm it and my shawl wasn't thick enough. I shivered. Without a word, Quin removed his coat and laid it around my shoulders. I smiled at him in thanks and caught Nathaniel watching us from beneath lowered lashes. I felt a twinge of regret that our friendship hadn't picked up where it had left off. He really had been very sweet on the ship and we'd talked into the evenings when we should have returned to our cabins. He'd even held my hand on that final night of the voyage as he promised to write to me.

Perhaps Celia was right after all, and I was too young and naive to be allowed so much freedom. She hadn't wanted me to travel with only Mrs. Dartmoor for company, but I'd insisted and Louis had taken my side, telling her I was mature and shrewd for my age. Clearly I wasn't mature enough or shrewd enough to know when a gentleman was merely dallying with me as opposed to having serious intentions.

I sighed, drawing the attentions of both men.

"Bored already?" Nathaniel asked with a supercilious smile.

"Not at all. It's just that there are an awful lot of books here. I can see why Myer gave up looking through them. It's rather like searching for a needle in a haystack. I'm glad we're only looking for general information on portals and disturbances and not the book of spells like you."

"Aye," Quin said. "Here, Cara. This one is useful."

He handed me a text with tanned leather stretched over the end boards. Images of the moon and stars were stamped into the cover and metal clasps had held it closed. The open page depicted a beautiful illumination of the Virgin Mary as a tree. Leaves grew from her toes and flowers bloomed from her fingertips. Except they weren't flowers but symbols. Some were swirls and patterns, others were simple drawings of animals. Seeing the Virgin Mary in a text on the paranormal gave me pause. It seemed unlikely at first, but I supposed it wasn't when one considered most medieval books had a religious purpose. But what did it all mean? I wanted to ask Quin, but not alert Nathaniel.

"You're wasting your time with that one," Nathaniel said. He couldn't see the page since I held the book up, so he must know it from the cover. "The book is full of images and symbols that nobody can decipher. "

"I thought you hadn't been here before," I said.

"I haven't." He returned his attention to the text he was studying. "It's one I've heard about, that's all."

I handed the book back to Quin and gave him a wry smile.

His eyes twinkled in response. What was he up to? He returned the book to the shelves and began flipping through another. I pretended to study a book on angels as he drew out text after text. He looked through each one for a few minutes then returned them too. Finally, he announced it was time to leave.

Nathaniel pulled out his watch from his waistcoat pocket. "But you've hardly been here an hour."

"Cara is cold and I'm growing restless," Quin said.

I handed him back his jacket and returned the book I was looking through to the shelves. "Good day, Nathaniel. I do hope we'll see you again."

He hurriedly stood, scraping the chair's feet on the floorboards. "As do I, Cara. Good day."

Quin waited for me to walk out of the library ahead of him. We left Nathaniel to his books and headed out of the coffee house. I waited until we'd reached the more open thoroughfare of Cornhill before peppering Quin with questions.

"Why that book? What about it piqued your curiosity enough to pull it off the shelf?"

"It felt different."

"What do you mean?"

He walked fast and I had to quicken my steps to keep up with him. "There was something about it that pulled me. I cannot explain it well with words you would understand."

"Do you mean there was an energy about it? An otherworldly essence, as it were?"

"Aye."

"I felt nothing."

"You're not a warrior."

"A fair point." It began to drizzle and we'd not brought umbrellas. Quin pulled me into the large recessed doorway of a bank and shot a frustrated glance at the gray sky.

"Clearly you found something important in the book," I said. "But I couldn't make any sense of it. Nor could anyone else according to Nathaniel."

"The symbols on that page I showed you were a code."

"And you were able to decipher it in that short time?"

"It's a code I've seen before."

"Where?"

"Never mind."

I clicked my tongue. "Quin, if we are to be partners in this search, you need to keep me informed."

"I don't *need* to do anything."

I crossed my arms and very nearly stamped my foot on the ground in a show of petulance. Obstinate man.

"You're angry with me," he said idly.

"Yes. I understand that you wish to keep details of your life to yourself. I'll grant you your privacy there. But this is different. You need to trust me, Quin, and talk to me. If we are to find the book of spells, we need to work together."

As my tone grew more brisk, his face softened until he was actually smiling. "I was always going to tell you what the symbols meant," he said.

"Oh. Very well. Continue."

"The image of the Virgin Mary means creation, new life. The symbols growing from the tree meant something in my time, but it's possible their meaning has been lost."

"That would explain why Nathaniel didn't recognize them. Or Myer for that matter."

"Some of the symbols describe demons and evil spirits while others told of the spells used to control them."

"Incantations," I whispered. "But those aren't secrets. Myer has used spells to bring demons here. George, Emily and Jacob have used another to send them back."

"Aye, but they all originally came from the book we seek,

115

and that book contains many more than just those incantations."

"I see. So that image is referring to *our* book."

"And its original creator."

The door behind us opened and a gentleman stood there. He hesitated, a wary eye on Quin, then noticed the rain. He put up his umbrella and stepped into the street.

"Who created it?" I asked, my heart thumping a little heavier.

"There were symbols I recognized that belong to the human world, not the supernatural. Specifically a particular coat of arms. An eagle, which means redemption and resurrection, and the thistle, meaning pain and suffering."

"Which family uses those symbols in their coat of arms?"

"De Mordaunts," he said darkly.

"You knew them?" I could barely speak above a whisper. It was strangely fascinating to think that here was another link to his past life.

"Edward de Mordaunt was a friend to my brother." He stepped out into the street, leaving me standing in the doorway, staring after him. "Come, Cara. We have to find his descendants."

"Wait. What?" I ran after him. The rain had stopped, but the air hung damp and ponderous around us, promising a heavier downpour. "Your brother's friend lived hundreds of years ago. He might not have any descendants."

"Or he might. The book in the library is proof that the book of spells was created by the de Mordaunt family. It's something highly prized and therefore highly protected. I'd wager it's been passed down through the generations and is still in their possession."

I lifted my skirts and stepped around a puddle. Quin walked right through it. "You expect to see it in their private library? You expect them to just show it to you?"

"No."

"Then how shall we see it?"

"I'm yet to form a plan. First, we must find out where the seat of the de Mordaunt family is now located."

What if there were several seats? I'd mentioned the problem of no living descendants, but what if there were dozens or even hundreds? And what if the book hadn't been given to the eldest son and heir, but a second son here, a third son there, followed by a daughter? The possibilities were endless, the task daunting.

Another problem struck me. "The abbot of Frakingham Abbey was once custodian. That implies the book left the de Mordaunt family before the fifteen-thirties."

"Unless he was a de Mordaunt too."

"But what if he wasn't?" I dropped my skirts and didn't care if the hem picked up mud and muck off the street. I was lost in the hopelessness of it all.

Quin slowed his pace and crooked his elbow. "Come, Cara," he said gently. "Don't be troubled. We're further in our search than we were this morning."

I took his elbow and gave him a grateful smile. "You're right. I should stay optimistic. We'll find every single de Mordaunt living today and ask them about the book. It's possible they don't know the value of it, particularly if they have no interest in the paranormal."

"We will ask your niece and her husband if they know them."

I couldn't help laughing. "Quin, you have seen how many people live in this city, haven't you? Emily and Jacob don't know everyone, let alone those in other parts of the country."

"Edward de Mordaunt was an important knight, close to the king."

"That doesn't mean his family is still important. But I do know how to find out."

"How?"

"*Debrett's.*"

* * *

WE ARRIVED BACK at the Belgravia house and asked Watkins to inform Emily and Jacob that we would be in the library. They arrived just as I finally found their copy of the latest edition of *Debrett's Peerage*, the authority on all persons of note in Britain.

"You two look industrious," Emily said, breezing into the library in a sleek cream and green day dress. On closer inspection, however, there were food stains at the shoulder and her fingers were covered in chalk. She'd been helping out the nanny in the nursery again.

"*Debrett's?*" Jacob said with a nod at the book in my hand.

"We have a slender idea on how to find the spell book," I told him. "Very slender."

"That's better than no clues at all." Emily signaled for me to set *Debrett's* on the large hexagonal table, and she and I sat while Jacob and Quin stood behind us.

I explained what Quin had discovered in the society's library and how we hoped to find a descendent of the de Mordaunt family. "As I said, a slender way forward."

"But a way nevertheless. Well done, Quin." Emily flipped the pages, searching for surnames beginning with D. *Debrett's* listed all the peers beneath their rank, but also provided a separate alphabetical list of surnames and titles.

"I don't know any de Mordaunts," Jacob said, leaning over his wife's shoulder. "But I'm not familiar with every peer of the realm."

A thorough search did not reveal any de Mordaunts or Mordaunts. "They may not be peers," I said, shutting *Debrett's* with a sigh. "Just because the fellow Quin knew was a knight doesn't mean his descendants took advantage of that and made something of themselves."

"We could try the General Register Office," Jacob suggested. "They record all births, deaths and marriages," he explained to Quin.

Quin looked astounded. "All of them?"

"Yes, but it only began earlier this century. Prior to that it was up to the parish record keepers. A search through the current names should tell us if there are living de Mordaunts."

"Or Mordaunts," I added. That got me thinking. It was common for medieval names of important families to be of French origin, since most had followed William the Conqueror over from Normandy. But many Anglicized their names over the centuries, changing spellings entirely. Quin's own surname, for example, was commonly changed to Sinclair.

I reached for *Debrett's* again. "Our de Mordaunts may have an alternative spelling now."

"Good thinking." Emily leaned in to me, Jacob and Quin too until Jacob ordered Quin back. Quin hesitated then obliged after a moment, moving only an inch or two farther away. If Jacob was dissatisfied, he didn't get a chance to say so. Emily was speaking.

"What would be some variations, do you think?" She was engrossed in our search once more and oblivious to the power struggle happening behind us.

"Mordane," I suggested. "Mordette, Mordred, Mordent—"

"Mordant!" Jacob reached between us and furiously flipped the pages. "Specifically, one Byron Mordant-Turpin." He stopped and stabbed the page with his finger.

Emily gasped. "Lord Alwyn! I know his wife, Lady Alwyn."

I scanned the entry. According to *Debrett's*, Byron

Mordant-Turpin was the eighth earl of Alwyn. His ancestry could be traced with certainty to one Henry Mordant, born in 1423, and with less certainty to the de Mordaunt family before that. "According to this, Gilbert de Mordaunt may have come over with William the Conqueror in 1066, since he was granted lands soon afterward. Alwyn must be from the same line as your friend, Quin. To have separate de Mordaunts living at the same time here in England would be highly unlikely."

"He was not my friend," Quin said with a bitterness I hadn't expected. "He was my brother's. Where can we find this Byron Mordant-Turpin? Does he live here in London?"

"He does," Jacob said, nodding eagerly. "He's a hopeless gambler and rakehell and rarely visits his family seat in Derbyshire anymore. There's little to occupy him, so he says. Rumor has it that he's run the estate into the ground with debts."

I shook my head. "Why do so many men do that?" It was how August Langley had been able to buy Frakingham House from Lord Frakingham. The earl's father had racked up debts so enormous that his son had needed to sell off the family estate to pay them.

"Lady Alwyn is no better," Emily said. "She throws parties in their townhouse most weeks, and she always wears the latest fashions from France. Her cook and lady's maid are French too."

I ran my palm over the warm leather cover of *Debrett's*. "Let's hope they haven't sold off their library to make ends meet."

"Introduce me," Quin said to Jacob.

"Of course, since you ask so nicely. He's probably not out of bed yet. He keeps late hours. I'll ask around this afternoon and see if I can discover his movements for this evening."

"That suits me," I said. "I'm a little tired myself and wouldn't mind a nap."

Jacob angled himself between Quin and I. "Why are you tired? Didn't you sleep last night?"

"Of course I did. Quin and I were up late talking, that's all."

"Talking about what?"

"That's none of your affair," I said.

Quin crossed his arms and arched his brows in challenge.

Jacob's nostrils flared and I worried that he would explode in anger. Fortunately, Emily knew how to manage her husband. She laid a hand on his arm and stood, but stumbled. He caught her and his frown quickly went from glaring to concerned.

"Are you all right, Em?"

"Yes, thank you. Let's see to the children before you go in search of answers to Alwyn's whereabouts."

"But Cara…"

"Sylvia will return soon. Can your nap wait for her?" she asked me. "She'll probably be needing a rest too."

I nodded. "Where is she?"

"Shopping. Tommy and one of our footmen went with her to help with the packages."

"You let her go shopping without supervision?" I laughed. "I do hope she didn't spend too much."

"Does Langley hold the purse strings tightly?"

"Jack does. He manages all the family's finances. While he's away, Samuel has been helping Bollard with the task, but neither have been around much."

"Then Sylvia has picked the right time to go shopping."

"No wonder she was so keen to come to London."

Emily took her husband's arm, but Jacob seemed reluctant to leave. He took Louis' trust in him very seriously, and I felt a little sorry that I was causing problems.

"Quin and I will remain here until Sylvia returns," I assured him. "Perhaps you could send in a footman with some tea and ask him to stay with us. Will that appease you, Jacob?"

"Hardly," he growled, not taking his bold gaze off Quin.

"Jacob!" Emily cried.

He had the decency to look away, although I didn't believe for a moment that he'd backed down.

"Emily, you'd better take him away before they engage in battle," I said. "You know how difficult it is to remove blood from rugs."

She smiled, and Jacob rolled his eyes. "Very amusing, Cara."

"I am not going to harm her," Quin assured them. "My honor forbids it."

"Your honor means little to me since I don't know you well," Jacob said.

"Does the honor of a knight mean more?"

"Knight? Do you mean to tell us that *you're* a knight?"

"Good lord," Emily muttered, blinking at Quin.

I expected I must have looked as awed as her. It was one thing to have an otherworldly warrior in my presence, but for him to be a knight as well was quite thrilling. "Does this mean we should have been addressing you as Sir Quintin all this time?"

One side of his mouth kicked up. "Quin will suffice."

"Well, Jacob?" Emily asked her husband. "Do you trust him now?"

"If I must," Jacob muttered. "Although I don't see why ladies find knights so interesting. I know many, and none deserve this sort of reaction."

"But they're not *medieval* knights. Knights were so chivalrous back then," Emily said dreamily.

"Romantic stories only. I'm sure reality was quite different."

"How do you know?" She slipped her arm through his and directed him toward the door. "Were you there?"

He grunted. "Do I need to remind you that viscounts outrank knights?"

"You're not a viscount yet." She grinned at me over her shoulder. She was only teasing him and Jacob was taking it in his stride, his temper seemingly dampened by her manipulations.

Quin finally lowered himself into the leather armchair near the fire once they were gone. "He doesn't like me."

"He's worried about me being alone with a...man." I was about to say handsome, powerful, mysterious and compelling man, but thought better of it. I wasn't sure what Quin's reaction would be to my admitting that I found him to be all those things, and more. I wasn't sure I dared find out. "It's not personal."

"How can I convince him that I won't harm you?"

"Try to be a little less..." Wonderful. "Difficult. Try not to butt heads with him so much."

"Butt heads?"

"Yes, like goats do." I made two fists and knocked them together. "He's used to being the strongest and most powerful man in this household. And now you've come along and suddenly his authority seems to be in doubt."

He stretched out his long legs and crossed his ankles. Aside from when he was lying in bed, it was the most laid back pose I'd ever seen him adopt. He must be feeling as tired as me, or he had simply grown comfortable in the house now. "It is not in doubt. He's your guardian and the head of this house. I respect his position."

"You do? You don't necessarily show it all of the time."

He thought about it then conceded my point with a nod.

"I must apologize to him then. I'm used to giving orders, not taking them from anyone less than a king."

I blinked slowly. "Whom did you give orders to in your time?"

He closed his eyes and tipped his head against the chair's backrest. "No questions, Cara."

I bit my tongue to stop my retort. He looked worn out after our nocturnal wanderings and early morning start. I was no longer feeling tired, however. Something had just occurred to me. I turned to *Debrett's*, still sitting on the table before me, and as quietly as possible turned the pages until I came to the list of surnames beginning with S.

CHAPTER 9

"*T*here you are!" Sylvia burst into the library and handed her hat and gloves to Watkins. A footman followed behind her, carrying a tray with teapot and cups.

Quin sat up and I pretended that I hadn't been looking through *Debrett's* for any St. Clairs, Sinclairs or variations thereof. My quick glance had proven futile. If Quin had descendants, they were not important enough to have an entry in *Debrett's Peerage*.

"Emily told us you've been shopping," I said, accepting the teacup from the footman. "Tell us what you bought."

She launched into a list so long that I began to worry Jack would grow angry once he found out. "I've also ordered invitations for the ball and new gowns to be made up for both myself and Hannah. I do hope she doesn't mind, but timing is crucial and all the best *modistes* are busy. If we waited for Hannah's return, she would never have anything made in time."

"You know her size and what she likes?"

"The *modiste* has her measurements already, so unless she ate too many French pastries while she was gone, she ought to be the same. And with her red hair, she can wear so few colors, so I chose a lovely shade of green and black. Her hair is regrettable, but does make it easier for me to choose in her absence."

I tried to hide my smirk, but failed. "I'm sure she'll be very pleased with your choice, Sylvia. Come and have some tea and let us tell you everything that happened this morning."

* * *

I AWOKE from my afternoon nap to see Sylvia still asleep beside me on the bed and Quin dozing in an armchair nearby. He'd shed his jacket, waistcoat and tie, and his booted feet rested on a chair opposite. With his arms crossed over his chest and his eyes closed, he looked at peace. I didn't want to wake him. For one thing, he needed to rest if we were to be out late again that night and, for another, I just wanted to keep staring at him.

I was struck again by how handsome he was. While Nathaniel had the fine bone structure and coloring of a gentleman usually found in libraries and drawing rooms, there was nothing refined about Quin. His face and body could have been hewn from granite and chiseled by a sculptor. It was hard and uncompromising, even in repose. His only soft features were his lips and the long dark lashes that fanned his cheeks. With his callused palms and scarred back, there was nothing gentlemanly about him. Not in the modern sense of the word. To think that he was a medieval knight! I was beginning to think that Jacob was right when he said knights weren't the romantic figures stories made them out to be. My medieval knight was every bit a warrior. He made libraries and drawing rooms seem small and dull.

A brisk knock on the door woke Quin and Sylvia. She

snapped at the visitor to go away, while Quin jumped to his feet and answered it, fully alert.

Jacob stood there. His face darkened upon seeing Quin's state of undress. "Do I need to remind you that you should dress appropriately while in the presence of ladies?"

A muscle in Quin's jaw worked, but instead of snapping back, he gave a slight bow. "My apologies."

Jacob looked taken aback. I suspected he'd prepared himself to be hit with either a fist or an argument. "Accepted. But I must insist."

"Do you know where Alwyn will be tonight?" I asked before Quin decided he no longer cared if he were on Jacob's good side if it meant biting his tongue.

"The Brickmaker's Arms. It's a tavern where illegal prize fights are held once a month."

Sylvia made a whimpering sound from the bed. "You can't possibly go, Cara. It sounds much too dangerous for a lady."

"But Alwyn is a peer," I protested. "It can't be all that bad."

"It can and it probably is," Jacob said. "I agree with Sylvia. You'll stay home."

"No." Quin gave an emphatic shake of his head before I could protest. "I'm going so she must come."

"You don't have to, St. Clair. I can ask Alwyn for you."

"No."

"Why do you insist?"

Quin's gaze lowered. I exchanged frowns with Jacob. "You can trust Jacob," I said. "If Alwyn has a library worth searching, Jacob will convince him to allow us access to it."

"No," Quin said again. "I'll go tonight. Cara will dress as a boy to avoid attention."

I wasn't sure whose protest was loudest, Sylvia's or Jacob's. I simply laughed and declared that it sounded amusing. The protests died down when I walked out. "Let's let Emily decide, shall we?"

"That's not fair," Jacob muttered. But he followed us anyway and we found Emily in the small sitting room, eating cake with the two eldest children. I received their sticky-fingered hugs and joined them.

"Emily, tell Cara she cannot go to the boxing tonight," Sylvia said, reaching for a piece of cake.

"Boxing!" Gabe shouted. He set down his cake and punched an imaginary opponent. "Can I come too?"

"No," his mother said. "Run along and see if Nanny can play with you while Matthew sleeps."

Emily waited until two sets of little feet could be heard pounding down the hallway. Then she picked up her teacup. She didn't seem in the least surprised that we were talking about me attending a prize fight. She and Jacob must have already discussed it. "I'm not going to ban Cara from attending," she said. "If Quin wishes to go then so must she."

"But it's not a sport for ladies' eyes!" Sylvia cried, pulling a face. "All that blood and foul language."

"Agreed," Jacob said without taking his gaze off his wife. "I forbid it."

"Come now, Jacob. No harm will come to her with both you and Quin there. I have complete faith in your ability to frighten off would-be thugs, my darling."

"Flattery won't work, Em."

"Then perhaps reason will. Quin can't leave Cara and I suspect he wishes to ensure Alwyn agrees to let him see his library."

Quin nodded. "Thank you. I will take good care of your aunt."

"You don't understand, Em," Jacob said with barely disguised patience. "These illegal bouts can attract a rough crowd. Even the authorities give them a wide berth."

"She will not leave my side," Quin assured him. "Dressed as a boy, she will be left alone. I'll see to it."

"Cocky, aren't you?" Jacob muttered.

"He's no different from another gentleman I know," Emily said pointedly.

Jacob's blink was all innocence.

"You seem to be forgetting something," I told them. "I survived on the streets as a child, and I'd wager the things I saw and experienced then were far rougher than what I'll see at The Brickmaker's Arms tonight."

The fact that Quin didn't ask me what I meant was telling indeed. Not only did he know about the evil spirit I'd summoned into another person's body when I was ten, but he must also know about my childhood. I hadn't been an orphan, but close to it since my sick mother and mad father were incapable of caring for me.

"Good point," Emily said.

I smiled at her. It looked like I had won and had her to thank. I'd known she was the adventurous sort before she married, and I supposed I was a lot like her in that regard. The fact that Jacob didn't put his foot down and insist I do as I was told meant he knew it too and understood that stifling me would never work to his advantage.

"You ought to take Tommy, just to be sure," she said.

Sylvia coughed, spitting cake crumbs into her hand. "Have you all gone mad?" she asked when she recovered. "Why do you need to go to The Brickmaker's Arms at all? Why not simply call on Alwyn at his home?"

"Because he's never at home," Jacob told her. "I asked around at my club, and it was agreed that this was the best way to speak to him."

"I called on Lady Alwyn this afternoon and she claimed not to know when her husband would next appear," Emily said. "She seemed completely unconcerned too. In fact, she was far more interested in the ball you'll be throwing, Sylvia."

"Indeed?" Sylvia's face brightened, her anxiety over my impropriety forgotten. "Should I invite her?"

"I'm not sure. She has a tendency to take advantage of one's hospitality and linger after an invitation has expired."

"Did you speak with her about her husband's library?" Quin asked.

"I did, but she claimed to know very little. She told me, quite proudly, that the last time she was in their library at their country house was three years ago and that was only to search for a tiara that had gone missing."

We ate dinner in a state of nervous anxiety. Or at least, I did. Jacob and Quin looked quite composed. Afterward, Emily and Sylvia helped me dress in clothes borrowed from the housekeeper's nephew. The twelve year old was my height and since I wasn't very big in the chest, they fitted. With my hair pinned up beneath a large hat, I could pass as a boy, if I kept to the shadows.

We set off by coach and drove into the East End, an area I'd not returned to since I was a child. It was still a slum, with the poorest of the poor living cheek by jowl in houses that were only standing because their equally perilous neighbor had not yet fallen down. The coach picked its way carefully along the street, stopping outside a tavern with the sign of The Brickmaker's Arms swinging in the breeze. Smelly muck clogged the gutters and my nostrils, and most of the street lamps didn't work.

"This isn't going to be a lark, Cara," Jacob said grimly. "Just because a peer of the realm attends the fights doesn't mean it's safe or legitimate."

"I know that." He'd already told me—twice—that bare knuckle boxing was no longer the popular sport supported by the rich and titled fancy. Since the introduction of rules and gloves, the bare knuckle fights had been relegated to the rookeries where London's poorest eked out an existence amid disease and filth. It would seem Lord Alwyn was one of the few gentlemen who frequented the illegal fights nowadays.

"I still cannot believe I allowed you to come," Jacob muttered as he climbed out of the coach. "What was I thinking?"

"You were thinking that you wished to stay on Emily's good side. No harm will come to me, Jacob. I'll be beside Quin the entire time and keep my head low."

Tommy jumped down from the footman's seat at the rear of the coach and held his hand out to me. He snatched it back as he realized a boy wouldn't need help. It was unlikely anyone had seen. The only other sign of life was another coach that passed us and continued around the corner. It didn't have its lamps on, and it seemed ghostly in the darkness.

Jacob's coach rolled away and the four of us entered the tavern. The smell of ale didn't quite cover the undercurrent of sweat and urine that leeched out of the shadowy corners. A handful of heavy-browed types, holding tankards in dirty hands, narrowed their eyes as we passed. Their gazes sent icy prickles down the back of my neck. Jacob spoke to the keep behind the bar. After a brief exchange, in which Jacob handed him a wad of money, the keep directed us to a door that led out the back. A sound like a wave crashing on a distant shore came from the other side. The noise became louder as the keep opened the thick door and led us through to a storeroom, lit by a single hissing lamp. Behind a wall of barrels was a trapdoor in the floor. The keep left us and we descended down the steps into the bowels of the tavern.

The basement was filled with perhaps a hundred men, roughly arranged around a near-empty square that was best viewed from the steps. There were no barricades around the crude boxing ring, not even a rope. It was simply a vacant space surrounded by all but two men who were in it, fighting. Behind the crowd were stacked barrels, and broken tables and stools, which had been pushed out of the way to make room. If the police arrived, they could be quickly arranged in such a manner that would make it look as if the room was simply another storage space.

Inside the central square the faces and fists of the two bare-chested men were covered in blood. One punched and the other ducked, but he was too slow and received a blow to the jaw that sent him reeling back into the crowd. Dozens of hands pushed him forward again, into the fists of his opponent. With one eye swollen shut and blood pouring from his nose and mouth, he was too injured and dazed to put up much of a fight. Another hard punch to his stomach had him doubling over and collapsing to the floor. A mustachioed man I'd not seen before bent over him and appeared to be saying something to the boxer. When he received no response, he declared the fight over.

A segment of the crowd rushed into the ring and circled the victor, while most of the others exchanged money with a few large men with thick necks and bruised knuckles. Moving through the throng, with the confidence of a general surrounded by his loyal army, was an extremely tall fellow sporting a stomach that tested the seams of his well-cut suit. A fat cigar dangled from his wide, fishy lips as he spoke with a round fellow with a scar pinching the skin above and below his eye, as though someone had tried to slice right through it. The cigar smoker was the only one dressed as a gentleman; he must be Lord Alwyn.

A bald man with no facial hair tapped Alwyn on the shoulder and pointed at us. The earl pulled the cigar from his mouth and gave Jacob a shallow nod of greeting.

"Is that Alwyn?" Quin asked Jacob.

"Yes. Let's go talk to him then get out of here."

We made our way down the steps into the throng. If I'd thought the smell upstairs was bad, it was positively putrid in the basement. I didn't even want to try and identify what might be causing it. We moved slowly through the crowd. Most people paid little attention to us; one or two sized up Jacob and Quin, but Tommy and I were overlooked. Perhaps they thought us the servants of wealthy gentlemen and not worth fleecing. Somewhere off to our right, an argument broke out and we were forgotten entirely as the protagonists were encouraged with shouts and the sort of language a lady ought not to hear. In front of me, Jacob's back stiffened, but he did not turn around. Behind me, I felt Quin's solid, comforting presence draw closer.

I was determined not to be afraid. I had wanted to come and experience the illegal fighting scene. It was too late to back out now.

"Beaufort," Alwyn said to Jacob as he joined us. "Never thought I'd see you here."

"I'm looking for you. You're a hard man to pin down."

Alwyn's lips stretched into a grimace without dropping his cigar. A clump of ash fell off the end onto his stomach. He brushed it off absently and I saw that his waistcoat was already stained. "I find that makes it easier to stay one step ahead of the creditors, don't you?" He spoke to Jacob, but his attention was on Quin. He looked over the top of me and eyed Quin with a thorough, assessing gaze.

"I have a strange request to ask of you," Jacob said. "Indeed, my friend, St. Clair, does."

Alwyn thrust out his hand to Quin and Quin shook it. "Strong grip." Alwyn nodded in approval. "Big fellow. Ever been in the ring before?" He let go of Quin's hand and clasped his shoulder instead. I got the feeling he was assessing Quin's form, like a horse trainer checks over a thoroughbred.

Quin jerked away. "I want to talk to you about your library,"

Alwyn snorted. "My *library*? You don't look like a bookish fellow."

A roar went up around us and the crowd suddenly surged, jostling for position. Another bout must be about to begin. I was too short to see anything except backs and heads.

"We'll talk between fights." Alwyn moved off. "Come down to the front and place a wager before the first punch is thrown."

Quin and Jacob exchanged glances as Alwyn set off, not looking back to see if we followed. Seeing no other choice, we snaked our way through the crowd and stood at the edge of the square. Jacob angled himself in front of me, while Quin and Tommy stood behind.

"Since this is your first time, Beaufort, I'll give you some advice." Alwyn removed his cigar with stubby fingers and licked his lips. "See how that fellow limps?" He pointed his cigar at one of the fighters. "Put your money on him."

"Isn't the limp a sign of weakness?"

"It's a sign of strength. The victors don't escape injury, but the losers rarely fight again." He said something to the hairless man beside him and he in turn signaled to one of the thugs collecting money. It wasn't just one thug who descended on us, however, but six. They formed a ring of protection for one another. In a place like this, it must be necessary.

Jacob handed over some money and one of the men passed him a ticket before they all moved off. Alwyn slapped Jacob's shoulder and glanced at Quin again. He returned his cigar to his mouth and smiled around it before turning back to the ring.

The referee called the fighters to start and the crowd

roared again. They surged against us and punched the air, much like little Gabe had done that afternoon. Some held tankards and spilled ale over their shoes, but none cared. The fight had begun.

I watched the crowd. Most were young men dressed in dusty, old clothes; the soles of their boots were worn down and their lank hair skimmed dirty collars. They cheered every punch, and some swayed drunkenly against their shouting, laughing companions. I was surprised to see a handful of women mingling with the patrons, though perhaps I shouldn't have been. From their exposed décolletages and painted faces, they were clearly as much part of the entertainment as the boxers. But even they were forgotten when the first drops of blood spilled in the ring.

The crunch of bone on bone had me focusing once more on the fight. I flinched and shut my eyes as blood sprayed in an arc from one fighter's nose. Fingers pinched my arm, forcing me to reopen them.

"Watch, lad," Alwyn shouted over the cheers. I was startled that he'd even taken notice of me. "Pretty boy like you needs to learn." He turned back to the fight.

Behind me, Quin rested a hand on my hip. The gesture was possessive, intimate, and a risk considering I was trying to hide my gender. It lasted only a moment, but the sensation remained. It was as if I could still feel the weight of his hand there.

One of the fighters fell to his knees amid cheers and jeers from the onlookers. The referee moved forward, but the boxer waved him away and stood on wobbly legs, causing an even louder eruption from the patrons. To my complete shock, another man stepped into the ring—a dead one. He faded in and out as all ghosts did, as if he were half in this world and half in the next. He was bare-chested, like the fighters, and blood stained one side of his face, ear and neck.

He was intent on the fight, even throwing a punch in his enthusiasm, but his fist traveled through the boxers.

I watched him rather than the fighters. If he were still haunting this realm, he mustn't want to cross yet. Sometimes I would speak to spirits and find out what troubled them. Merely the act of telling their problems to a living person helped them to finally move on to the afterlife, but not always. Some were too deeply troubled and did not want to leave, preferring to haunt those who'd harmed them in life. It was difficult to tell which sort this spirit would be, and considering the dangers of revealing my talent in such a crowd, I didn't want to find out.

As if he could sense me looking, he glanced up. I quickly focused my gaze on the fighter once more falling to the ground, but it was too late. The spirit approached.

"You can see me," he said in a thick Irish accent. He leaned down and peered into my face. Then he sniffed me. I leaned back into Quin's chest. "Well, well. If only they knew you is a girl, and a toff one at that. Never seen a brown toff before."

I didn't answer him. Speaking to someone nobody else could see would be foolish. Instead, I signaled for him to go away with a jerk of my head that could pass as a twitch if anyone saw.

He didn't move. "That used to be me in there," he said, pointing at the fight. "I died here. Not in the ring in a fair fight, but out there in the alley where there ain't no refree. It were him that killed me." The spirit jerked his chin at Alwyn.

I swallowed heavily. I didn't want to know anymore, but I knew it was foolish to pretend that Alwyn was a gentleman who followed the same code of conduct that decent men like Jacob did. Alwyn was not decent, I'd already realized. I had to hear out the spirit. He hadn't been able to tell anyone his story, and now that he had a captive audience, he wasn't going to let the chance go.

He bared his teeth at Alwyn and hissed. "I was supposed to throw me fight that night, see, but I wouldn't. If I can win, I win. I don't go down for nobody. The toff lost a large sum on me, so he got Sweet Moll to trick me into followin' her outside then set his men on me. I'm a good fighter, but there was six of 'em, all big bruisers. They left my body in the alley as a lesson for others. Alwyn wanted everyone to know that if he tells you to lose, you lose."

I blinked back at him, trying to convey sympathy without actually speaking. He seemed to understand my dilemma and nodded. "Stay away from him." He sauntered off and rejoined the fight as it entered into the final stages. He jeered along with the crowd as the injured man collapsed. Any sympathy I'd felt for him vanished. He was as bloodthirsty as the rest of them.

"Your library," Quin began as soon as the fight was declared over.

"Steady on," Alwyn said. "Need to collect my winnings first."

He was the first one the money thugs approached. Indeed, it wasn't he they approached, but his bald friend.

"Your ticket, Beaufort," Alwyn said cheerfully. "Show them your ticket, man. Our bruiser won."

Jacob gave the men his ticket. After the transactions were completed in silence, the thugs moved off into the crowd, doling out money as winning tickets were shoved in their faces.

"Now, what do you want with my library, St. Clair?" Alwyn seemed in a jolly mood after his win, but I couldn't help wondering if he'd paid the loser to fall. I looked around for the spirit but he'd vanished.

"I'm a historian with an interest in old books," Quin said. "It has come to my attention that you may possess a manuscript I've been seeking. Its last known whereabouts was in the hands of your ancestors."

"Bloody hell, is that so? This book worth anything?"

"Only to historians."

Alwyn's cigar and jowls sagged in thought. "I sold some old books off not long ago. Had some debts to pay and a priest came knocking, saying he wanted to buy 'em. It was probably among that lot."

"Priest?" Jacob echoed. "What was his name?"

But Alwyn didn't get a chance to speak. The crowd parted and spat out the fat man, with the scar across his eye, who Alwyn had been talking to upon our arrival. He was short, only my height, but was as wide as three men. The scar was a red, jagged line of puckered flesh that pulled his eyelid shut. It looked as if it had been inflicted recently. His bushy moustache curled back and he emitted a low growl in Alwyn's direction.

"You bloody cur," he snarled.

Quin, Jacob and Tommy bristled, but Alwyn pulled his cigar out and clasped the lapels of his jacket. He didn't look in the least concerned. "Bains, come and meet my friends."

Bains's gaze flicked to Jacob and Quin then back to Alwyn. "I'm not here to meet your friends, you dog, I'm here to warn you." He stabbed a fat finger into Alwyn's chest. "Don't do that again."

The same thugs who'd collected tickets and money ranged behind him in a wall of muscle and fierce scowls. One pulled back his jacket to reveal a blade tucked into the waist band of his trousers.

"Come now, Bains," Alwyn said, throwing an arm around the shorter man. "You have no proof of foul play."

Bains pushed Alwyn's arm off. His good eye narrowed, disappearing into the heavy flesh of his face. "You think I need proof?" he said, voice a low warning.

Alwyn's smile vanished, replaced with a cruel sneer. "You do if you wish to accuse me. I can crush you and your tavern with a dash of my pen." He straightened and the smile returned, but it was as false as my disguise. "If anyone threw the fight, it's they you must punish, not me. I'm an innocent gentleman enjoying a night out." The smile turned hard. "Understand?"

Bains stared him down for a moment before backing away with his men. The crowd closed around us again, thicker and closer than before. I felt their cloying breaths in my hair, and their stench hung in the airless basement. I wanted to leave. Jacob asked Alwyn for the name of the priest again, but Alwyn didn't answer. His attention was back on the ring.

"Blast," he muttered as the referee introduced two bare-chested men with shoulders as big as Quin's. "He got to him."

"What's going on?" Jacob shot Quin a glance over the top of my head. Quin gripped my elbow, ready to steer me away from danger if necessary.

"Bains swapped fighters," Alwyn snapped. "That's bloody what." A string of curses followed then he shouted, "Bains! Where's Gibson?"

"Gone home to his mother with his tail between his legs," Bains said, laughing. "Old Filth here agreed to step in."

"We don't want 'im!" someone shouted. "We want to see a good fight!"

"Aye!" came the roar from the crowd.

Bains looked worried, but he stuck to his guns. "There ain't none here who's the right size except Old Filth."

Alwyn's gaze slid to Quin.

The spirit joined the men in the ring. He took one look at Alwyn and laughed. "Bains is onto him now," he shouted at me in triumph. "Ever since me death, he's been watchin' Alwyn, and now he's doin' somethin' about it. Y' see, Alwyn's

139

been payin' fighters to throw matches, but Bains didn't know. It were me who told him. I weren't afraid of Alwyn. Alwyn can make a man's family suffer if he don't do what he wants, but I had no family in England. He couldn't get to 'em, so he killed me instead. Only Bains knows it now, and he won't stand for Alwyn throwin' fights and takin' all the winnings. You watch, girlie."

I did, but it was doubtful the fight would even go ahead. The crowd roared their disapproval at the last minute switch. They jeered and threw their ale onto the floor, calling for the vacant-eyed fighter named Old Filth to get out of the ring and Gibson to return.

"They want the fight to go ahead as planned," Quin said.

Tommy leaned close so that we could hear him over the jeers. "Bains has taken Gibson off, the fighter he thinks Alwyn paid to lose, and replaced him with Old Filth. Only no one else knows Alwyn rigged the fight and since Gibson is the better boxer, the crowd want to see him in there. They want a good show and won't be happy unless Gibson comes out."

"How do you know all this?" I asked.

"It wasn't that many years ago that I came to places like this to pick up a bit of extra coin in the ring. Old Filth was past it even then, but Bains would put him forward now and again and me and Jack learned it only happened when someone paid a boxer to throw the fight."

"We're going," Jacob announced, turning to us, his face pinched with concern.

"No," Quin said. He pinned Alwyn with a stare, willing him to turn around. But Alwyn was intent on the ring and the crowd, calling for Gibson. Quin swore in French. "I need that book."

"We'll wait until the morning and send a message to Alwyn's house. Now that he's met us—"

"I've waited too long already."

I frowned. Had I misheard him? From the desperate glare he bestowed on Alwyn, I didn't think so. He spoke as if he had wanted—needed—the book for much longer than he'd known me.

"The crowd is getting restless," Jacob told him. "It's too dangerous for...the lad."

Quin's gaze shifted to me. He blinked rapidly, dispersing the shadows that had banked in his eyes. "Aye," he murmured so quietly that I almost didn't hear it over the noise swelling around us. "Your safety is most important."

I felt numb, not able to think clearly. Quin had come to this realm to find the book and cure me—hadn't he? Or was there another reason he needed the book? His expression was unreadable as he gained Alwyn's attention.

"The priest," he said to the earl. "What's his name?"

But Alwyn simply smiled and gripped Quin's shoulder. "Bains!" he shouted, signaling for the proprietor to join him. "Bains! I have a proposition for you." As Bains waddled over, Alwyn lowered his voice and said to Quin, "You will fight and you'll lose. Understand? Or I won't tell you a damned thing."

CHAPTER 10

I gasped and silently appealed to Jacob, but he was already ahead of me. "No," he said to Alwyn. "He won't fight for you."

Alwyn bit down on his cigar and arched an eyebrow at Quin. "Well?" It was clear from his smug half-grin that he knew what the answer would be.

Quin removed his hat and unbuttoned his jacket.

I caught his arm, but he shook his head in warning. People were watching us now as Bains approached. The eerie silence was deafening after the roar of protests over the switch.

Tommy took Quin's jacket, hat, tie, waistcoat and shirt. At the sight of Quin's muscular frame, the audience became intrigued. Their hushed whispers rippled through the room and some tried to get closer, but Alwyn kept them at bay with a few barked orders.

"Why should I trust your friend?" Bains asked darkly.

"That's your choice." Alwyn chomped down on his cigar. "But I think your customers would like to see him fight, and as a shrewd businessman, I'm sure you want to keep your audience happy. Imagine the mischief they could get up to if denied their sport."

Bains glanced around at the patrons as the whispers became shouts. They called on him to let Quin fight and bayed for his blood if he did not. Someone had already led Old Filth away and the other opponent stood waiting. He was huge with a mean sneer that revealed large gaps between his teeth. I didn't want Quin to fight him.

But he did not meet my gaze and I didn't dare throw myself at him and plead with him to refuse. That wouldn't do either of us any good.

"You don't fight fair," Bains said to Alwyn. From the resigned way he said it, we all knew he'd given in.

"Sometimes it's not about fighting fair. Sometimes it's simply about showing up." Alwyn grinned wolfishly.

"Get in there," Bains growled at Quin. Before Quin could move off, Bains grabbed his arm. "And if I find out you threw it, I'll mess up that face of yours so bad your mother won't recognize you."

The crowd roared its approval as Quin joined the other fighter in the ring. I felt sick.

"He'll be all right," Jacob whispered to me as the other fellow threw a punch and Quin easily dodged it. "He's strong and has good instincts."

"Yes, but he has to lose, or Alwyn won't tell him the priest's name."

"Then he'll go down before he gets injured."

"You think so?" I said wryly. "I hope you're right." But I had a horrible feeling that Quin would want to put on a good show. His masculine pride would forbid him to give up easily.

We watched as Quin dodged a few more punches before finally getting in one of his own. The blow to the other man's stomach sent him reeling backward into the crowd who only shoved him forward again into the ring. He gasped for air and Quin allowed him a moment to recover before repeating the punch.

"Why is he hitting him in the stomach and not the face?" I asked.

"Because bare-knuckle fighting is not the same as boxing with gloves," Tommy told me. "Punching the hard bones of a jaw or skull will hurt Quin's hand just as much, maybe even break it. But punching a soft belly will wind his opponent and save Quin's hands. It's the better strategy." He nodded in approval. "Your warrior knows what he's doing."

He was also the better fighter. Everyone there recognized it. He had a longer reach and was faster, getting in blow after rapid blow, but dancing away from the other man's fist as he wound up to punch. Quin was going to win, and win easily. The crowd knew it, and Bains knew it, going by his triumphant smirk in Alwyn's direction. The only people who didn't seem to think Quin would win were Alwyn and me. Quin wanted that book at all costs.

But not because of me.

"My God," I heard Jacob say. "He's damned good." He sounded impressed and a little awed.

Quin finally went down after a blow slammed into his stomach. He had not defended himself or tried to get out of the way, and his body took the full force of the other man's punch. He did not get up.

"Quin!" My cry was lost in the angry shouts of the spectators. They knew he could have avoided his opponent's fist if he'd wanted to, and they suspected foul play.

Quin's pride had won out. He'd obeyed Alwyn's orders while proving that he could have won the fight.

"Fool!" Alwyn threw his cigar onto the floor where it sizzled in the spilled ale before getting trodden on. "Your friend is a damned imbecile, Beaufort! He's put us all in danger."

Bains met his gaze from across the ring and shook his head. He might have caught Alwyn out at his game, but he had not won, either. The drunken crowd's objections grew louder, echoing around the basement. They called for Quin's blood and blamed Bains for the farcical result. The referee appealed to Bains just as a stool was flung into the ring. It smashed near Quin's head, and he leapt to his feet. Seeing him healthy and alert riled the spectators more.

"Bloody cheats!" one shouted.

"Bains! You owe me a quid."

"You better pay up or your dog won't get out alive."

Oh God. "Quin!" I ran toward him, but Jacob and Tommy held me back.

"We have to get you out of here," Jacob growled. "Up the stairs! Now!"

"I can't go without him." It wasn't simply that I didn't want to leave him behind, I couldn't. Not if I wanted to survive the curse.

We headed into the ring. The crowd grew thicker around Quin and Bains. The money collectors formed a ring around their employer, but not even they could hold back a hundred men intent on revenge and havoc.

We pushed into the ring, or what was left of it, and joined Quin. His gaze connected with mine then quickly roamed over me, to check that I was unharmed perhaps, or still in disguise. I touched my fingertips to his ridged stomach where he'd been hit. A bruise was already blooming.

"You couldn't lose properly?" Tommy snapped. He must be panicked or he wouldn't have spoken so candidly. "Fine mess you've landed us in."

The crowd shouted at Quin and Bains, and some argued among themselves too. Ale and entire tankards were thrown in our direction as we backed into the center of the ring. Our party and Bains's formed a cluster surrounded by the angry mob.

"Bains!" Jacob called. "You have to offer them their money back."

"It's not my bloody fault! It's Alwyn's. He should pay 'em."

"Alwyn has gone." It was true. I only hoped he would still give us the name of the priest in the morning when we called on him at home.

If we got out of the tavern alive and unharmed.

Quin gripped my arm and roughly pulled me behind him. He looked ready to take on the entire roomful of drunks. I wondered if he were capable. He had, after all, sent dozens of demons back to the otherworld single-handedly.

"Giving them their money back won't be enough," Bains said, puffing like a steam engine. He wiped the sweat off his brow with the back of his hand. "I should thrash you for that pathetic act," he growled at Quin.

Another stool was lobbed from the back of the crowd. Quin and Jacob fended it off before it hit us, but the crowd cheered. They'd found a new sport and the tide began to shift away from us and toward the walls where the furniture and barrels were stacked. Our exit, however, was still blocked.

My heart hammered in my chest and a tremble rippled through me. Quin, standing at my back, must have sensed my fear. He circled his arm around my middle. "Stay close to me."

I wanted to believe he could protect me, but there were so many.

"Calm down!" Jacob shouted at the crowd as he punched away a flying table leg. "Bains will give you your money back!"

Bains made a hissing sound, but grudgingly nodded. He

put up his hands, placating. "Anyone who bet on St. Clair to win will be reimbursed."

Half the crowd quieted, but not all. They had been cheated of their entertainment and wanted to see a fight. It no longer mattered if it didn't take place in the ring.

"Go upstairs!" Jacob ordered them. They were at least quieter so that he could be heard. "If you leave now, I will buy you all an ale."

"Two!" someone called back.

Laughter and echoes of agreement rang around the basement.

"Two then," Jacob agreed.

"It'll cost you a fortune, sir," Tommy said.

But it had worked. The spectators put down their weapons and surged up the staircase to the trapdoor. Quin let me go when the last of them disappeared. I drew in a long, measured breath and exhaled slowly. That had been too close.

"Send the account to my house," Jacob told Bains. "Eaton Square."

I wasn't sure if Bains heard him, however. His one eye pinned Quin with a steely glare. His lips peeled back and he bared his teeth. "You could have ruined me! I hope Alwyn is paying you well to dance for him."

Quin ignored him.

"That's it? You almost start a riot in my tavern and you think you can walk away?"

"It's Alwyn you want to talk to," Jacob said. "We needed something from him and struck a deal. Now, if you'll excuse us."

"Excuse you! You think I care about your deal? Alwyn is not here. You are."

Jacob squared up to him, apparently oblivious to the

thugs backing up Bains. "There was no riot, Bains. The trouble is over. Chalk it up to a bad experience and move on."

"Move on! A bad experience!" Spittle flew from Bains's lips and splattered on his massive chest. "My reputation is ruined! If you think I'll let you walk away from here after that, you're mistaken. I don't care who you are, toff, you're not in your big, fancy house now. You're in my den. We play by my rules here."

As if he'd given them a signal, his men produced knives from where they'd hidden them beneath jackets and waistcoats. I gasped and found myself once more being roughly pulled behind Quin.

"Bloody hell," Jacob muttered. "Emily's going to be upset when she learns what happened here."

Tommy grunted. "I won't tell her if you won't inform Miss Langley."

"I'm afraid they'll probably find out somehow, Dawson. Women always do."

With a sudden burst of speed, Quin charged into the group. Jacob and Tommy followed. Both were armed with knives. Where had they gotten those? Quin, too, wielded a dagger. He easily dodged the first thug's wild slash, and kicked him away.

"Get back, Cara!" he ordered.

"Cara?" Bains frowned at me. "You're a woman!" He advanced on me as his companions kept Tommy, Jacob and Quin busy. I wanted to help, but I felt utterly useless. Why hadn't I thought to carry a knife too?

"Stay where you are," I warned Bains. I backed into a stack of broken stools near the wall, but he kept coming and coming. His small, pink tongue wet his lips like a dog that had sniffed out a piece of meat.

"Got you now," he said with a twisted grin.

I gripped a stool leg behind me, but I wasn't sure if I could hit him hard enough to make him stop. The stool leg was small and he was very large. A lump formed in my throat and I swallowed it down; now was no time for fear. The others were still occupied and I was hemmed into a corner with the slavering Bains advancing on me. I needed a cool head and a steady hand.

The spirit of the Irish fighter suddenly appeared near Bains. "Aim for his knees." He rubbed his bruised and bloodied hands together in anticipation of some violence.

"He has weak knees?" Forget keeping my talent a secret. Bains already knew I was female, he might as well know I was a medium too.

Bains looked around. "Who are you talking to?"

The Irishman chuckled. "The knees are weakest. Don't have to hit a man hard there to make him lose his balance. And a fat pig like Bains loses his balance easy. Wish I could show you."

"You can. You can pick up one of these stools and use it on him."

"I got no beef with Bains."

"You're mad," Bains said, laughing. His tongue darted out again and slid along his top lip. "Come here, Mad Cara. Let Bains give you something to ramble about."

Ugh. The man was disgusting. The fight behind him was drawing to a close. Three thugs lay on the ground, and Jacob, Tommy and Quin battled with one last opponent each. Quin spotted me and quickly ended his fight with a fist to the other man's jaw.

"It's all over," I said to Bains.

"Can't be." He spun round to see for himself. He muttered a curse then looked to me again. He reached for me, perhaps planning on using me as a bargaining chip with a fast approaching and very fierce looking Quin.

I didn't give him a chance. I smacked the table leg into his knee. He screamed in pain as his leg buckled. He lost his balance and toppled to the floor, landing with a bone-shuddering thud.

"Good girl!" the spirit said with a nod of approval. Then he vanished.

"Cara!" Quin had barely gotten my name out before his fingers wrapped around my arm. He steered me up the stairs, his grip bruising.

I glanced back to see Tommy and Jacob following, having dispensed with the remainder of the men. Bains hauled himself to his feet, grunting and sweating like an animal.

We wound our way through the crowded taproom. Quin received the occasional jeer or punch on his shoulder, but he forged ahead with single-minded determination. He had not let go of my arm. We were about to exit when I recognized the face of someone I'd never expected to see there.

"Nathaniel?" I stopped and Quin did too, following my gaze. "What's he doing here?"

"Following us." Quin spoke in dark, guttural tones. His temper hadn't yet dissipated and I grew worried as he carved a path to Nathaniel.

When the man Nathaniel was speaking to nodded at us, Nathaniel's mouth flopped open and his eyes bulged wide. He broke away and made for the door, albeit in a circuitous pattern to avoid us. But he wasn't fast enough to beat Quin, despite him drawing me along in his wake. He grasped Nathaniel's collar. "Why are you following us?"

"I'm not!" Nathaniel's eyes bulged even farther and his face turned purple. He gasped for air and flailed pathetically at Quin.

The patrons around us went quiet, but none intervened. They were finally getting the sport they'd been denied downstairs.

"Quin," I said. "You'll strangle him."

"That's the idea." Nevertheless, he let him go. "Answer me."

Nathaniel spluttered and coughed, but fortunately his face returned to its natural pallid color. Behind us, Jacob had caught up, while Tommy peeled away and headed for the door. He still carried Quin's clothes.

"This is Nathaniel Faraday," I said to Jacob. "We're about to discover what he's doing here."

"Nothing!" Nathaniel squeaked. He rubbed his throat and coughed again. "I swear to you, I wasn't following you. I happened to be driving past when I spotted you getting out of a coach," he said to Quin. "I went on my way, but couldn't help wondering what you were doing in this place. After I concluded my business, I returned via this route and decided to find out. I was asking after you just now." He blinked owlishly at me. "I admit to being surprised at seeing you, Cara, particularly dressed as a...er...country lad."

"I don't believe you," Quin snarled.

Nathaniel held up his hands. "It's the truth! I'm a scholar, and scholars become curious about these things. I thought it an odd place for a man like you to be seen." His gaze flicked to me. "I admit that I'd hoped to inform Cara that you liked to frequent these sorts of dens. I hadn't expected her to be a party to them."

"Why would you do such a thing?" I said.

He straightened his crooked tie. "Isn't it obvious? I can see that St. Clair and you are...well, acquainted. I had hoped... that is, I wanted to renew my...friendship with you."

"By disparaging Quin?" I shook my head. "That is not the right way to go about renewing our friendship."

Nathaniel conceded the point with a nod. "Forgive me. I'm not very adept at wooing."

He'd been quite good at it on the ship. I wasn't sure what to say to his response so I said nothing. He wouldn't meet my gaze and began to edge away from us.

Beside me, Quin stiffened. He still looked furious, but he let Nathaniel go.

Jacob watched him leave with a bemused expression. "I'm not sure what you see in him, Cara."

We left The Brickmaker's Arms a moment later, before the crowd finished their two free ales and decided to pursue further compensation. I was sandwiched between Jacob and Quin. Outside, there was no sign of Nathaniel. The Beaufort coach pulled to a stop and Tommy jumped down from the back. He handed Quin his clothes and we piled into the cabin.

"You too, Dawson," Jacob said.

Tommy climbed in behind us and shut the door. Quin put his shirt on, but not his jacket, waistcoat or tie. I blew out a breath as the coach rolled off and flopped back against the leather seat. What a night!

"Do you think Faraday was lying?" Jacob asked.

"I'm not sure," I said, answering at the same time as Quin. "Aye."

"You think he was spying on us?" I shook my head, but I suspected he was right. "For himself or for Myer?"

"It doesn't matter," Jacob said. "If he was spying, that means he probably knows you're after the book of spells and not simply curious about the supernatural."

Quin closed his bruised fist on his knee. He still seemed wound up like a tight coil. It wouldn't take much for him to unravel. "We'll visit him tomorrow."

"No." I removed my oversized hat and shook my hair free. "If he was following us on behalf of Myer, then we should pretend we're none the wiser. We may need Myer's help again, and I'd rather keep him on our side. If he suspects that we know he sent Nathaniel, he'll be on his guard. Besides." I flicked my hair over my shoulder. "Nathaniel may be telling the truth. He may simply be trying to woo me again."

"You're not going anywhere near him," Jacob growled. "I don't trust him."

"Aye," Quin said. "He's not suitable for you, Cara."

I sniffed. "I see you two can finally agree on something."

"I suspect there's something else we agree upon," Jacob said. "You're quite a fighter, St. Clair."

Quin grunted.

"You're clearly experienced in hand to hand combat."

"I've been involved in many fights." He turned away to look out the window, even though there was little to see in the dimly lit streets.

Jacob appealed to me, but I merely shrugged. I was in no mood to coax answers out of Quin. Not even the answer to one burning question—was he after the book for his own reasons? My body hummed with the excitement of the evening and I felt too restless even to sit still for the journey home.

"Do you think Emily will still be awake?" I said as we drove around St. James' Park.

"Yes," Jacob said heavily.

"Miss Langley too," Tommy said, equally as heavily.

"What shall we tell them?"

"Nothing." I glanced at each of them, trying to assess how they'd fared in their fights. "Is anybody injured?"

Jacob shook his head while Tommy showed me a rent in his sleeve. Dried blood crusted around a small flesh wound. It wasn't too deep and could be easily hidden from Sylvia or Emily.

"We'll tell them everything went well and we got what we needed." The last thing I wanted was Emily forbidding me to go anywhere ever again. She had taken my side against Jacob so far, but if she found out what had transpired at The Brickmaker's Arms I suspected she would want to keep me protected as much as he did.

"I don't want to lie to my wife," Jacob said.

"Then let me do it."

We arrived back at the house. The windows were ablaze with light when the rest of the street was shrouded in shadows.

"Someone's here," Quin announced.

Jacob couldn't get to the window fast enough. He shoved Quin out of the way then growled low in his throat. "Alwyn."

We climbed out of the cabin and that's when I saw what he'd seen. The escutcheon painted on the side of the other coach contained both a thistle and an eagle. The de Mordaunt crest. It would seem those elements had remained with the family through the centuries.

"Stay back with Tommy," Jacob said to me. "Quin, with me."

He and Quin approached the coach parked on the other side of the road. It wasn't so far away that I began to feel ill, but I wanted to hear what Alwyn said so I faked symptoms of fever. Tommy crossed the road with me.

"Coward," Jacob spat through the window. I couldn't see Alwyn, and I suspected he wouldn't show his face. He knew how well Quin could fight now and wouldn't risk his wrath. Anger vibrated off Quin in waves.

"You put on a poor show," Alwyn told him.

"I fulfilled my end of the bargain." Quin kept his voice low, but the threat in it was unmistakable. "Tell me the name of the priest or I'll tear you apart."

I could hear Alwyn's nervous swallow from where I stood. "Why do you think I'm here? To congratulate you on such a spectacular failure?"

Jacob grunted. "If you think that was a failure then you weren't watching the same fight I was. Tell us, Alwyn. That was the agreement."

"Of course, of course. The priest's name is Father William. He's from the Catholic church of St. Etheldreda in Ely Place."

"How did he know about the book we seek?" Quin asked.

"I don't know if he did. He came to my man of business, a week or two ago, and asked if I'd be interested in selling off some books that have been in my family for generations. Very humble fellow, apparently. I agreed, since I have no need of them and he offered a nice sum at a time when my creditors were becoming insistent. He mentioned no specific book as far as I am aware."

"Did he say anything else?"

"How should I know? The entire transaction was done through my man. I never saw the fellow. Now, if you don't mind, I must seek out another den that will satisfy my thirst for blood sports and gambling. Don't think Bains will let me back in, and I'm not as good at disguises as your little lass."

Jacob and Quin turned to me then had to jump back away from the wheels as Alwyn thumped the cabin roof and the coach lurched forward.

I quickly headed back across the street and up the front steps to the house. Both Emily and Sylvia met us at the door. They must have sent the servants to bed as none were about.

"Well?" Emily said, clasping Jacob's arm, her eyes bright with excitement. "How was it?"

"Entertaining," he said without inflection.

She turned to me. "Cara?"

"Oh yes, very entertaining."

Sylvia put her hands on her hips and eyed each of the men. "You look more disheveled than when you left, and Quin is half undressed. Again."

Emily's eyes narrowed as she too took in the appearance of each man. "Jacob, have you been fighting?"

He gave her an innocent look. "Why do you say that?"

"Don't answer me with a question."

"We got our answer from Alwyn," I told her. "That's the important thing. It turns out the book may have been sold with some others, but he did give us the name of the priest who bought the collection."

"That's promising." Sylvia seemed to have moved on from the topic of the fights, but Emily continued to watch her husband from beneath lowered lashes. I suspected he would have to answer a few questions in private.

"We'll seek out the priest tomorrow," Quin said. "It's late. Cara must retire for the evening."

"But I wanted to find out more about prize fights," Sylvia protested. "How many people were in attendance? What were the fighters like? Was it particularly bloody?"

"I'll tell you tomorrow." I yawned for good measure. Hopefully she would have forgotten all about it by then. I could probably distract her with talk of the ball.

I didn't think Jacob would get off so lightly, however. Emily continued to watch him through hooded eyes as we left. Not that I expected her to become angry with him, as she had supported my desire to attend, but I suspected he would tell her everything after all. Honesty was an important part of their marriage.

I sighed. At least that made one honest man that I knew. Quin was being positively mysterious. Being mysterious and handsome were turning out not to be the alluring combination I'd originally thought.

Once again I waited for Sylvia and Tommy to fall asleep before I got up and sat on the edge of Quin's bed. He was already sitting, apparently expecting me.

"I want the truth this time, Quin," I whispered. "Do you want the book so that I can be cured? Or are you after it for your own reasons?"

CHAPTER 11

uin became very still. "Those are two different questions. Answering aye to one does not mean answering nay to the other."

"Then answer them separately," I hissed.

In the darkness, I could just make out his head shaking. "Don't, Cara."

I threw up my hands. "Is that all you have to say?"

His dark eyes glistened like polished jet as he stared back at me. I began to cry. It was silly, but I couldn't help it. The combination of excitement and fear from our adventure, and my frustration with Quin, played havoc with my emotions. And at the back of my mind was the even more palpable fear that I would not be cured.

"Cara." The combination of his accent and leonine voice sent a thrill through me. He scooted down the bed and touched my cheek. His thumb wiped away tears I'd hoped he couldn't see. "Don't cry." He pressed his lips to my forehead and didn't draw them away for several beats of my heart.

"Stop it," I mumbled. "Stop being so nice."

He tucked my hair behind my ear and drew back. "I don't

tell you everything because not knowing keeps you from being afraid. Do you understand?"

"No." I swiped at my tears with the back of my hand. "I want to trust you, Quin. Tell me I can."

He hesitated and my stomach plunged. "I told you," he finally said. "I have done bad things in my life. You're right not to trust me. But I won't allow any harm to come to you, Cara."

"How can you say that and then tell me I shouldn't trust you?"

"Because…I…" He muttered something under his breath in a language I didn't understand.

"Quin?"

"You must have faith in your own feelings, Cara. You know in your heart what the truth is. I know you do."

He was talking in riddles. "What does that mean?"

He shook his head and twisted away to lie down. A small grunt of pain escaped his lips.

"Your injuries," I said, reaching for him without thinking. I touched his chest and felt my way down to where the other fighter had bruised him. "Does it hurt?"

"More than I remember."

That almost encouraged a smile from me, despite my heavy heart. "You don't feel pain when you fight the demons?"

"I do while I'm here, but it vanishes as soon as I return to the other realm and heal. My visits here are usually too brief for me to feel pain for long." He sucked air between his teeth as my fingers pressed into the bruised area.

"Sorry," I said. "I'm checking for broken ribs."

"And punishing me for my secrecy."

"You're behaving like a child."

He huffed out a breath and remained silent as I continued my assessment. I gentled my touch and ran my hand over the ridges of hard muscle and warm flesh. My fingers roamed up his chest, through the scattered hairs, to his shoulders. I traced a strap of corded muscle and found a small moon-shaped scar. It reminded me of the larger scars on his back and I opened my mouth to ask him how he'd gotten them, but shut it again. He wouldn't tell me.

"Cara," he murmured thickly. "We must not."

But I wanted to. Despite his secrets and continued warnings that he couldn't be trusted, I wanted to explore his body further. I wanted to kiss him as we'd kissed outside Myer's house. I wanted to go on a scandalous adventure with him.

But he was right. We couldn't. For one thing, if we were discovered, it would shame Emily and Jacob. For another, it could ruin my life. Nothing could come of Quin and me. He didn't belong here. Besides, I was supposed to find a gentleman and settle down; I wanted to, although with one of my choosing. Lying with Quin would take away my best bargaining chip—my virginity—and limit my choices. I was no fool.

I pulled back and returned to my bed. I crawled under the covers where Sylvia's warmth provided little comfort. On the other side of the screen, Quin's deep sigh echoed mine.

I shut my eyes but didn't fall asleep for a long time.

* * *

I KNEW something was wrong with Quin before we reached Ely Place. He wouldn't sit still in the coach, either fidgeting with his tie or trying to find a comfortable position for his long legs. He didn't meet my gaze. When the coach finally pulled to a stop outside St. Etheldreda's Catholic Church, I could stand it no longer.

"Quin, what's wrong?"

"Nothing." His sullenness implied otherwise.

The footman opened the door and we alighted onto the pavement outside the ancient stone building. Nestled between rather plain modern terraces, it looked out of place but welcoming. I gazed up at the large stained glass window and was about to ask Quin if the building had been there in his lifetime when I heard his sharp intake of breath.

"Are you all right?"

He looked pale and hot, and his shoulders slumped as if he were caving in on himself. "Come, Cara. We must do this quickly." He walked off without waiting for me.

"Why? Quin, what's happening to you?"

"Nothing." But even as he said it, he groaned and clutched at his stomach.

I rested my hand on his back and tried to look at his face again, but he forged on, albeit more slowly. A passing gentleman eyed us with curiosity but did not stop to offer his help. Another crossed the street to avoid us, and a hansom cab pulled up a little way behind our coach, but no one got out. I registered all of this activity yet hardly took any notice. Quin's sickly pallor had me too worried to care what others thought of our odd behavior.

"If you don't feel well, we can come back another time," I told him.

"I'm not coming back." He stopped and squeezed his eyes shut. His mouth twisted into a hard grimace.

"Quin!" I directed him to rest against the church's low stone fence, but he shook me off. "Quin, this is madness. You're in no state to talk to Father William."

He bent forward and sucked in great gasps of air. I caught his hat before it fell to the ground and rubbed his back, but it was a useless gesture. His body began to tremble as if he'd been overtaken by a fever. But he couldn't have caught an illness so quickly; he'd been perfectly fine a moment ago. It was only as he'd gotten out of the coach and approached the church that he'd shown symptoms.

His illness wasn't a medical condition; it was a supernatural one.

I didn't know how to cure that sort of sickness. The only thing I could do was take him home. I was about to signal the footman to help me get Quin back in the coach when a man dressed in priest's robes emerged from the church. Beside him, the ghostly form of another, younger man lingered. He too was dressed in priestly robes, but his were caked in blood at his chest.

"May I help you?" asked the living priest, approaching. "Is he all right?"

"My friend has a stomach ache," I said, trying to ignore the dead priest as he approached Quin. "I'm going to take him home."

"No," Quin growled. He straightened, but it seemed to take considerable effort. His skin was as white as a porcelain doll's and his eyes were glassy orbs. He still trembled.

I took his hand and he gripped it in return, as if the contact helped. He rallied a little, even casting a small smile at the priest.

"Are you Father William?" I asked.

"I am. Father William Lockhart." The man had a friendly face and deep laughter lines radiated from the corners of his warm brown eyes. "Would you like to come inside and sit down, sir?"

"Christ, no." Quin glanced at Father William. "Apologies. No, thank you. This is close enough."

The ghost frowned and squatted in front of Quin. He rubbed his jaw, causing it to shift into an awkward position. It must have been broken during his death. I tried not to look at him, but it was difficult not to as he suddenly gasped and scurried back from Quin. He crossed himself, twice.

I couldn't speak to him and alert him that I was a medium for fear of upsetting Father William. While many people despised mediums, either through fear or distrust, I'd found the clergy were the worst. Ever since one particular Catholic priest in Melbourne had called me a demonic creature, I'd been sure to hide my talent from them. I wasn't about to risk Father William dissociating himself from us before he could help.

"Perhaps if you wouldn't mind getting a glass of water for Mr. St. Clair," I said to the priest. "We would be most grateful."

"Of course, of course. I'll be right back." For an elderly man, he moved rather swiftly into the church. The ghost remained, albeit at a wary distance.

"Good morning," I said gently to him.

Despite my politeness, he lost his balance in his shock and fell against the church wall.

"Who's there?" Quin asked me.

"A ghost. A priest, I think. I'm a medium," I told the spirit. "My name is Cara Moreau."

"Father Ignatius," he said with a nod of greeting that had his jaw swinging like an unhinged sign in the breeze. "You should not be here."

"We need to speak to Father William," I said. "It's very important, but my friend cannot seem to enter the church without feeling ill."

"Cara," Quin snapped. He looked as if he were about to say something further, but he doubled over again as another wave of pain gripped him.

I removed my glove and rested my cool hand on the back of his neck. He was so hot, and had begun to shake again. I didn't think we could wait for Father William to return. Quin needed to get away from the church now.

"Do you know anything about his illness that can help us?" I asked the spirit.

Quin groaned again and reached for me. I clasped his hands in mine and squatted before him. "Can you stand?" I asked him gently. "We have to get you away from here."

He shook his head. "A few more moments."

The spirit edged back toward the church door, crossing himself the entire time. "The devil is in him." He pointed a shaky finger at me. "You are the devil's whore for cavorting with him."

"I am not cavorting. Oh, never mind. If you're not going to help then leave us in peace."

"You should not be here." It wasn't clear if he was speaking to me or Quin. Either way, Quin couldn't hear him. "You belong there. Go!" He made a shooing gesture at Quin. "Go back, Devil."

I stood and marched over to Father Ignatius's ghost. He wasn't much taller than me, and was just as slender with a rather boyish face. "He is not the devil," I snapped. "He is an otherworldly warrior and has battled demons in this realm to keep it safe. He deserves your thanks, not your accusations."

The priest switched his narrow, beady focus to me. "If that is so then he should certainly not be here. Warriors are never let off their leash. Never." He blinked out of existence.

I stared at the space where he'd been, unable to focus on anything except Quin's groaning behind me. The spirit's words were a confusing mess in my head. I couldn't sift through them, let alone determine what he meant.

"Cara." Quin's appeal was laced with pain.

I turned back to him and my stomach dove. His face was twisted, a picture of torture, and his lips had turned blue. He shook violently, but did not take his eyes off me.

I took his face in my hands and searched his clouded,

pain-filled eyes. But what I saw wasn't the devil described by the priest. I saw a frightened and vulnerable man who was not used to either emotion.

"If he doesn't return soon, we'll send Jacob here," I said. "You have to leave." I helped him to his feet just as Father William returned carrying a cup of water.

"Here," he said, handing it to Quin. He rested one hand on Quin's shoulder as he drank greedily. "There, now. Can I help you get him back into the coach, miss?"

"No, thank you." I signaled for the footman, who'd been watching and waiting by the coach's door, to come and assist Quin. "We're here to ask you something, Father. We had word from Lord Alwyn that you purchased some books from him recently."

The footman steered Quin away from me toward the coach, but Quin shook him off and waited to hear Father William's answer.

The priest nodded. "As a matter of fact, yes, I did. Some old books that had belonged to his family for centuries. He had them transported from his Derbyshire estate a few days ago."

"Is it possible to see them? There's one in particular that we're interested in viewing. Mr. St. Clair is a historian, you see, and he's come all the way from Melbourne to find a particular book that we know was compiled by Lord Alwyn's ancestor."

The priest's gaze widened. "I know the one. There was a very rare book in that collection, most likely written by a de Mordaunt. A beautiful and very old item, it was, and probably quite valuable. Mr. Ludlow from Hatchard's was excited to find it and learn more about it."

"Hatchard's, the bookshop on Piccadilly?"

"The one and only," he said with a smile. "Mr. Ludlow had

heard of Lord Alwyn's collection and commissioned me to approach him and broker the purchase."

"Why you?"

"I'm an expert on old and rare religious texts. He wanted me to verify that the books in Lord Alwyn's collection were indeed genuine, and to value them. I was happy to confirm their authenticity and Lord Alwyn eagerly accepted the price, even for that particular book. I admit to being surprised that he didn't want to keep it in the family."

I glanced at Quin, slumped against the church wall. He gasped out labored, shallow breaths and sweat beaded along his hairline. He folded his arms over his stomach and closed his eyes as another wave of pain hit him.

"Thank you, Father," I said quickly. "You've been most helpful."

"You're welcome." He approached Quin and rested his hand on his arm. "Go to the doctor, sir. And may God bless you." He formed the sign of the cross and muttered a short prayer in Latin.

Quin grunted like an injured animal and bolted for the coach. He climbed inside, unassisted, and slunk into the shadows on the far side.

"You really ought to get him some medical help," Father William said to me, with a worried shake of his head.

"I will. Thank you again. You've been most helpful." I hurried to the coach and the footman assisted me inside before shutting the door.

"I do hope you find your book before it's sold," Father William called out.

"What do you mean?"

"Mr. Ludlow had a buyer in mind when he commissioned me. I believe it was this buyer who brought it to his attention in the first place."

I thanked him again and sat back against the seat as the coach rolled forward. Beside me, Quin groaned. He doubled over, his head cradled in his hands. His body shuddered again and rocked against me in time with the coach's motion. I took him in my arms and stroked his hair until his shudders subsided. He remained there and I listened as his breathing slowly returned to normal and he no longer felt dangerously hot.

Without thinking, I kissed the top of his head and gently cupped his face, forcing him to look at me. He leaned away and his gaze met mine, wary, as if guarding himself against a barrage of questions.

"I won't ask you why that happened." I forced my voice to remain steady when my heart was jumping madly in my chest. "I know you won't tell me. And anyway, your answers aren't important. What is important is that you appear to be better." My determination to remain stern with him faltered, and a sob escaped. I pressed my lips together to hold myself in check, and managed not to let any further tears escape.

"Cara," he whispered gently, his eyes soft. He reached for me, but lowered his hand before making contact.

I slid across the seat and caught him in my arms in a fierce hug, impropriety and answers be damned. I just wanted to hold him and know that he was well again. "Don't do that again," I said on another sob. "If we have to go to any more churches, we'll send Jacob. I won't risk it."

He circled me in his arms and held me as tightly as I held him. It was difficult to tell who comforted whom, and which one of us needed the contact more. He buried his face in my neck and breathed deeply. He felt warm, but not hot, and so very, very good.

Neither of us spoke for several long, glorious moments. I didn't want to shatter the sweet peace or end the wonderful embrace. We sat entwined on the seat, gently swaying with the coach, and I had never felt so happy, as if I were exactly where I should be. In Quin's arms.

But the moment didn't last. We rounded a particularly sharp bend and Quin drew away, as if he'd suddenly realized he was doing something wrong. He leaned as far away from me as he could and did not meet my gaze.

I shifted along the seat and rested my hands in my lap. I studied my fingers and wondered if he had felt what I'd felt— a deep, strong bond that connected us as surely as the thickest rope. I didn't dare ask.

He cleared his throat. "We should go to the bookseller's."

"Yes, of course." I pulled down the window and gave instructions to the driver then leaned back again. I still could not look at Quin. I didn't want to see regret in his eyes.

Besides, I didn't dare let him see that Father Ignatius's words troubled me. The spirit had been afraid of Quin and called him the devil. What if he'd been right?

* * *

MR. LUDLOW WAS NOT in the bookshop. We left a message for him then returned to the Eaton Square house in silence. I could tell that Quin was frustrated by Ludlow's absence as much as I was, but it went further than that. He was troubled. By what, I couldn't say. He wouldn't have heard the spirit of Father Ignatius call him the devil, but from my half of the conversation, he perhaps knew what the nature of the discussion had been. He refused to look at me and focused his attention on the view out the window.

Tommy and Sylvia arrived at the house at the same time as us. They were a welcome distraction from the tension emanating from Quin. "We've been to the office of *The*

Times," Sylvia said in answer to our question. "Our advertisement for staff will appear in tomorrow's edition."

"Do you think you'll get many wishing to move to Frakingham?" I asked as we walked arm-in-arm to the drawing room. Tommy peeled off to inquire about luncheon and Quin followed behind us.

"They will if they don't know the house's history. And how can they, if they're not local? I do believe we'll have our pick of applicants." She sounded very pleased with herself.

"Has Tommy come to terms with not being promoted to butler?"

Tommy had wanted to fill the position of butler, but Langley and Sylvia had insisted he learn from a more experienced servant first. I didn't see that it was necessary, since he already performed all the jobs required of a butler—and performed them well—but Langley in particular wouldn't be swayed. He was determined to employ the best butler his fortune could buy.

"He says he has."

"What a pleasant outing you both must have had together. It's such a lovely day." I admit I was fishing for information on their relationship, but she gave nothing away.

"Very pleasant. Ah, here's Emily."

Emily joined us, along with the children, and we played with them as we discussed the implications of the book now being at Hatchard's. I didn't mention Quin's mysterious illness and he didn't speak much at all. He was too occupied with giving Gabe and Lizzy rides on his back while little Matthew clapped his hands and watched. I needed no more proof that Quin wasn't the devilish character Father Ignatius feared.

George Culvert arrived after luncheon, along with Jacob. We all retreated back to the drawing room, the children having gone upstairs, Matthew for a nap and Gabe and Lizzy to their lessons. George seemed unable to contain his excitement over something, but Jacob seemed guarded and a little uncertain. I caught him watching Quin from beneath lowered lashes several times.

"We found it!" George announced as soon as he'd greeted each of us.

"Yes," I said. "It's at Hatchard's."

He pushed his glasses up his nose. "What?"

"The book. We know it's at Hatchard's."

"It is?"

"George didn't find the book itself," Jacob said. "He found other books referencing it."

That got Quin's attention. He leaned forward, resting his elbows on his knees. "What did you learn?"

"It is not all spells and incantations. That's why it took me so long to find information about it. I was looking for references to an ancient book of spells, but I believe the book is primarily a treatise on the various realms. It is, however, very old, as you thought, St. Clair. That's why I disregarded those references whenever I read them over the years. I assumed it was long lost and therefore not helpful to my research. I'm damned annoyed at myself, let me tell you."

"Don't be too hard on yourself," Emily said. "You weren't to know it would be become important."

"That may be so, but I wish I'd taken more notice whenever I came upon a mention of it. It would have saved me some time now." He wrinkled his nose to keep his slipping glasses from sliding all the way down. He managed to stop them half way. "As far as I can tell, the book describes using the portals to travel between realms as well as the incantations that must be used to open and close them. It discusses demons and warriors too."

I frowned. He seemed not to be speaking to Quin at all, but to everyone else in the room. Jacob, however, continued to watch Quin with a wary gaze, as if he expected him to make a sudden movement.

"How will any of that cure Cara?" Emily asked, covering my hand with hers. "We don't care about accessing the realms, we just need to cure her."

"Among the limited number of incantations, I believe the book mentions the three that we know of and several more, all relating to curses. These curses were supposed to be used on demons, and other supernatural creatures emerging through the portals, to control them, not on humans. Although I found no reference to the specific curse that has been inflicted upon Cara, we must trust Quin when he tells us that there is indeed a counter curse contained within the book's pages."

We all looked to Quin. "You can trust me," he said. "I would not lie about something as important as Cara's life."

A lump formed in my throat. Not only was hearing him say it reassuring, but hearing him say it with such rawness in his voice filled my heart.

"You already knew most of what Culvert learned, didn't you?" Jacob asked Quin.

He nodded.

Jacob rested his elbow on the arm of his chair and stroked his top lip in thought. They locked gazes for a brief, charged moment, but it was Quin who looked away first.

George went on. "The book is supposed to be guarded by humans of impeccable character who will keep it safe."

"The spirit of Brother Francis told us his abbot was a guardian," I said. "What I don't quite understand is why *he* was a guardian when the book has been in the library of the de Mordaunt family and its descendants all this time?"

"Because it hasn't been there all this time," Emily whispered. Her eyes brightened with feverish excitement.

"Then where has it been?" Sylvia asked. "And how did it get *back* to Lord Alwyn's library?

"Good questions," George muttered.

"There is another one," I said. "How did Garrett get a hold of it? He must have seen that curse in the book or he wouldn't have known to speak it."

Quin nodded. "If the book has been in Lord Alwyn's library in recent years, Garrett must have been given access to it."

"Perhaps he learned of its location as master of the Society for Supernatural Activity and was granted access upon request. A small bribe would have been sufficient. Lord Alwyn didn't seem aware of the book's power and so wouldn't have minded giving him access."

"That also means that Alwyn probably isn't the one who returned the lost book to his library, if it had indeed been absent at all," Jacob said. "It happened earlier."

"Garrett may have found the same reference to the de Mordaunt family that Quin did." I looked at him. "He may have deciphered that same image and recognized Alwyn's family crest."

"If Garrett saw the book, wouldn't he have made a record of where to find it?" Emily asked. "Perhaps even have made copies of the spells and curses for members of the society to study?"

"It would seem he didn't," George said. "If Myer didn't know of its whereabouts, or the words of the incantations, then none in the society did."

Emily's hand, still covering mine, squeezed. "Thank goodness Myer and Faraday didn't understand the symbols in that text you studied, Quin. If Myer knew you had a clue to the book's whereabouts, he would have made sure to follow you."

I exchanged a glance with Quin.

"He did," Jacob said before I could. "He sent Faraday to follow us to The Brickmaker's Arms last night."

"And today to the church," I said. "There was a hansom cab parked a little behind us but nobody got out. I was a little distracted at the time and had forgotten all about it until now."

"Aye," Quin muttered.

"You two aren't the most alert couple," George said with a shake of his head. "Young people these days."

"You're forgetting that Quin is quite old," Emily countered.

"He's positively ancient," Sylvia chimed in.

We told them about our morning at St. Etheldreda's Church, leaving out the parts about Quin's illness and the spirit's reaction to him. I finished by telling them we hoped Ludlow hadn't already sold off the book.

"We must find out who the interested party is, regardless," Jacob said. "Nobody should have access to that text."

"Including us?" George frowned.

"I think we can be trusted," Emily said with a smile.

George stayed for the afternoon, and joined in playing with his niece and nephew when the nanny brought them in. The two children were besotted with Quin, however, and demanded more rides on his back. Quin obliged, much to Jacob's irritation. His frown did not leave his face as he sat beside me.

"There is something I need to tell you," he said quietly.

From the way he was no longer looking at Quin, I suspected it was about him. Fortunately Quin was preoccupied and didn't notice.

"Go on," I said.

"I think I know which realm he's from."

I twisted to look at him fully. My heart pounded once then stilled. "Oh?"

He met my gaze with his steady one. There was concern in their depths and sympathy too. "Today when you went to the church, did he become ill?"

I swallowed heavily and nodded.

"In that case, I'm positive."

"Where? Which realm?"

"Purgatory."

CHAPTER 12

*P*urgatory!

It was a Catholic concept, not believed by all Christian religions, let alone non-Christian ones. It was said to be the place between Heaven and Hell where sinners could redeem themselves and earn a place in Heaven. Souls that were sent there weren't deemed evil enough to go to Hell, but had committed sins that blocked their access to Heaven.

Quin had said he was from a realm 'in between'. He'd been telling me all along that he was from Purgatory, but I'd not deciphered his meaning and he'd not been willing to explain it. I knew from my interaction with spirits that after death, souls entered the Waiting Area or could choose to remain and haunt this realm. Those in the Waiting Area were then sorted into categories according to the life they'd led. I wasn't able to communicate with souls beyond the Waiting Area so I'd never learned anything more about those categories. It would seem the concepts of Heaven, Hell and Purgatory were accurate. There was, however, one other thing I knew about Purgatory: souls committed there had to endure pain and punishment to purify them of their sins and become worthy of Heaven.

Quin grinned as he scooped up little Matthew and tossed him in the air. I couldn't stop staring. Surely there'd been a mistake; surely he hadn't committed a sin bad enough to cause him to suffer in Purgatory for centuries?

"Cara." Jacob's quietly earnest voice had me turning toward him. "I know it's a shock, but you mustn't let him see that you know. We can't fully trust him. Do you understand?"

He was speaking to me like an adult to a child, but I wasn't outraged. At that moment, I *did* feel very childlike as I tried to take it all in. "I'll be careful."

"Good. We have to be, not only for your sake, but for everyone associated with you." He glanced pointedly at the laughing children as they gathered around the man who'd done something so terrible that, upon his death, he'd been sent to Purgatory.

His death. Quin was most definitely dead then. Even though he'd said as much, I hadn't really believed it before. There was no way around that fact, and no coming back from it.

Yet he didn't look dead. Everyone could see him, and he was as solid as me. It was all so confusing.

"Cara," Jacob murmured, "there is an incantation I now know can be found in the book that might become useful."

"What does it do?" My voice sounded small, lost. I tried to rally myself and fight through the fog in my brain but it was so *hard*.

"It destroys the portal forever."

His words slammed into me, blasting the fog away. I rounded on him. "No." I put as much ferocity behind my whisper as I dared. Fortunately Quin seemed not to notice, but Emily glanced our way. "We cannot use it. Quin will be trapped in...that place...and never be able to return." And visit me.

"He wouldn't be needed here if the demons are also trapped in their own realm."

A hot ball of tears clogged my throat. It was all too much. I wanted to question Jacob further, but the children's nanny arrived and collected them, relieving Quin of his horsey duties. He sat near me, oblivious to the explosive piece of news Jacob had just delivered. His eyes twinkled like bright stars and a small smile curved his lips as he told Emily that he believed Gabe would grow into a fine, strong man. There were no signs of his earlier illness. He looked every bit the fun, favorite uncle, and nothing like a soul trapped in the misery of Purgatory.

* * *

I WARRED with myself for the rest of the day and finally decided, as I lay in bed that night listening to Sylvia snoring, that I had to talk to Quin. Jacob hadn't wanted me to say anything, but I couldn't not ask him. He ought to know that we knew he came from Purgatory, and have an opportunity to explain.

I waited a little longer, until I was sure Tommy was also asleep, then rounded the screen. It had become a nightly event and Quin didn't seem at all surprised when I perched on the end of his bed.

He sat up and I could just make out the shape of his shoulders and chest. I blew out a breath in an attempt to stay focused.

"You have questions about my illness at the church today," he began. "Cara, please do not—"

"I know why you became ill." My heart fluttered a warning to proceed carefully.

He stilled. "Go on."

"You're from Purgatory."

His brief intake of breath was the only sound in the room, and even that was barely audible in the thick, heavy air. The silence stretched and suddenly it seemed like I'd made a terrible mistake.

"Say something," I urged him. "Please. Just…say something." *Deny it, tell me that I'm wrong. Tell me you weren't sent to a place of pain and suffering after your death.*

"Purgatory is one name for it," he finally answered.

Tears burned the backs of my eyes. It was the confirmation I'd dreaded. "Is it the same as what the Catholic religion teaches?"

"It is a place in between. A place where sinners are punished and given a chance to redeem themselves. Those that do may move on to a better afterlife. Those that don't go somewhere worse."

"But I don't understand. If you've been given a chance to redeem yourself, why haven't you? Why are you still there, after all this time?"

"I was given the opportunity to become a warrior and keep demons and other undesirable supernatural creatures from this realm." It wasn't an answer to my question. Had he chosen to become a warrior or was it foisted upon him? If he had chosen it, did that mean he didn't want to redeem himself and leave Purgatory? Did he believe whatever he had done to be so terrible that he deserved to remain there?

"But you are dead?"

"My life as a human ended, but I live on as a warrior. It was a position granted to me because of the unusual circumstances surrounding my death. I'm neither dead nor alive. I just…am." He spoke slowly, choosing his words with care. "Because of my state, I'm not able to enter sacred places. It hasn't caused me difficulty until today." He almost sounded amused by the notion.

"What unusual circumstances?"

"My death came about by supernatural means. That is all I can tell you."

"Will you be punished if you tell me more?"

He didn't answer.

"Quin, I don't understand." I shifted a little and my hip touched his feet beneath the covers. "I've seen you with the children. You're kind and honest. What sin did you commit to see you sent to Purgatory?"

I heard him swallow. "I can't answer that."

"Can't or won't?" He went to shift his foot away from me, but I clamped my hand down on it, trapping him beneath the covers.

"Cara, that is one question I will not give an answer to." He spoke harshly, his voice a low growl. He jerked his foot free and drew both knees up to his chest. "I'm in that realm for a reason. It is not a mistake. Do you understand what I'm telling you?"

My throat was too tight to answer him so I nodded. A single tear dripped down my cheek. I dashed it away with my shoulder. "But I don't believe that you committed a terrible crime."

"It was more than terrible. It was unforgiveable."

"It couldn't be unforgiveable, or you would have been sent straight to Hell, or whatever the darkest place is called. You weren't. They gave you another chance in Purgatory."

He rested his elbow on his knee and dragged his hand through his hair. "I told you not to trust me, Cara. I meant it. I am no angel."

"I would like to make up my mind for myself," I hissed. "Tell me what you did."

He turned his face away and buried his hand further into his hair.

"We're friends," I whispered, as more tears spilled down my cheeks. My hands trembled and I clasped them together in an attempt to regain some control. But it was useless; my heart was crumbling a little more with everything I heard, and with every answer he refused to give. "Friends don't keep secrets from one another."

"We *are* friends, Cara. I've come to value your friendship and I don't want it to end." He looked up at me and, despite the darkness, I could see the glint of pain in his eyes, the downturn of his mouth. "That's why I can't tell you. If you knew the truth you wouldn't want me as your friend anymore. I've lost too much. I…I couldn't bear to lose you too."

Instinct told me to hold him and be held by him. I reached out but he leaned back, avoiding contact.

"No." He spoke firmly but quietly. "Friends only. There can never be anything more between us." The breath he expelled was half growl, half curse. "Return to bed, Cara. Please," he added when I was slow to move.

The plea was too raw and desperate for me not to obey. I crept back into my bed and shed silent tears into the pillow. My heart ached and my head felt like it had been stuffed full of cotton. Everything was a mess. I'd wanted to break down the barrier between us by asking him about Purgatory. Instead, it had grown even higher.

I was dimly aware of another question I'd forgotten to ask him too, although I probably wouldn't have received an answer. Did his need for the book of spells have something to do with him being in Purgatory?

* * *

179

Mr. Ludlow requested our company at his bookshop early the next morning. Quin and I departed immediately and traveled to Piccadilly, in silence, by coach. I occasionally stole glances his way, and twice I caught him looking at me from beneath lowered lashes. I wasn't sure what I'd expected to happen after our nocturnal discussion. An apology? A return to the normal state of affairs? An explanation? Hardly. I supposed silence was better than anger, but I missed our easy friendship and his humorous observations of the modern world. I missed *him*.

It wasn't yet opening time, and up and down Piccadilly shopkeepers swept their porches or prepared window displays. The street itself was choked with morning traffic and driving up to Hatchard's was a slow process. The coach had just swerved out of the bustle to park at Hatchard's front entrance when Quin leaned closer to the window.

"Bloody hell."

I followed his gaze and gasped. "What's he doing here?"

Nathaniel Faraday was climbing out of a hansom cab. He nodded a greeting at us as if he'd expected to see us there. I opened the coach door myself as soon as we stopped, alarming the footman who wasn't fast enough to do it for me. I marched up to Nathaniel and stabbed him with a glare. I wanted to stab his chest with my finger, but a glare would have to do in a busy precinct like Piccadilly.

"You questioned Father William after we left, didn't you?" I snapped.

His gaze lifted as Quin came up behind me. The solid presence at my back was as much a distraction as a comfort this morning. "Answer her." Quin's voice rumbled in the still, crisp air.

Nathaniel coughed nervously and flattened his tie. "Yes, I did. What of it?" His question lacked the bravado necessary to intimidate a kitten, let alone Quin. "Father William was happy to oblige, although he was curious as to why so much interest in a few books. I arrived here yesterday after you, and left Ludlow a message. It seems he's decided to see us together to save repeating himself."

"You're not getting that book, Nathaniel," I said. "Myer cannot be trusted with it."

"Ha! You're worried about Myer? Perhaps you ought to fear someone a little closer to home."

I felt Quin stiffen. Nathaniel swallowed heavily and stepped back. He didn't take his gaze off Quin—he was afraid of him. Of course! He'd seen what happened to Quin at St. Etheldreda's church and had guessed that Quin's soul wasn't worthy of being in a house of God.

"Look." He held up his hands. "You have nothing to fear from me, Cara."

"Perhaps not from you, but we do from your patron."

"I prefer not to comment on him but, I can assure you, the book will be in safe hands if I get it first."

"You won't."

"What does Myer want with it?" Quin asked.

Nathaniel seemed surprised that Quin addressed him directly. He touched his tie again, flattening it when it was already straight. "That is not for me to say." He took another step back until he was flat against the window of Hatchard's. He stared wide-eyed at Quin, as if he dared not blink or take his gaze off him. "Cara, I would ask you to consider turning away now and going home. Let me retrieve the book. I'll make sure it's not used against anyone."

"How can you assure us of that?" I spat. "Myer is unscrupulous."

"And your companion is trustworthy?" he spat back. "Do you know what he is?"

"Yes."

"Oh. Well. Do you know what realm he's from and why he wants the book?"

"Come, Cara," Quin said, storming off toward the door. "Mr. Ludlow awaits."

I should follow him, but Nathaniel might have the answers I sought. "Tell me," I said quickly before Quin returned.

"He wants it for his own ends." Nathaniel seemed somewhat relieved that Quin had moved off, but he still watched him warily. "He needs it to get out of Purgatory once and for all."

I spun around, but I already knew Quin had gone inside. My head swam with dizziness and my temperature plunged. I began to shiver uncontrollably, but that may not have been entirely the fever's fault. The shock of hearing Nathaniel's reasoning had settled into my bones and shaken me up.

"Ask yourself, Cara," Nathaniel said quietly. "Why does a fellow need to get out of Purgatory using a spell from the book when he can do so by enduring the official trials? He seems strong enough and capable of enduring anything."

A lump swelled in my throat. "He doesn't want the administrators in control of Purgatory to know," I whispered.

"That's my reasoning too."

I raced after Quin, not wanting to risk growing too weak. He held the door open for me, as polite as any modern gentleman. But the simmering anger I felt radiating from him told another story. The ice-cold glare he pinned on Nathaniel, coming up behind me, could have frozen Hell itself.

I managed to keep my thoughts to myself as Mr. Ludlow greeted us. In truth, however, I was in turmoil and hardly heard the introductions. I suspected Quin had overheard us, but he hadn't told Nathaniel that he was wrong. It was as much confirmation as I was likely to get.

Quin wanted to use a spell in the book to free himself from Purgatory—without the administrators knowing. I knew it couldn't be the full story but I would save my questions for later. For now, we still had to find the book before we worried about who got to use it and keep it. I turned a smile on Mr. Ludlow and pushed my concerns about Quin to the back of my mind.

Mr. Ludlow reminded me of a bird, complete with beaky nose, lashless eyes and long, claw-like fingers. "The books arrived two days ago from Father William," he said in hushed tones, as if the deep leather chairs were occupied by readers. "I've been busy and only cataloged them yesterday. The book I needed was by far the oldest in the collection."

"You were commissioned to find that particular book?" Quin asked.

Mr. Ludlow winced at Quin's strong voice. "Yes and no. I was told to purchase a certain tome from Lord Alwyn, but the title and author were unknown. Only its location was certain. Or somewhat certain. There was a chance that it had left Lord Alwyn's library."

"How did you know it was there at all?" I asked.

"The gentleman who commissioned me informed me in his letter."

"Who was he?"

"I don't know. He didn't sign it."

"Isn't that a little odd?"

"Not at all. Sometimes buyers wish to remain anonymous, even from me." He smiled benignly. "After receiving the commission, I decided it was best to get my hands upon as many of Lord Alwyn's books as I could. I would send the one that best matched the gentleman's description to him, and keep the rest for myself, to sell in the shop. Not being an expert in holy texts, I approached Father William to be my intermediary. I've worked with him before, and his knowledge of antiquarian religious documents is second to none. He arranged to visit Lord Alwyn's library and purchase as many old books as he could. He told me his lordship was most obliging. Father William authenticated several from the collection and identified the most likely match to my client's needs." He bestowed another bland smile upon us. "I do hope that explanation has been of assistance to you."

"Thank you," I said, matching his polite smile with one of my own. "It was most helpful. But we do need to know the name of the gentleman who commissioned you."

The smile withered. "I'm afraid I can't give you that information, Miss Moreau. As I said, sometimes buyers—"

Quin's hand whipped out and grasped Ludlow by the throat. His mouth twisted into a cruel sneer as he towered over the smaller man. "I am in no mood for games. You must have some idea of who the man is."

"Quin!" I cried. "Let him go."

Nathaniel edged away. He wouldn't be any help if I had to wrestle Quin off Ludlow.

Quin's grip tightened. "My ledger," Ludlow gasped out. "An address."

Quin let him go and Ludlow slumped forward, rubbing his reddened throat. I eyed Quin, but he wasn't looking at me. Nathaniel had slipped farther away, out of reach.

When Ludlow had recovered enough to speak, he made his way past the reading tables and bookshelves to the counter near the back. He breathed deeply again, seemingly settling his nerves as he flipped through a thick, folio-sized ledger on top of the counter. Perhaps the musty, familiar scent of the books soothed him.

"I received some money up front with the original letter." He no longer seemed worried about not giving out the name of his client. Quin's threat had worked. I wasn't surprised. Being the object of Quin's black mood must be rather frightening. Nathaniel was wise to steer clear of him. Not even I felt entirely safe.

Ludlow pointed to a line scrawled in the ledger. "The rest will be sent to me after the book's delivery." He spun the ledger around so we could see the address. "I sent it off this morning."

The three of us crowded in to study the page. But it was me who muttered, "Bloody hell," much to Ludlow's horror. I apologized for my language and blinked up at Quin.

But he was looking past me. I turned to see the front door closing. Nathaniel had left, taking knowledge of the address with him.

"Thank you, Mr. Ludlow," I called back as Quin took my hand and dragged me out. "We apologize again for our obtrusive behavior, but I assure you it was necessary!"

Quin bundled me into the coach and directed the driver to return to Eaton Square posthaste. I instinctively tucked my feet away from him. He noticed, but did not say anything. Some of his anger seemed to have vanished, perhaps taken over by surprise. He wasn't the only one who was surprised. I couldn't believe it.

The book was on its way to the village of Harborough, near Frakingham House.

"We'll catch the next train," I said.

"What time does it leave?"

"I don't know," I snapped back. "I don't have the timetable memorized." I pressed my lips together, instantly ashamed at my outburst. "I'm sorry, Quin. I'm a little overwrought at the moment."

"You don't need to apologize to me." His gentle voice matched his concerned frown.

I supposed I didn't, considering. "You used me." I was tired and anxious and overwhelmed, but most of all I was sad. It welled inside me and turned my voice small and desperate. I hated hearing it. "You used me to get out of Purgatory so you could get your hands on the book."

He turned to look out the window, allowing me the privacy to wipe away my tears. His voice, when he finally spoke, was as quiet as mine. "I warned you not to trust me."

I'd wanted him to tell me Nathaniel had been wrong or at least that he was sorry and would not take the book from me. But he didn't say anything for the rest of the way home.

CHAPTER 13

*T*he household was thrown into turmoil when we told Jacob, Emily and Sylvia what we'd learned from Ludlow. All the maids and footmen were directed to help us pack. Sylvia and Tommy would return with us, and we needed to get to the station as soon as possible. According to the copy of the timetable pinned to the board in Jacob's study, the next train left in an hour.

"Do you know the proprietor of The Red Lion?" Jacob asked Sylvia as she drew on her gloves in the entrance hall.

"As well as one can know an innkeeper," she said with a sniff and tilt of her chin.

"Tommy will," I said. "He'll speak to him for us."

Quin paced the tiled floor, glancing every now and again up the staircase as we waited for the servants to come down with our luggage. I half expected him to run up and take over the task himself. "I'll force him to tell us," he growled.

"I'd rather not frighten the poor fellow half to death," I said. According to Ludlow's ledger, the book of spells had been put on the early train to Harborough. Its final destination was listed as The Red Lion Inn, room number three.

Quin blew out a long breath and finally stopped pacing. He stood directly in front of me, his usually bright blue-green eyes inky and huge. He looked at me with such pain and misery that I regretted my distrust of him and harsh tones. He made me feel like we were the only two people in the room.

But we were not. Quin opened his mouth to say something to me, but Jacob got in first. "I'm coming with you."

"Why?" I asked.

He fixed his steely gaze on Quin. "To keep your *friend* on a leash."

It reminded me of something the spirit of Father Ignatius had said at the church: 'Warriors are never let off their leash.' It was just another confirmation that Quin was operating outside the laws of Purgatory. It was looking increasingly likely that he should not even be here at all. Oh God. What happened when one defied the administrators? The thought chilled my bones.

Jacob and Quin stood toe to toe, equally fierce and determined expressions hardening their features. Quin was a little larger and taller, but I knew Jacob wouldn't back away.

"Stop it," Emily snapped. "Both of you. Jacob, you can't go. Have you forgotten that important business meeting?"

"I can reschedule it," he said without looking away from Quin.

"It's too important to change at such short notice. Besides, let Cara handle Quin her way. He hasn't harmed her yet, and I'm sure he won't start."

"I won't," Quin said. "Thank you, Emily." Then he did a remarkable thing. He stepped away, essentially conceding to Jacob. "I would never harm her." It wasn't clear whether his quietly spoken words were directed at Emily, Jacob or myself. He didn't look at me, but I had the distinct feeling that I was the intended recipient.

"Damnation," Jacob muttered quietly. It would seem he had also conceded so that neither man had won the argument. "Dawson," he said as Tommy came down the stairs carrying luggage in both hands. "Be sure that Quin continues to behave as a gentleman ought."

Emily rolled her eyes. Like me, she was probably wondering how Tommy could stop Quin if he decided to behave any differently.

Tommy, however, nodded in earnest. "I will, sir." Behind him, other servants filed down the stairs. They headed out the front door and went about tying the cases to the roof of the coach.

We exchanged quick but heartfelt goodbyes in the entrance hall. The children had come to see us off and I enveloped each of them in big, but brief, hugs. Quin, however, took his time. He squatted in front of Gabe.

"Continue to practice your swordplay," he said to the boy. "One day, you will be a great warrior like your father."

The admiration in his voice took all of us by surprise. Jacob's brows almost shot off his forehead, but Emily only smiled. Perhaps it shouldn't have surprised me. Quin knew about my past, so it stood to reason that he knew Jacob and Emily's too.

"And you, little princess," Quin said to Lizzy. "If you try very hard, and ask clever questions, you'll continue to grow into a rare diamond like your mother and Aunt Cara."

"How do you know?" she asked, blinking those huge brown eyes back at him.

He kissed the top of her head. "I just do."

They waved us off from the top step as our coach rolled away. "We'll see them again soon, at the ball," Sylvia assured me, patting my hand.

"I might return here before then. Once all this is over." I

lifted my gaze to Quin sitting opposite, only to see him staring back at me.

"I do hope we get to the book before Faraday and Myer," Sylvia said with a grim sigh.

My concern wasn't in beating them, it was more in convincing Quin not to take the book at all.

* * *

WE DIDN'T SEE Nathaniel or Myer in first class. That didn't mean they weren't on board elsewhere, although I admit to being surprised. A man as wealthy as Myer wouldn't travel any other way on the train.

Unless they hadn't gone by train but by coach instead. It seemed like a foolish plan, however. Horses couldn't go as fast as a steam engine.

"Perhaps they simply missed the train altogether," Sylvia said, as the four of us settled into a private berth. "I must say, I'm glad. I do not like Mr. Myer, and I'm wary of anyone who works for him. I am sorry, Cara. I know you like Nathaniel."

"I don't."

Quin's lips flattened as he turned to look out the window. He was, however, still watching me in the reflection.

"I mean, I do like him," I clarified, "but not in the way you think, Syl. I believe he's an honest man but Myer employing him to find the book has clouded his judgment somewhat. I'm sure he'll do the right thing in the end."

"Perhaps he already has," Tommy said. At our questioning looks, he added, "That could be why they're not on board. Faraday may have delayed telling Myer on purpose to cause him to miss this train."

It was a possibility. "He left Hatchard's very quickly." I shot Quin a pointed look in the window's reflection. He seemed surprised that I'd caught him watching me. He blushed. "Although that might not have been because he was in a hurry to tell Myer about the book."

Sylvia and Tommy seemed unaware of our silent exchange or my double meaning. I hadn't told them that Quin was from Purgatory and it would seem that Emily and Jacob hadn't either. It was probably just as well. It would only add extra pressure to Tommy's already considerable burden of protecting us from a man stronger than himself.

Sylvia sighed. "I'm glad to be returning home."

"I thought you enjoyed London," I said.

"Not as much this time."

"Oh? Why?"

She sighed again. "When I told people where I was from, most of them gave me a sour look. One or two turned their noses up or made cruel comments to their friends."

I smiled sympathetically. "The reputation of Freak House is far-reaching, I take it."

"I do hope it won't stop anyone from coming to the ball."

"I'm sure Emily's influence will ensure a good turnout."

We talked some more until she yawned and announced she wanted to sleep for a while. I closed my eyes too, but although I was tired I couldn't sleep. I was all too aware of Quin's knees, only inches from mine, and his warm gaze watching me from beneath lowered lids. I was grateful, however, that I was prevented from talking to him. I no longer knew what to say.

* * *

THERE HAD BEEN no time to telegram ahead and warn Mr. Langley of our return, which meant there was no coach waiting for us at the station. The inn was only a short distance away, however, so we left our luggage in the station-master's office and walked to The Red Lion. Located on a busy corner in Harborough, the imposing building with its spacious taproom was filled with patrons of mostly humble background. It seemed half of the male population of the village had stopped by to enjoy a drink or two. Conversation dried up like a blocked stream as we entered. All heads turned toward us, but it was difficult to tell who was more of a curiosity—Quin, the large stranger, me with my exotic looks, or Sylvia, who had probably never before stepped foot inside such a common place.

It was she who picked her way carefully across the ale-slicked floor to the innkeeper, however. With her handkerchief pressed to her nose, and in her snootiest voice, she demanded to know who was staying in room number three. I groaned inwardly. It wasn't the best way to get served in a place like The Red Lion.

To my surprise, the innkeeper smiled. He told her to wait a moment then left through the door behind him. He returned with a ledger that he showed to her. "Mr. John Smith," he announced. "See for yourself." His smile turned smug. He knew it was a false name as much as we did.

I peered over Sylvia's shoulder at the book. Sure enough, Mr. John Smith had signed in the day before.

"Did he receive a package earlier today?" Quin asked.

The innkeeper shrugged. "Not sure it's my business to say, sir."

Quin's eyes darkened and his jaw hardened. Oh no. Starting a fight in The Red Lion would not serve our purpose of finding Mr. Smith before he used the book.

"Sylvia, give the innkeeper some money," I whispered.

"No!" She looked horrified. "We shouldn't encourage him."

Tommy, however, was holding most of her money in his inside jacket pocket. He smacked a bank note down on the polished surface of the bar. Sylvia stamped her hands on her hips and glared at him.

The innkeeper slid the money into his pocket and smiled. "A parcel from a bookshop in London arrived for him early this afternoon."

"Thank you," I said, as Quin took off for the stairs.

"You won't find him up there," the innkeeper called out. "He left a short time ago."

"Where to?"

The innkeeper shrugged.

I looked to Quin, my heart in my throat. Mr. Smith must have already gone to the abbey ruins at Frakingham—and the portal located there.

"We need a ride to Freak House," I announced to the drinkers who had all been openly following our conversation.

"Don't call it that," Sylvia said with a pout.

"I'll take you," said a man getting to his feet. He nodded at Tommy. "For a price." Tommy gave him some coins. "Come wiv me."

The cart was large enough to take all of us and our luggage as well, but the problem with large carts is that they are slow. It seemed to take forever to reach the stately iron gates of Frakingham. I craned my neck to catch a glimpse of the abbey beyond the oaks lining the drive. From a distance, the broken walls looked like a folly, perched as they were in prime position by the lake. But the ruin was as real as the house itself, an oppressive and bleak structure looming at the end of the drive.

"Can you see anyone?" Sylvia asked, also trying to peer down to the ruins.

"There's no coach," I noticed.

"There!" Tommy pointed to a figure wandering around the stones. "Stop, driver."

Quin leaped down before the horse pulled up. He took off at a run, leaving us following in his wake. The stocky figure had his back to us and hadn't seen our arrival. His hat sat on a large stone and his head was bent over something in his hands, but the sound of pounding footsteps must have caught his attention. He turned, gasped, then he looked down at the book in his hands and his lips moved in quiet speech.

"Lord Malborough!" I instinctively slowed at the sight of the gentleman who'd almost ruined Sylvia's reputation, killed Samuel, and harmed Charity only two weeks prior. I'd hoped never to see him again but it would seem his father, Lord Frakingham, couldn't keep him in check like he'd promised.

Sylvia stumbled and stopped. "Tommy! Go no farther!" Her piercing cry startled a bird in the treetops. They would have heard her from the house. "Please! You know how dangerous he is."

But Tommy didn't listen. He streaked after Quin. Between the two of them, they could easily tackle Malborough.

Unless Malborough finished the curse first. He was chanting something from the book of spells. I didn't need to inspect it to know that he held the most dangerous text in the world.

"Stop!" I shouted. "Lord Malborough, you don't know what you're unleashing!"

But Malborough's lips kept moving. Quin seemed to fly across the grass toward him, but I knew in my heart that he wouldn't be fast enough. Sylvia and I both screamed at Malborough, begging him to cease chanting.

But it was too late. The air around him grew murky, thick, as if a cloud had descended on that small area. Lightning ripped through it, renting a hole like shears through fabric. Malborough swiveled and fell back in shock, losing his balance. The black hole yawned above him, sending him scurrying away to a safer distance. When he realized he was in no immediate danger from the hole, he turned to us and laughed. "I told you this was my house. I told you I would get it back somehow."

"This is madness." Tommy slowed and raised his hands to calm Malborough. The air continued to crackle and a strong breeze swirled. "Do you know what will come through that portal?"

Quin strode toward Malborough. Where Tommy took a diplomatic approach, Quin took a soldier's and charged forward. "Give me the book," he demanded.

Malborough made to fling it through the dark, fathomless hole. Quin stopped. "Come any closer and I'll throw it!"

"Don't be a fool!"

"*Me* a fool? *You* are all the stupid ones. You don't deserve this book," Malborough spat. "Even Myer couldn't find it. *I* did, and it was so simple. A child could have succeeded where you failed."

"Tell us how," I said. Perhaps if we distracted him, Quin could tackle him.

"Myer told me that the dead man, Garrett, probably knew about the book of spells, but he'd not confided its location to anyone before his death. So I simply sought out his widow when I returned to London. She was still alive and happy to speak about her husband's movements all those years ago. Most of what she said was simply the ramblings of an old woman but there was one thing that had stayed in her mind. He'd gone to visit Lord Alwyn's library. She remembered because her husband had been so excited and Lord Alwyn is a memorable fellow." Malborough shrugged. "I decided to commission Ludlow to sift through the library and find the book I needed. His presence in a library wouldn't raise any suspicions whereas mine would. He told me it should be easy to find such an old and rare text among the more modern books." He laughed. "Look at your dull faces. Do you see how easy it was?"

Quin edged forward, but Malborough lifted the book, preparing to fling it through the hole. When Quin stopped, Malborough chuckled. "Big, strong fellow like you is afraid of losing this little book, eh? Interesting. What do you want it for?"

Quin didn't rise to the bait. His eyes were hard diamonds as he pinned Malborough with his glare. Every muscle in his face set firm, his body went taut, as if he would spring at any moment. But he was too far away to reach Malborough, even if he leapt.

"For God's sake," Sylvia cried. She clung to my arm with trembling hands. "Close the portal, Douglas. Please, close it before something comes through."

Malborough's wild eyes became black, swirling pools. "Why would I want to do that?" He grinned. "This is *my* house, you silly twit. It's *Frakingham* House and belongs to a *Frakingham*. The creatures that come through there will do my bidding and destroy you and your pathetic uncle. You're insignificant nobodies. Upstarts like you need to be taught a lesson. You should not try to take what isn't rightfully yours."

The entrance to the portal crackled again and flames licked at the edges. The wind grew stronger, whipping up leaves and dirt and sweeping them into its whirlpool.

"Whatever comes out of there will kill you too," I told Malborough. "The last time it opened, Garret and another man who summoned it died here. Demons killed them."

"I can control them. I've memorized the chants."

"The chant will help you control one or two, perhaps, not many. An abbot died here too, because he thought the same as you." The abbot and many of the abbey's brothers, and the king's soldiers too. It had been a chaotic, frightening hell, as scores of demons had been unleashed into the human world.

Oh God.

Malborough seemed to register my warning just as the

wind grew stronger. It battered against him, blowing his hat off the stone and sending it tumbling end over end toward the lake's edge. My hair was pulled from its pins and whipped about my face. Sylvia put her hands up, as if that would shelter her. Tommy moved back, protecting us with his body.

"Say the damned spell to close the portal!" Sylvia shouted at Malborough.

Quin spun round to us, registering the same thing that I had.

"He can't," I said. "It's not in the book. We have it."

But we also had the spell to open it, so how had Malborough known the words to chant? Had the book contained more than one?

There was no time to ask him. A creature shot out of the black hole. It landed on its huge, hairy feet near Malborough. It was hideous. Its teeth and claws were jagged blades, its body covered in patches of coarse brown hair. It had no nose, and saliva dripped in slimy globs from the slit of a mouth. The small, yellow eyes focused on Malborough and it growled.

Malborough stumbled back. "Jesus Christ!" But he quickly recovered himself and began to read from the book in a high-pitched voice. Through his words, he directed the demon to switch its beady glare onto us.

"Get back to the house!" Quin ordered. "All of you! Lock the doors and windows."

"I'm not leaving you!" I shouted at him.

"GO! This is what I do, Cara. I'm the warrior, forever and always." He was no longer shouting and his voice was tinged with a hint of sorrow. His gaze did not flinch from the beast. The creature blinked slowly, as if waking from slumber, and lowered itself into a crouching position.

Quin matched the stance. The demon charged.

CHAPTER 14

*T*he demon tried to use its claws, but Quin dodged its wild strikes and captured its wrists. The demon retaliated with a growl that bared both rows of vicious teeth. It attempted to bite Quin, but he slammed his forehead against the creature's and shoved it away. Malborough swore loudly and continued his chant.

"My God," Tommy muttered in admiration. "Those creatures are bloody strong and he batted it away as if it were a teddy bear."

The demon picked itself up and lowered its stance to attack again. Just then, another creature emerged from the portal.

Sylvia screamed, drawing its attention. Tommy put up his fists. This one wasn't under Malborough's control. He could only manage one at a time with his chants. The second demon was free to kill as it pleased.

"Dawson!" Quin shouted, kicking the second demon in the jaw before it could leap. "My sword!"

"Come, ladies!" Tommy grabbed both our hands and

dragged us along behind him at a run, back across the grass to the drive. But we were slow in our heels, petticoats and skirts, not to mention the tight corsets that made deep breathing nearly impossible.

No, not the corset, the illness. I glanced back at Quin, some twenty feet away. Too far. The effects of the curse took hold, weakening me. Tommy and Sylvia seemed to have forgotten in their fear and haste.

"We'll follow," I told Tommy. "You must go."

He cast a worried glance at Sylvia, then another back at the ruins, and sprinted ahead.

"Sylvia," I gasped, taking her hand. My head felt dizzy and gaining a full breath was so hard, but I mustn't let her know. "Where is the piece of parchment from the book?"

"In my things."

She ran after Tommy and I followed her, stumbling and falling to my knees. She helped me up and together we joined Tommy. Our luggage lay at the side of the drive where the cart driver had left it before leaving.

Tommy ripped open Quin's case and hefted the sword out, then ran back past us toward the ruins. I dared glance at the scene and was sickened by what I saw. There were four demons now, surrounding Quin. Malborough crouched behind a wall, unnoticed. Only his pale face was visible. He'd stopped chanting, perhaps because the creatures seemed to be following one another and focusing only on Quin. They no longer needed direction; instead they were learning from one another and growing stronger with every passing moment in this realm. Another demon emerged from the portal as I watched, joining its companions as two of them flung themselves at Quin.

He thumped them both away with his fists, but not before the claw of one scratched him across the chest.

Sylvia rifled through her valise, sobbing as she flung her belongings, including unmentionables, onto the ground. "I can't find it!"

I fell to my knees beside her and pushed through the pain in my head and chest. I performed a more methodical search until my shaking fingers closed around the rough wooden tube. "Got it!"

"Thank God," she sobbed.

I pulled the scroll out of the tube then felt for the small knife I'd tucked into my skirt pocket. Ever since the fight at The Brickmaker's Arms, I'd decided to carry one.

I stumbled back to the ruins until I was close enough to Quin. My fever instantly subsided and my breathing returned to normal. I wiped sweat from forehead with the back of my trembling hand. "Go to the house," I told Sylvia. "Tell your uncle and Bollard what's happening and lock all the doors."

"I can't leave you!"

"You have to. The fewer of us at the ruins, the less people Quin has to protect. I'll stay back while I speak the spell, but I suspect I need to get closer than his."

She seemed to be considering her options when I spotted Bollard coming out of the house. He waved his arms and ran toward us. He appeared to be holding something.

"Go to Bollard." I gave her a shove that was stronger than I intended. She stumbled but quickly righted herself and ran to her uncle's assistant.

I raced back toward the ruins. Quin now had his sword, and stood between Tommy and the demons. There were eight of them, all snapping teeth and sharp claws. Quin easily carved through two and their bodies disintegrated into a cloud of dust. But just as he did so, another two spewed from the portal, then another and another. They streamed out, a river of otherworldly animals maddened by hunger and confusion, desperate to fill their bellies. And they had their sights on Quin.

I began to speak the chant to close the portal, attracting the attention of two of the demons. They turned feral eyes on me and charged. Quin was quick to respond, blocking them both and dispensing them with two blows, only to have more demons take their place. His brow was slick with sweat. His clothes were shredded and damp with blood, some of it his. I began to fear that being here in our realm had weakened his strength to human levels. There were too many for him to fight off alone, but that no longer mattered. I finished the chant. All would be calm again.

Nothing happened.

The wind continued to swirl and howl like a localized tempest, expelling more and more demons from its eye.

The spell hadn't worked.

Tommy looked to me, confusion and fear warring in his eyes as they searched mine. I shook my head. "I don't understand," I said, my voice high and panicky.

"Say it again," he urged.

I was about to when Quin grunted. He fell onto his knee as three demons lunged at once. They descended on him, their claws lashing at his shoulders, their teeth snapping. Oh God. Quin. Tommy ran to help, kicking one of the beasts out of the way, allowing Quin to rise again and fight off the other two. His sword slashed and sliced, cutting them both down, only to have another two take their place. Tommy helped him as best he could, but he only had fists and feet, and human ones at that.

I began the chant again. Out of the corner of my eye I spotted Bollard lumbering toward us. He wielded a knife and I suspected it was Jack's mother's, the one forged in the demon realm. I finished the spell, but still the portal remained open, spitting out more and more demons. Soon there would be too many. Why wouldn't the damned thing close? The spell was the right one, according to the title on the page. Had my accent been wrong, or my inflection? Perhaps speaking one word incorrectly could cause the entire thing to fail.

I wanted to ask Quin but he was too busy. A moment's distraction would certainly end badly for him. He needed to concentrate on his task. He didn't appear to be tiring, but it became clear he was heading toward a wall of the ruins. Did he plan to hide behind it to give himself a moment to regroup?

Malborough's head popped up from behind the wall, his lips moving again. Then it dawned on me. Malborough had stopped the chant that directed the demons and was now speaking the words to keep the portal open. That's why my spell to close it wasn't working. It was being overridden by the one already in full swing. He had to be stopped first, and Quin planned on doing just that. But he was struggling to make any headway through the swarm of demons, even with Tommy and Bollard's help. So why hadn't he directed me to do it?

To protect me.

He couldn't do it all. There were just too many demons now, and his progress had halted entirely. I picked up my skirts and circled the fight scene. I was behind Malborough and he didn't even know. I fished the small knife out of my pocket and gripped the handle so hard my fingernails cut into my palm. I could do this. I had to. Perhaps I wouldn't need to kill him, just injure him or scare him.

I blew out a breath and ran at him.

I don't know what alerted the demon. Perhaps it was my sudden movement or the rustle of my skirts, or even Quin's quick glance in my direction. The creature's yellow eyes honed in on me. Its lipless mouth pulled apart to reveal monstrous teeth. It lumbered toward me, surprisingly fast, sending Malborough spinning around to see what it had seen.

"Get away!" he screamed. "Get away from me!"

He had stopped chanting. I quickly resumed the spell to close the portal. His face turned white, realizing his error. Not only had my chant taken over from his, but he was between me and the demon. The creature kept coming, its attention now on Malborough, the closer of the two of us.

He gave a strangled cry then flipped the pages of the book in his hand. He stumbled over some strange words as he resumed his chant. The demon switched its focus to me, under Malborough's direction.

It came straight for me. Its teeth gnashed in a starving frenzy, and globs of saliva dripped from its mouth. My stomach dropped and I wanted to throw up, run, and scream for help. Fear squeezed my chest and turned my voice hoarse. I trembled all over, barely able to keep my grip on the parchment. But I continued to chant; I had to finish it. If I did not, the portal would continue to spew out more creatures and my friends would die. Quin could not hold off many more, barraged as he was by dozens already. It was a simple mathematical equation, the result being our deaths.

"Cara!" Quin's voice was panicked. He seemed to gather more strength from his fear and slashed through two demons in quick succession to clear a path to me.

But he could not reach me in time.

The demon ran past Malborough as if he weren't even there and headed straight for me. I steeled myself as it raised its massive claw to swipe. At the last moment, I ducked and rammed home the knife in my right hand, straight into the soft belly of the creature.

It screamed in pain and reared backward, stumbling over its own feet. I hadn't killed it—I couldn't with only an ordinary blade—but I'd injured it enough to give myself precious more seconds.

I finished the spell just as the creature got to its feet again. Behind it, the black, swirling well of the portal snapped shut.

Malborough suddenly stopped. He seemed unsure whether he should continue with the chant to control the demon or the one to reopen the portal. He swore as Quin dispensed with demon after demon with renewed energy. His sword seemed to have taken on a life of its own, flying through the air as if it were a living entity. Malborough flipped back through the book's pages again, cursing over and over.

The demon hesitated. Awareness flared in its eyes where before they were cloudy from Malborough's control. They weren't clever creatures when they first came to our realm. They needed to feed their ravenous appetite to regain their wits. This one seemed to become aware of two things at the same time. Firstly, that it was separated from its group, where danger lay in the form of Quin, and secondly, that I possessed a weapon that had already harmed it, whereas Malborough did not.

It charged at him. I shut my eyes the moment it sank its teeth into Malborough, but I couldn't block out his screams. I forced myself to reopen my eyes and maintain awareness of my surroundings and all of the demons. Many of them now swarmed the ruins, all centering around Quin, Tommy and Bollard. But at the sound of Malborough's screams, some peeled away from the main group. They must have sensed an easy meal. Malborough fell silent, but the other demons still came. I backed away.

Quin said something to Tommy and Bollard, and they left the main fight and chased after the creatures heading toward me. They mowed most of them down without any problem, and the last two stopped to feed on Malborough.

Bollard turned them to dust with Jack's knife and Tommy limped over to me. One of his eyes was starting to close over and his right arm hung loosely at his side. But he was alive. I flung my arms around him, and then Bollard, when he joined us. He handed me the book and I clutched it to my chest.

Together we watched as Quin dispensed with the final demon. He slumped to one knee near the pile of dust, leaning heavily on his sword.

I ran to him and caught him in my arms as he swayed. His chest heaved with labored breathing and he was covered in blood from head to toe. I didn't care. He was alive. We all were.

I began to cry.

"Cara," he murmured, wiping my tears away with the pad of his thumb. "My brave warrior."

I copied his gesture and wiped away the blood on his face. His bright blue-green eyes blinked back at me, swirling with an intensity that sent my heart soaring. Every nerve ending sizzled with burning desire. I ached for his kiss, his touch, and saw that ache echoed in his eyes as they turned smoky. He captured my face in both his hands and his eyelids lowered.

"St. Clair," came Tommy's sharp voice behind me.

Quin let me go as if touching me stung him. He swallowed heavily and dragged his hand through his hair.

"Mr. Beaufort has asked me to protect Cara from you. I cannot ignore his request. I'm sorry," he added, sounding genuinely apologetic.

He held out his good hand to me and I took it. I stood and so did Quin, avoiding my gaze. Sylvia and Langley joined us. She pushed her uncle's chair across the lawn. Her face was streaked from her tears, but she was smiling, mostly at

Tommy. Langley signed something to Bollard who answered with a nod. They exchanged relieved smiles.

"You're alive," Sylvia said, starting to cry and laugh at the same time. "Everyone's alive and well."

"Except Malborough," Langley pointed out.

She shuddered and turned away from the scene of the mangled, half-eaten body.

"Who was he?" Quin asked.

"Lord Frakingham's son and heir," Langley said.

"Lord Frakingham sold the house to Uncle August," Sylvia explained. "Douglas—Lord Malborough—never accepted it. He believed the house should belong to him. This is just the last in a long list of despicable things he's done to try and get it back."

I circled my arm around her waist. "At least it's over now. He won't be troubling you again."

Langley sighed. "I'm not going to enjoy explaining this to Lord Frakingham. How did Malborough get the book?"

"Garrett's widow told him that her husband visited Lord Alwyn, twenty-two years ago, before he came here with the other members of the society," I said. "Lord Alwyn was in possession of the book but didn't know it. Garrett and the society already had the parchment." I held up the scroll. "He must have followed the same line of investigation as we did and searched through the society's library to find any mention of the book in other texts. It's likely he recognized Alwyn's family symbols in the same book Quin did, setting him on the path to Lord Alwyn's library. Once he found it, he must have memorized some of the curses contained within it, including the one that made me ill."

"What a relief," Sylvia said cheerfully with a nod at the book in my hand. "You can find the counter-curse and be well again."

I nodded and walked across the lawn toward the house

with them. If anybody thought it odd that I didn't respond, they didn't say. Speaking the counter-curse now would mean saying goodbye to Quin. The administrators would call him back to Purgatory. Not speaking it, however, meant he had a chance of snatching it and removing it from my possession altogether. Neither option sounded particularly welcoming.

I wasn't yet sure if I could trust him, despite everything he'd done to save us. A kernel of doubt lingered, made worse by the fact he wouldn't look at me. I couldn't make out what he was thinking behind his hooded eyes.

"St. Clair," Langley said as we rounded the side of the house to enter through the courtyard out the back. "Thank you. It's because of you that we're here now."

Quin nodded. "Your thanks are appreciated, sir. But I am the warrior, and fighting off demons is what I do."

It was the second time that he'd said as much and it sounded equally forlorn as the first. I frowned and willed him to look at me and explain, but he did not.

"I want to offer my thanks too," Tommy said. His face was pale from pain and loss of blood, but he managed a small smile. "It's been an honor to know you, sir."

Sylvia too gave Quin a smile. "Farewell. We do appreciate all that you did here today and over the past several days. Cara is very special to us, and you've saved her life. Thank you."

"He's not going just yet," I said before he could say anything. "He's much too filthy." It was a ridiculous notion that he couldn't return to Purgatory covered in blood, but neither he nor the others pointed it out. Sylvia's smile turned pitying.

Quin wouldn't bathe in the privacy of the bathroom, claiming all the blood would ruin the tub. Instead, he scrubbed himself clean in an empty stable stall while I sat on a stool on the other side of the doors. His shredded clothes couldn't be salvaged so Fray, the Frakingham driver, and the stable lad were sent to retrieve the luggage from the side of the drive.

Bollard refused to clean up while I was present and Tommy was too injured to perform the task alone, so they trooped inside the main house like battle-weary heroes returning from war. I heard Sylvia speak to either the housekeeper or maid, who'd begun wailing hysterically. Her crisp but sympathetic tones set tasks for everyone in the household, from fetching Dr. Gowan and Inspector Weeks to boiling water and preparing wound dressings.

With everyone occupied, Quin and I were left alone in the stables. Not even Tommy seemed to recall his duty to protect me from the warrior.

I listened to the splashing of water as Quin washed himself. I didn't need to see him to picture the straps of thick muscles across chest and shoulders, and his ridged stomach. It would seem the memory of his masculine perfection would remain with me for quite some time, even after he was gone from my life and this realm.

His sharp intake of breath had me rising from the stool, but I quickly plopped back down again as I heard the water splashing once more. I wanted to inspect his injuries but, of course, there would be no point. They would most likely heal quickly once he'd returned to Purgatory.

I clutched the book closer to my chest. I should look for the spell to break Garrett's curse, but couldn't bring myself to even open the book's plain wooden cover. I would. Soon. Just not yet.

Fray returned with a towel, shirt and trousers, then left again, plunging us once again into silence. We had experienced many tense moments together of late, but this silence was denser than the rest. There were so many things I wanted to say to him, yet I voiced none of them. I was afraid; not only of his reaction, but of mine. If I begged him to kiss me, what powerful emotions would we unleash? I would never be able to close them off the way the portal had been sealed. What if he pushed me away instead? How could I hold my head up through my shame and heartache? Even worse, what if he pried the book from my hands? He could do it easily enough. Such a betrayal would devastate me.

The splashing stopped and I listened as Quin dried and dressed. Then there was total silence in which the only sound was my own breathing. I bent over and peered under the stall doors. Quin was sitting on a dry patch of floor, leaning back against the wall. His eyes were closed and his head tipped back. Water dripped from the ends of his hair onto his bare shoulders. He clutched his scrunched up shirt in his fist as if he'd been about to put it on but decided against it and slumped to the floor instead. The smooth planes of his face weren't as hard as they had been during the fight, but were now pinched and pale.

With the blood cleaned away, I could take stock of his injuries, at least on his right side. Scratches marked the flesh on his arm, from wrist to shoulder. A purple bruise darkened his jaw and a cut sliced through his lip. Worse than all of those were the three deep gashes across his chest. A demon's claws had struck him, and the wounds still bled.

I ached to go into the stall and see to it, but I didn't dare get too close to him while we were alone. There was no telling what might happen between us, or what he might do.

"Are you all right?" I asked, straightening.

Several beats passed before he answered. "Aye." He came out of the stall and I saw that his left side fared as badly as his right.

I felt sick. "Oh, Quin."

He looked down at the claw marks on his chest where the

blood began to congeal in droplets. "I didn't want to stain the shirt."

"Come to the house. Sylvia will dress the wounds for you."

"You can do it." His gaze held mine for a long moment. I felt like I was falling into their depths, sucked in by the compelling force of Quin himself. Then his gaze dropped to the book.

CHAPTER 15

I tightened my hold on the book and stayed out of reach. Quin did not try to force it from me, but I knew from the hungry way he looked at it that he wanted it. I was quite sure he wouldn't take it before I spoke the counter-curse to cure myself, but I would not give it to him after either. I would ensure that he didn't leave Purgatory through any means other than official ones. The administrators would release him when he'd completed sufficient penance. Going against their wishes would be unwise if we didn't know the consequences.

"You haven't spoken the curse yet," he said simply.

"No."

The next most logical questions would be to ask me why, but he didn't. He simply nodded. "It would be difficult to explain my sudden disappearance to the servants."

It wasn't the reason I hadn't spoken it, but it was one I could cling to when asked.

I strode out of the stables, glancing back over my shoulder every three steps to see how close he followed behind me. That intense green-blue gaze connected with mine each time, as if he could hypnotize me into giving the book to him.

Doctor Gowan was just arriving through the front door as we entered through the rear. He was brought into the kitchen where the others had congregated. He inspected Tommy's arm first, and his grave face told us what we dreaded to hear before his words did.

"The wounds are extensive," he said gently. "Come to my surgery first thing in the morning and I'll do my best to patch you up. I'll give you something for the pain now, and then you must rest tonight. I warn you, however, that the recovery will be long and arduous."

Tommy nodded and closed his eyes. The muscles in his jaw worked, as if he were bearing down against the pain. His face went even whiter as the doctor cleaned and dressed the wound.

"He *will* recover fully, won't he?" Sylvia asked, her face as pale as Tommy's. She had balled her hands into fists on the kitchen table, but now opened them and reached for Tommy's good hand, resting on the surface. Their fingers closed around one another.

Langley's nostrils flared as his gaze zeroed in on their linked hands. Bollard, standing behind Langley's wheelchair, touched his master's shoulder briefly before resuming his stiff-backed stance.

"It's too early to say," Dr. Gowan said. "But you must prepare yourselves for the worst."

"You mean he may lose some strength in his arm?" Her voice was soft, as if she didn't dare ask the question but needed to know the answer regardless.

"I mean it may never function again."

Tommy let go of Sylvia's hand and rubbed his bloodless lips. She began to reach for him, but pulled back and simply stared instead. I dragged my chair closer to her and circled my arm around her waist, but I wasn't sure if she even noticed.

The doctor finished bandaging Tommy and gave him something for the pain before sending him to bed. He wanted to inspect Quin next, and eyed the gashes on his chest, but Quin insisted Bollard be seen to. Most of his wounds were superficial and would heal as long as they didn't become infected.

"You must rest too," Langley told Bollard.

Bollard shook his head and signed something.

"I can push myself around," Langley said in that indomitable way of his.

Bollard huffed out a breath and he too left the kitchen.

The doctor finally inspected Quin. "You must come to my surgery tomorrow too. These are deep and require suturing."

Quin glanced at me, but said nothing. Whether he would still be in this realm in the morning remained to be seen.

The doctor left and Detective Inspector Weeks replaced him. He and his men had been investigating the ruins and the body. "I have some questions for you," he said with a twitch of his ratty nose.

Langley rubbed his forehead. "Get it over with, man. Everyone's tired."

Weeks cleared his throat and asked us where the dogs had come from and disappeared to after the attack. His forehead glistened with sweat by the time he finished, and he watched Langley anxiously, as if expecting him to erupt in anger without warning.

"They came from out of my woods, Inspector," Langley said. "There were perhaps half a dozen or so."

"I see. And now where are they? I don't see their bodies, sir."

"I threw them into the river," Quin said. "The scent of their blood might have attracted others."

Weeks switched his slick gaze to Quin. "And who are you?"

"Quintin St. Clair."

"He's a guest here," Sylvia cut in quickly. "A friend of Miss Moreau's from Melbourne. On the other side of the world," she clarified when he frowned at her.

"I know where it is," he said mildly. "Just a few more questions—"

"No." Langley wheeled himself to the door, showing Weeks out. "No more questions. The members of this household have endured enough for today."

"Right, sir. Of course. My apologies, Mr. Langley, Miss Langley." Weeks tucked his hat under his arm and bowed to Sylvia, before scurrying out of the kitchen.

Quin got up to inspect his wounds in the light coming through the window. Dusk had descended quickly and the kitchen was darkening. Langley wheeled himself out without another word to anyone.

Sylvia leaned closer to me. "Why haven't you spoken the counter-curse yet?" she whispered.

I nodded at Quin's back. "I thought it would be difficult to explain his sudden disappearance, particularly if he is scheduled to see Dr. Gowan in the morning."

"You're planning on letting him stay so the doctor can suture his wounds?"

"I...I admit I haven't thought it through yet. But I do think it best that we wait until the eyes of Harborough and the police force are no longer on Frakingham."

She pressed her lips together, flattening her smile. "I see. It has nothing to do with any feelings you two may have for one another?"

"Don't be absurd. We can't be together."

"That doesn't mean you don't want to be." She leaned

closer and her smile vanished. "The real question is, can you be trusted in the same room for one more night?"

I was glad she didn't know about Quin coming from Purgatory or his need for the book. She wouldn't be so willing to let him stay longer in the house if she did, let alone in our room. "Of course. I'm no fool when it comes to gentlemen."

"What about otherworldly warriors?"

* * *

I DID NOT LET GO of the book. I placed it on the stool beside the bath as I bathed, and in my lap when I ate. Quin and I hardly spoke all evening and he seemed to be avoiding my gaze. It was horrible but I had no idea what to say to him anymore. He seemed to accept that he would spend the night in this realm, although what he thought of that was a mystery. Perhaps he was in conflict, like me. I very much wanted him to stay, but I needed him to go.

We met Sylvia coming down the hall toward the bedroom. She'd been to see Tommy and taken him something to eat. Her presence was a welcome distraction from Quin.

"How is he?" I asked her.

"In pain, but otherwise showing remarkable spirits, considering."

"Considering he may never be able to use his arm again, you mean?"

She nodded and her lower lip trembled. "Oh, Cara. If he becomes a cripple, what shall he do? Where will he go?" She clasped my hand in both of hers. "He won't be able to work, and if he can't work...he'll wind up in the poor house."

"Sylvia, calm down. Jack wouldn't allow that. Neither

would your uncle. Whatever happens, Tommy will be well taken care of."

She sighed, not quite appeased. "He'll hate being a charity case. He'll want to work."

"We'll have to find something else for him to do."

"Like what?" She sighed again and I had no answers for her either. She looked to Quin as he opened the door. "What happened to men who lost the use of their limbs in your day?"

He lifted his gaze to hers. "You don't want to know."

"It was a much harsher time," I said before she could become upset.

We prepared for bed, Quin on one side of the screen and us on the other. There would be no Tommy to protect us tonight, but nobody seemed to think it necessary.

"Have you looked through it?" Sylvia asked, nodding at the book that I'd set down on the bed.

"Not yet."

She pulled it to her and carefully opened it as if it were made from eggshells. "It smells old."

"It is old. Look." I pointed to the lines of text on the first page. "I think this means it was written by or for Gilbert de Mordaunt. According to Jacob's copy of *Debrett's*, Gilbert came over with William the Conqueror and earned himself lands and accolades."

"His knowledge of the supernatural must have been extensive for him to have compiled this book."

"I wonder how he gathered all this information in a time when there were few written documents."

"Good lord." She studied the pages with their beautiful illuminated images. The gold leaf gleamed in the lamplight and the colors were as bright as if they'd been mixed recently. "It's remarkable."

I was just as entranced. A great deal of effort had been

spent on it in a time when texts were written by scholar-monks and few people could even read.

"Here's your spell," she said, tapping a page. "Thank God." She eyed me, as if expecting me to announce I would read it then and there.

On the other side of the screen, Quin hissed out a breath.

"Are you all right?" she asked him.

"Aye."

"Is it the scratches?"

He hesitated before answering, "Aye."

"Dr. Gowan will fix you up tomorrow," she said. "If you're still here then." She gave me a sympathetic smile as she settled under the covers. "Don't stay up too late."

I turned back to the book and continued to look through the spells and other information contained within its pages as she fell asleep. The writing was difficult to understand with its odd spellings and intricate lettering, but I managed to decipher most of it. I found the spell Quin needed to get out of Purgatory. I read through the words at the top of the page, and my blood ran cold.

Speeke these words at ye peril,

Or Almighteye wrathe will conquer the forbidden soulle.

Surely anyone banished to Purgatory was a forbidden soul. I was already quite certain that Quin didn't have permission to be searching for the book to achieve his own ends, but now I was equally worried that his plan to leave that realm would result in more problems for him.

I read on, and learned more about the other realms and the links between them. The book contained information on demons and spirits that I already knew, plus some facts that were new to me. I was thoroughly absorbed in it, so that I didn't notice Quin until he appeared beside the bed with the blanket wrapped around his waist. His wounds looked angry and sore.

I shut the book and clasped it against my chest. His eyes shuttered and his shoulders slumped a little.

"I won't take it," he said simply.

I eyed him closely as he sat on the end of the bed.

He sighed. "Cara, I've never done this before. Never cured anyone of a supernatural illness. But I fear I'll disappear from this realm as soon as you speak the counter-curse."

I bit my lip. "We don't know that for sure. You may have a choice in the matter."

"I doubt it," he said wryly. "Choices are not easily granted in my realm."

"Then we should say our goodbyes first. But not tonight. I'm…I'm not ready. Tomorrow."

He rubbed a hand covered in scratches over his jaw. "I'm telling you this now so that you understand the need for me to hold the book while one of us speaks your counter-curse."

"I don't think that's wise."

He pressed his lips together as if forcibly stopping himself from shouting or swearing. "Why not?"

"Think about what you're doing. What you want is dangerous. The book itself warns of an almighty wrath if that spell is used by…by the wrong person."

"We don't know that for certain, or what that wrath will entail." He did not ask to see the warning, which meant he already knew about it.

"Quin, you're in Purgatory. You cannot get out without disrupting the natural order of things. Of course there will be consequences."

"Perhaps."

"And you're still willing to try?"

He splayed his fingers on the bedcover, as if stretching out the tension and forcing himself to remain calm when all he felt was anger. "Cara, I *need* the book. I'm tired of being a warrior and they will not let me stop."

My heart leapt at this new information. It was just one more piece of the puzzle. "Why not? Why can't you earn your way out?"

"My situation is unique. It's not like any other. The rules are different for me."

"Tell me, Quin. Just tell me why you're in Purgatory and I will consider whether to give you the book."

He shook his head. "I can't. You'll hate me. Fear me. I already hate myself." His voice was so quiet that I had to strain to hear the last part. It chilled me to hear that he considered his actions so despicable, shameful, that he could not speak of them after hundreds of years.

I adjusted my grip on the book. "I'm scared that if you do this, something worse will happen to you. At least this way, you can come and go through the portal. You can come to me."

He shook his head sadly. "Only when there is real need, like there was today. They won't let me see you again unless the situation is dire. Please, Cara, let me hold the book."

I shook my head and edged back from him, even though he made no move to lunge.

"Please don't fear me, Cara." The raw pain in his voice clawed at my already aching heart. The plea in his eyes made it break. "I will always protect you. You hold all the power over me. Do you understand? I cannot harm you."

It was too much. I felt like I was falling apart. My tears spilled down my cheeks and onto my hands, which were crossed over the book.

He shifted toward me, but I inched back again, clutching the book to my chest. My wariness made him wince.

"I don't fear you, Quin, but I will not give you the book. Please don't ask again."

He lowered his head. His damaged chest rose and fell with his labored breathing. "Very well," he muttered. "You've made yourself clear. I apologize for the position I put you in."

It was my turn to wince. I didn't want regret and apologies. I wanted...I wanted him.

I watched him rise and walk away from my bed. I climbed under the covers with the book and listened to him moving about on the other side of the screen. He finally settled around the time my tears dried up. He was silent, perhaps asleep.

I lay awake all night.

* * *

DR. GOWAN TENDED to Quin's chest wounds before taking Tommy through to the room he used for surgery. We were told to return in a few hours.

"A few hours!" Sylvia clicked her tongue as she watched the doctor's assistant wheel a very pale Tommy through a door. Seeing him so weak and in pain worried me. His blood loss had been substantial and the risk of infection from such deep wounds was high. I was surprised Sylvia hadn't shown the same concerns this morning. She seemed very brusque and matter-of-fact about the whole thing. "What are we supposed to do in the mean time?"

"Walk," I said. "A leisurely one." Quin may seem as robust as usual with most of his cuts and bruises hidden beneath his clothes, but I didn't want to exert him too much. While he was in this realm, he was subject to infection too.

When he returned to Purgatory, I suspected the physical injuries he'd incurred here would fade away. It was now only a matter of *when* he returned. I still wasn't ready to send him off, and he didn't seem eager to go.

We hadn't spoken to one another all morning, but Sylvia didn't seem to notice. She'd not stopped prattling since breakfast, her topics far-reaching and dull. The one topic she hadn't discussed was Tommy's surgery. Its omission was like a beacon in the dark. At least to me.

"Yes, a walk," she said now with a sunny smile. "A marvelous idea. Tommy is in good hands, and when we return, he'll be ready to come home." She gave another click of her tongue. "Dr. Gowan should have tended to him up at Frakingham like I'd wanted. People like us ought to get home visits."

"This was too complicated to do at home. Dr. Gowan needed his instruments." I touched her elbow and steered her out to the street. "You know all this, Syl. We explained it to you earlier."

She sniffed. "Yes. Well." With her chin and chest thrust forward, she headed off down the hill, away from Dr. Gowan's surgery, into the heart of the village.

"She's just a little worried about Tommy," I said to Quin.

"I understand."

"She doesn't know how to react outwardly so she's resorting to aloofness and nonchalance."

"I know, Cara. I've observed how they are together."

I glanced at him, and took proper stock of his appearance for the first time that day. He looked much better than the day before. If he were in pain, it didn't show on his face. The cut on his lip was swollen, but the bruises didn't appear as dark now, nor did he move gingerly in deference to other cuts on his body. He looked as if he could enter the boxing ring and fight.

I clutched the sack that held the book in it against my side. I'd decided to keep it on me at all times, even though I was with Quin. It was safe from him while it was with me. If he were going to wrestle it off me, he would have done so already. There were no guarantees that he wouldn't take it if I set it down, however.

We wandered along the High Street and peered into the shop windows at the displays. Sylvia didn't want to go inside, despite me asking her whenever we passed a shop that would usually catch her interest. Not even the new fabrics in the draper's could tempt her, nor the various shopkeepers who followed her up the street, touting the wonders of their latest product.

She smiled politely at them, and at other passersby, but said very little beyond the required pleasantries. I was about to suggest we detour to the public gardens some streets away when I spotted a spirit at the front of the butcher's shop. He appeared to be a lad of about sixteen and his method of death was unclear, although his face had a gray pallor to it that suggested some kind of illness. He had large protruding front teeth and darting eyes that peered through the butcher's window.

"Quin, would you mind if I had a quiet word with Sylvia for a moment."

"Of course not."

He lingered at the draper's while I took Sylvia's hand and dragged her to the butcher's, two shops down. It was far enough that Quin couldn't hear us, but close enough that I felt no onset of the supernatural fever.

"What is it?" she asked. "Has Quin said or done something?" She gasped. "He hasn't *kissed* you, has he?"

"It's not you I wish to speak to." I thought it best not to answer her question directly, since I would have to lie. "There's a spirit here and I need to ask him a question."

"Now?"

The ghost gave a start. "You can see me?" His nose twitched and eyes blinked, a nervous habit he'd not shaken off even in death. With the large teeth, he resembled a rabbit.

"I'm a medium," I told him.

Sylvia glanced up and down the street then sidled closer

to me. "Cara, I may be growing used to you stopping and speaking to every ghost you come across, but do we have to do this out here in public?"

"Yes, we do. Pretend I'm talking to you."

"I'm no good at pretending."

"Just nod and smile occasionally as if I've said something interesting." To the spirit, I said, "Would you mind helping me with something? And perhaps I can help you in return."

"I could try, miss, but don't know what help I'd be to the living. Can't do much." He swiped his hand through Sylvia to show me. It was fortunate that she had no idea or she would have been outraged at the indignity.

"It's not in this realm I want your help, but in the Waiting Area."

"That place with all them other spirits I went to after me death?" His nose twitched again. "I don't like it. Too crowded and everyone's real sad to be there."

I gave him a sympathetic look. "I can imagine. It must be a confusing time for you." I needed to get him on side quickly before Quin became suspicious or restless. "Do you see that gentleman behind me?" The ghost squinted at Quin. "His name is Quintin St. Clair and he's an otherworldly warrior."

"Blimey."

"Can you ask around up there for any information about him? He's very old. He died in the twelfth or thirteenth century and he's been a warrior ever since."

"That were a long time ago. Not sure any spirits up there would have known him. They died recent, far as I know."

"You're right. I was actually thinking that you could ask the administrators of the Waiting Area for me."

"Them in charge? They won't speak to the likes of me, miss."

"You can only ask. If you tell them it's for Cara Moreau, then that may sway them. I helped them out some years ago along with Emily Chambers and Jacob Beaufort. Perhaps mention their names if they refuse your request for information."

His mouth twisted to the side and one eye twitched rapidly.

"Please," I added. "I really need your help. And when you get back, I can help you." I nodded at the butcher through the window. "Do we have a deal?"

He narrowed his gaze at the butcher as the fellow caught sight of Sylvia and I. He also had protruding front teeth, and similar eyes to the lad. He held up a joint of meat with a hopeful smile to tempt us inside. "All right," the boy said. "Say them names again."

I repeated mine, Emily's and Jacob's then promised to return later. He cast a frown at the butcher then blinked out of existence.

"Was that wise?" Sylvia said as we walked slowly back to Quin.

"Why wouldn't it be?"

"Because Quin is going back and you're staying here. Learning about his past makes no difference to the current state of affairs."

I sighed. She was right, and I did not have a good reason for finding out more about him behind his back. But I couldn't help it. I needed to know everything I could about him.

We rejoined him and I suggested we head to the stream for a gentle stroll along the bank. Thankfully Sylvia chattered endlessly about nothing in particular so Quin and I didn't need to speak, or even listen for that matter. I had nothing to say to him, and he seemed just as disinterested in talking to me. If he was curious about when I would speak the counter-curse and send him back, he didn't ask. Thankfully. I wasn't sure what answer I would give. I felt no more ready to say goodbye to him than I had been yesterday.

We didn't reach the stream, however. We got only as far as The Red Lion. Quin halted and put out his arm to stop me. I followed his gaze and my stomach did a little flop.

Nathaniel Faraday and Everett Myer stood on the front steps of the inn and squinted into the sunlight at us. Myer hailed us and headed our way. Faraday hung back, his slack-jawed stare aimed at Quin.

I tightened my hold on the book in the sack, tucked under my arm, and had the sickening sense that my delay in speaking the counter curse might prove to be a mistake.

CHAPTER 16

"*T*he book!" Myer said as he marched across the street to us. "Where is it?" His unblinking, beady eyes settled on the package under my arm. "Is that it?"

"No," I said, edging back. "This is a new pair of gloves."

Myer kept coming as if he hadn't heard, or didn't care.

Quin stepped in front of me. "Stay back," he growled. "Leave Cara be. We no longer have the book."

"What?" he cried. "Faraday! Here! Now!"

Nathaniel rushed up behind Myer and offered me a nervous smile as I stepped out from behind Quin. His smile quickly vanished, however, when Quin turned the full force of his glare onto him.

"You told me we left London ahead of them," Myer spat at him.

Nathaniel put up his hands. "I was under that assumption, sir! I came to you as soon as I learned that the book was here."

"When did you arrive in Harborough?" Myer snapped at us in a voice that wasn't at all like his usual calm one. I'd never seen him so angry before. He was usually charming and conciliatory, his occasional frustrations taken out on his wife only.

Behind him, Nathaniel shook his head at me. It would seem he had decided to do the right thing and delay his employer's chase so that we could keep the book out of his hands. His actions were commendable, and it seemed fair that he not be punished for them.

"We traveled overnight by coach," I said. "And arrived early this morning. Nathaniel wasn't to know that we'd already left." I prayed Myer didn't return to The Red Lion and question the landlord.

He didn't. It would seem he had other plans to learn the truth. "Listen to me," he said, his voice gentler but no less commanding. Alluring. "Listen to my voice and only my voice."

A humming noise set up in my head, turning me a little dizzy. I fought against it, clamping my hands over my ears. Beside me, Sylvia did the same. Nathaniel looked somewhat panicked, as if he wasn't sure what to do.

Myer took a breath to continue his hypnotic words, but Quin grabbed him by the throat, cutting him off. Nathaniel closed his eyes in relief and breathed deeply as if he were glad the confrontation wasn't left to him. My head cleared and I lowered my hands.

"Be quiet," Quin growled. "Or I will snap your neck."

Myer's face turned dark red and he made a gurgling sound that Quin took for assent. He let him go and Myer lost his balance, falling back against Nathaniel. He rubbed his throat and coughed as Nathaniel righted him.

"I can move faster than you can speak," Quin told him. "So save your voice and listen to *me*. I drove last night and hid the book along the way. It was dark and nobody knows which route I took. I am the only one who knows the book's location, so using your powers against anyone to find out the information will not work. If I learn that you have tried, I will ruin your life. Do you understand?"

Myer's hand stilled at his throat. He swallowed, nodded, but I didn't think he would give up that easily.

"You shouldn't be so desperate for it," Sylvia told him, hands on hips. "It's a dangerous thing. It's best left hidden."

Myer continued to rub his throat and took a moment to answer. "With respect, Miss Langley," he rasped after a moment, "I think I do know. I only wish to study it, not use it for any wrongdoing."

Wisely, she didn't respond. Making a bigger enemy of Myer than we already had could prove dangerous.

"Nevertheless, the book is safer hidden as it is," I said. "Only Quin knows where."

"And I suppose he'll take that information back to Melbourne with him. When do you leave, sir?"

I arched an eyebrow at Nathaniel. He hadn't told Myer that Quin was from Purgatory? The omission was rather a large one, considering his employer would undoubtedly be enthusiastic about the idea of studying Quin.

Nathaniel gave me a small shrug and I offered up a smile of thanks for his discretion. Perhaps, like us, Nathaniel had come to learn how ruthless Myer could be when it came to the supernatural and had decided to be selective with the information he passed on to him. It would seem Nathaniel wasn't quite such a sycophant after all.

"I will be leaving Frakingham House in the morning." Quin spoke to Myer, but I felt as if he were addressing me. He expected me—*wanted* me—to speak the curse this evening. "My ship departs in two days. The information about the book's location goes with me. I'll alert the authorities here to the danger you pose to Cara and the others. If anything happens to them, you will be the first one they question and I will be the first one they notify. I'll return and make good my promise to hunt you down and destroy you. Understand?"

I could see Myer digesting the threat. Whether he believed Quin or not wasn't clear, but he did seem genuinely concerned about his own health. He rubbed his throat, still red from where Quin had grabbed it.

"No harm will come to these ladies because of me," he said. "You have my word."

It was the most we could hope to get out of him. I didn't like the fact that he could hypnotize me once Quin was gone, but I did believe that he wouldn't harm any of us. We were more useful alive and in good health. I began to form a plan that would save me from telling him where the book was while under hypnosis.

Myer bowed shallowly. "I wish you safe travels, sir. Miss Moreau, Miss Langley, I hope we'll see one another again under more pleasant circumstances." His smile was forced, his words false, but at least he left, and Nathaniel went with him.

"Good riddance," Sylvia muttered as she watched them return to the inn. "Do you think he believed you, Quin?"

"Perhaps. But you are vulnerable now. He may still try to hypnotize you."

"That's why we're going to stop at the post office and send a telegram to Samuel," I said. "I hope he'll be free to leave immediately."

"Good thinking." Sylvia walked off toward the post office. "That way he can arrive tonight before Quin leaves."

I hazarded a glance at Quin and caught him doing the same to me. We didn't need words to say what needed to be said. We both knew that I had to speak the spell soon so that the book could be hidden. We couldn't risk Myer getting hold of it.

"What do you think of Nathaniel not telling Myer that we'd left London yesterday morning?" Sylvia asked, breaking into my melancholia as we walked.

"It was a wise decision," Quin said. "But I still don't like him."

"Of course you don't," she quipped.

"What do you mean?"

Her arm tightened in mine. "It means that Nathaniel likes Cara and you are protective of her. That's all."

He grunted. "She can do better than Faraday," he muttered. "Much, much better."

My face heated and I studied the ground hard.

"I agree," she sang. "Although he is very handsome. We must learn what his connections are before we dismiss him altogether, however; particularly in light of his noble gesture in not telling Myer. It would seem he's rather a good egg after all. Don't you think, Cara?"

"I, er, he is very handsome, yes, but there is more to a man than his face, Sylvia. And his connections."

"Hmm."

We arrived at the post office and sent off our telegram to Samuel. It began with the word URGENT.

"Come, let's return to Dr. Gowan's rooms." Sylvia was already striding off in that direction before I'd stepped onto the pavement. "Perhaps he's finished and we can speak to Tommy."

I hurried to catch up and looped my arm through hers. "Even if he is finished, Tommy may still be under sedation and unable to communicate. But if you want to return, then we'll just wait in the waiting room."

That reminded me. It was unlikely that the spirit had learned anything from the Waiting Area yet, but I wasn't sure when I'd get another chance to speak to him. We walked via the butcher's, but he wasn't there and Sylvia was in no mood to linger. We continued on to the surgery and were directed to sit down and wait.

We waited a few more hours and were finally allowed to see Tommy mid-afternoon. He was a little tired and heavily bandaged, but otherwise in good spirits. Sylvia fussed over him, ensuring the blanket was tucked tightly around him and he was comfortable. The doctor allowed us a few minutes and then his assistant shooed us out. Quin was the last to leave, and I waited at the door while he spoke a few quiet words to Tommy then shook his good hand in farewell.

I blew out a measured breath. It was becoming more real now. The goodbyes had begun. A lump formed in my throat and remained there the entire journey to the house.

I napped for two hours in the afternoon while Quin sat in the armchair near the door, reading a book about Captain Cook's expeditions that he'd borrowed from Langley's library. I still felt tired when he woke me with a gentle shake of my arm.

"We have a visitor," he said.

I yawned. "Who is it?"

"Gladstone."

"Already?"

We went in search of him and found him with Sylvia, talking in the drawing room. He told us he'd left as soon as he'd got our telegram and had run to catch the train. Sylvia had already informed him about meeting Myer in the village and of Quin threatening him.

"I'll hide the book," he said. "I agree that it's the best course of action, with Myer on the loose. Until he loses interest in the book, I must be the only one to know of its whereabouts. I won't even tell Charity."

We separated to dress for dinner and reconvened outside

the dining room when the bell was rung by the housekeeper. She and Maud delivered the dishes too, but did not serve. Langley had decided to have an informal meal where we served ourselves.

"We're practically all family anyway," Sylvia said with a smile. She'd been smiling rather a lot since returning from the village. It was good to see her anxiety had dissolved after seeing Tommy on the mend. Despite outward appearances, it was obvious to me that she liked him beyond what was acceptable between mistress and servant. I worried for her, however, if that was the case. Worried for both of them. Theirs was an impossible situation.

It seemed Sylvia had already told her uncle and Bollard about meeting Myer and Nathaniel in the village, as well as informing them of our plan to give the book to Samuel after I'd used it.

"I've been thinking," Langley said as we tucked into our first course when the servants had left. All except Bollard, that is. He remained behind his master's chair, standing like an automaton that only worked when wound up. "You will need to make provisions in the event of your death, Gladstone."

"Uncle!"

Langley gave his niece a curious look, as if he didn't know what he'd said wrong. "Death comes to us all, my dear. This book is too important to lose track of completely. Gladstone, like all of us, must consider his mortality and what it means for the book."

"I will see that a letter detailing its location is left with my lawyers," Samuel said. "I'll take the book in the morning. Will that be enough time, Cara?"

I nodded and risked a glance at Quin. He set his fork down, his fish uneaten, and laid his palm flat on the table-cloth. It was not like him to abandon his food.

232

"Yes," I said quietly. "I'm sure it will be."

"I think we ought to consider using another spell from the book," Sylvia said, also setting down her cutlery. She gave each of us a determined look. "The one that permanently closes the portal."

"No!" I cried.

"Cara, I know you want to keep it open, and I know why." She didn't have to look at Quin for me to catch her meaning. Whether Langley or Samuel knew he was the reason I wanted it left untouched, however, I couldn't tell. Neither of them asked her to explain. "I think we must consider it. There have been too many escaped demons lately, and I'm not sure how much longer we can go on pretending the attacks are the work of wild dogs."

"But all those demons were let loose either by accident or by wicked people," I said.

"And they will continue to be released as long as that portal is accessible."

I shook my head. "Not if Myer is banned. Everything will be well again soon, Sylvia. These past few months have been an aberration."

"Cara, I adore you and I respect you, but in this you are wrong. Remember, *you* won't be living here. I will."

"And you forget that it's my house," Langley snapped. "I will decide what's to be done."

Sylvia bit her lip and my anger dissolved. She hadn't deserved that admonishment. She wasn't known for giving thoughtful opinions on difficult topics, and she ought to be commended for thinking for herself and coming up with a reasoned argument, not be treated like a child. I only wished I could support her, but I couldn't. Destroying the portal would mean saying a permanent goodbye to Quin. Even though he'd said he would only come back if a dire situation called for it, there was still hope. Closing the portal forever would destroy that hope.

Speaking of destruction, I remembered something Myer had said. "Destroying the portal might cause Frakingham House itself to be damaged beyond repair. You would lose your home, Sylvia."

"It's only bricks," she muttered. "Not a life."

"I'm not sure I could afford to rebuild on this scale," Langley told her, taking stock of the dining room's elaborate gilded ceiling rosette and cornices, the marble mantel, and the carved wooden wall panels. "I would have to borrow a large sum and I'm not sure if we could repay it. I don't want to leave you and Jack in debt."

Bollard blinked rapidly but otherwise remained immobile.

"Oh." Sylvia looked down at her lap. "Well, I don't mind." She shrugged off her concerns. "As I said before, it's just bricks and plaster and things, not people."

We all blinked at her. I'd wager nobody could believe their ears. When I'd first met Sylvia, she wouldn't have entertained the notion of losing her home. She was somewhat selfish, and liked her comforts and the status the house gave her. It would seem she'd changed.

"I'll speak with Jack upon his return," Langley said.

I shot to my feet, grabbing the book and its carry sack as it slipped off my lap. "No! Stop this talk at once. You can't go destroying portals and changing the way things are and have always been. It's madness! You don't know what the repercussions will be."

"Cara, calm yourself," Sylvia soothed.

"Not until you've given me an assurance that you won't destroy the portal, or the book, or…or anything!" I heard the rising panic in my voice, and I tried hard to swallow it, but couldn't.

"I know this is about Quin—"

"It's not! It's about not interfering with things we don't fully understand." But she and I both knew that wasn't entirely true.

His hand closed around mine. "Do you want to leave?"

I shook my head and plopped back down in my chair. Sylvia was my friend and I wouldn't allow this to come between us, nor would I insult her by storming out of her dining room like a petulant child. Perhaps we could discuss it again when we had both calmed down.

I forced myself to eat, although I was merely going through the motions and hardly tasted the food. The conversation turned to safer topics. It seemed Sylvia had read her mail before coming into the dining room. Jack and Hannah had written to say they would be arriving home within the week, paving the way for Sylvia to set a date for the ball. She settled on three weeks hence.

Other mail had come from applicants responding to her advertisements. One looked particularly promising for the position of butler. This time, nobody argued that Tommy could perform the duties admirably. His injuries would see him out of action for some time, perhaps indefinitely. That topic was avoided altogether.

I retired early, claiming exhaustion. I *was* tired, the nap hardly making up for having been awake for much of the previous night. Sylvia decided to read for a little while in bed, and Quin lay down on the truckle. I heard his clothing and bedcovers rustle beyond the curtain and regretted that tonight would be our last together.

But there would be no talking this time. Our nocturnal rendezvous were over. A sharp pang of regret and sorrow stabbed my chest where the book rested against it. It was bad enough that I may never see him again, but it was so much worse that I'd decided not to say goodbye. It was too much of a risk—he could either overpower me, or talk me into handing the book over. There was no doubt in my mind that he had the capability to disarm me completely and convince me that he should hold the book while I spoke the words of the counter-curse. I wouldn't risk it.

I must have slept for a few hours because when I awoke, it was dark and Sylvia was asleep, tucked up in bed beside me. I listened for Quin, half expecting him to be awake, but his breathing had the rhythmic cadence of someone in deep slumber.

I climbed out of bed and threw a wrap around my shoulders. I slipped into a pair of velvet slippers and winced at the soft thud of my first footstep. Quin made no sound on the other side of the screen. I warred with myself as to whether I should take a peek at him, but desire to see him one last time won out over common sense in the end.

I peered round the screen and instantly regretted my decision. Seeing him again made it so much harder to part. The covers were bunched at his hips and his arms crossed over his bare chest. His face wasn't so hard and unforgiving in sleep, but it was just as handsome. Or perhaps that was my imagination, because it was too dark to see his features clearly.

I closed my eyes against the sting of tears, and forced myself to turn away and not lie down beside him. With the book under my arm, I fled silently along the corridor. I felt the first tugs of the illness when I reached the stairs. My face became hot and my chest tight. I had only a narrow window of time in which to act.

I reached the library as the fog hovering at the edges of my consciousness began to roll in. My skin was warm and clammy, yet it felt like ice slid through my veins. I shivered uncontrollably.

I set the book down on the table and lit the lamp. It hissed and spat into life and cast out enough light for me to see the words by. I flopped into a chair, exhausted. My throat began to close, but whether from my unshed tears or the ravages of the illness, I couldn't tell. It made breathing difficult and speaking almost impossible. I fought against the weight pulling at my limbs and pressing down on my chest, and used every last ounce of energy to open the book.

Where was the damned counter curse? I flipped pages back and forth, unsure of which one it was on. The fog in my head thickened, making thinking difficult and my trembling fingers slow.

I stopped. Breathed. I could do this. I *had* to. I couldn't make it up the stairs and back to the bedroom now. I was committed to speaking the counter curse here in the library, alone.

With my nerves a little steadier, I flipped the pages again and found the spell. I wasted no time in speaking the first line, but the words came out rasping, strangled. My tongue was too thick and my mouth too dry. I couldn't understand myself. Would the curse work? I hadn't a clue, but forged on until the end.

Nothing happened.

My head still ached and now my body too. Exhaustion called to me like an irresistible siren song and I set my heavy head down on the book. I felt like Atlas, with the entire world on his shoulders. Yet unlike Atlas, I lacked the strength to carry it. My chest felt like it would burst beneath the great weight pressing down on it. Tears rolled down my cheeks and dripped onto the page. I closed my eyes. It was the only movement I could manage.

Then the weight began to lift and the fog cleared. The ice in my veins thawed as if a blanket had been thrown around me and wrapped me up in a cocoon. I stopped trembling and spun round.

Quin stood in the doorway, dressed only in trousers. His bare chest rose and fell with his ragged breathing. His face was a picture of fury, his fists like rocks at his sides. He strode into the library, coming straight for me with fierce determination.

At that moment he looked every bit the warrior, and he was angry.

CHAPTER 17

"Cara," he ground out. As he drew closer, I could see the muscle pulsing in his jaw, and something in his eyes that I hadn't seen from a distance. Concern.

I swallowed the lump in my throat and placed a protective arm over the book. He paid it no attention. He dropped to his knees in front of me and clasped my face in both his hands.

"Cara, why?" But he didn't wait for my answer. He pressed his forehead to mine and stroked my damp cheeks with his thumbs. His breath warmed my lips.

Then he closed the gap and kissed me. It wasn't gentle. It was filled with his lingering anger, and perhaps some frustrated desire too. He nipped my lip with his teeth, and when I gave a small gasp, his tongue pushed into my mouth.

The kiss quickly gentled, but the intimacy grew fiercer. It fueled my own passion and I kissed him back. I gripped his shoulders, digging my fingers into his smooth skin because I was afraid of floating off on a cloud of desire. He grasped the back of my head, his fingers in my hair, holding me there. I needed no such encouragement. I wasn't going anywhere.

This was where I wanted to be—in Quin's arms, his lips on mine. If we lay together, what would happen? Would he be allowed to stay in this realm? Could he make me with child?

It was scandalous thinking, but I didn't care. I wanted to be with him in that most shockingly intimate way. I fumbled with the fastening of his trousers.

He sprang back from me and I almost toppled forward off the chair. We were both breathing heavily as we stared at one another. The shock of what we'd almost done registered in his eyes and was perhaps visible in mine. My wantonness surprised me, but my lack of regret surprised me more. I would have lain with him and accepted whatever consequences came my way, and done so happily.

I wasn't sure Quin felt the same way. He had, after all, been the one to back out. He shook his head and rubbed the back of his hand over his mouth.

"You could have died," he muttered. So he'd chosen to discuss that and not the kiss. Very well. I would too.

"I saw no other choice." I placed my arm over the book, but he made no move to snatch it. "I didn't know if I could trust you not to take it."

He lowered his head and his hair fell across his face, hiding his eyes from me. "I told you I would not. Not before you were well again."

"I don't want you taking it afterward, either. I had hoped to get farther away from the house, but I felt too ill to continue and I knew there would be lamps in here."

"You could have died," he whispered again. He swore in French and pressed the heel of his hand to his forehead.

I half-rose to go to him but sat back down again. There could be no more intimacy between us. It only caused problems and heartache.

He blew out a long breath and squared his shoulders. He looked directly at me and I could see that he'd come to a decision. "If you don't want me to have it, I won't take it. Begin the spell."

I blinked at him, trying to determine if he was merely telling me what he knew I wanted to hear or if he was genuine.

When I didn't speak, he said, "Cara, you cannot leave me again before the curse is broken. You won't have the strength to speak the entire spell and make it understandable. You must say it with me present, and that means you must trust me now."

He was right. I knew it, yet I still hesitated. It wasn't just because I didn't fully trust him. It was also because this was it, the end. I had kissed the most wonderful man, the only man I could ever see myself being with—and now he was going back to a place where he was already dead.

Saying goodbye didn't seem enough.

"If it's your wish that I don't take the book, I won't take it," he said again, misunderstanding my hesitation.

I turned to the book, but did not speak even the first line of the counter curse. "Am I doing the right thing, Quin?" My voice sounded small, childlike.

"You ask me now?"

I turned back to him and nodded. "I hate going against your wishes, but I believe what I said earlier at dinner. We shouldn't interfere with the supernatural. The portal shouldn't be destroyed, and you shouldn't be allowed to leave Purgatory in any other way than the natural one. It could prove to be dangerous in ways we are yet to realize."

"So it's not just because leaving Purgatory means I will move on to a place where I cannot return to this realm?"

He had said it to gently tease me, but he watched me closely and I suspected my answer was important to him.

"I hope you will one day leave Purgatory. I hate to think

of you there. But not through untried ways that may incur the anger of the administrators."

He nodded grimly. "That's why...why I like you so much, Cara." His smile was sad, his eyes swimming. "Even though you are too educated for a wench."

I spluttered a watery laugh, and he responded with a brief grin that was all teeth.

"You are a strong, brave woman, Cara, and you're not in the least devious like I first thought."

"Thank you. I think."

"I regret that I lied about the book." He spoke softly, but in earnest. "I am truly sorry for my trickery. I admit that I saw your illness as a way of being granted access to this realm. Once it was explained to the administrators that you were cursed through no fault of your own, they agreed that I could help. But I had every intention of taking the book from you, after you were cured."

I went to reach for the book, but held myself back. He had told me he wouldn't take it and I believed him now. He needed to know that.

"I knew the moment I met you that you would affect me," he went on, "but I had no notion then that your life would become precious to me."

My lower lip wobbled. I bit it hard.

"You've made your choice about the book based on what your heart and mind tell you, Cara. I ask for nothing else from my brave little warrior. Speak the counter curse now and have no regrets. You are probably right, anyway, when you say we shouldn't go against the order of things. I should never have allowed myself to hope."

A sob escaped my throat. "Oh, Quin."

"No, Cara. Stay there or...or parting will just be harder."

"But...will I ever see you again?"

"I hope not, because that will mean you are in difficulty

again and I want you to be safe. I want you to live a full, happy life, free from curses and demons. That's the life you deserve."

My heart thundered against my ribs and my throat burned. How could I do this? How could I send him away?

"You must," he whispered, as if he read my mind. "Speak it now. Go on."

I drank in the sight of him one last time—his beautiful face, his changeable blue-green eyes, now bright with emotion; his wicked mouth that tasted so delicious. Then I turned and began the counter curse to cure myself.

I was half way through when I became aware of him standing behind me. His presence was a reassurance rather than a threat. I no longer feared that he would snatch the book. I kept reading. When I reached the last line, I felt his hand on my hair. He stroked the tresses, let them slide through his fingers. The tears that had been hovering on the brink of my eyelids finally spilled, and it was an effort to say the last word. As I whispered the final syllable, I felt his lips against the top of my head, his hand on my shoulder.

I spun round, hoping that I'd been wrong and he would still be there. But he was gone. The air where he'd been standing swirled with a gentle breeze. His scent lingered a moment more, then it too disappeared.

I moved to the deep wingback by the fire and tucked my feet beneath me. I clutched the book to my chest and cried until I fell asleep near dawn.

* * *

SYLVIA HAD my own bedroom made up for me and I retreated to its solitude, remaining there all of the following day and night without coming out. I needed to be alone, although Sylvia had difficulty understanding that at first. I think she only came to terms with it because Tommy came home and she had somebody else to fuss over, although she did pop in to see me from time to time and bestow sympathetic looks upon me.

"I know how you feel," she said once with a deep sigh.

I refrained from snipping back that she couldn't possibly know since she'd never sent anyone back to Purgatory, and certainly not anyone she'd kissed.

I rallied the following day, only because I wanted to return to London and Emily. I needed her now more than ever. But first, I had a spirit in the village to see.

I found the lad outside the butcher's shop again, peering through the window with a surly frown. I leaned against the lamppost, opened the newspaper I'd brought with me for the purpose of hiding behind, and surreptitiously beckoned him over once I was certain no one was about.

"Aha," he said when he appeared at my side. "I was worried you weren't coming back."

"I'm very sorry for the delay. Indeed, I've been thinking that I don't need your help after all, and I came to tell you not to concern yourself."

His mouth drooped around his big front teeth. "But you promised!"

"I'll still help you," I assured him. "That's why I'm here."

"But I worked hard to find out what I could. Don't you want to hear it anyway?"

I hesitated. I admit to still being curious, even though I'd resolved not to chase after the information anymore. It no longer seemed right to find out what I could about Quin without his knowledge; it felt devious. I smiled. He'd been wrong to absolve me of that flaw. It also no longer seemed necessary to find out more. I would never see him again, so what did it matter?

I fought to close the pit in my heart as it threatened to

open again. I managed it without spilling a tear, although they welled close. "Tell me what I can do to help you. Since you're here, I suspect you died somewhere nearby?"

He nodded. "I were on me death bed when I came here, hoping to speak to him." He jerked his head at the butcher's window. "But I never made it. Died out the front."

"I am sorry. I do hope I can help you move on now. You'll be much happier once you cross over to the afterlife. Do you want me to say something to your father? Perhaps tell him you love him—"

"Love him! Why would I want to do that? He's a prick, he is, and a liar. He wouldn't acknowledge me when I were born, wouldn't help out me ma. Said I were another man's whelp."

It was impossible to believe that anyone would think the lad had been fathered by another man; he looked just like the butcher. Perhaps as a baby the resemblance hadn't been so marked and it had been easier to lie about a connection between himself and the boy's mother.

"She died working herself to the bone just to feed me. He ruined her and now look at him, all fat and jolly."

I lowered the corner of the newspaper. The butcher smiled at me through the window. He did look cheerful. "You should join your mother now," I said. "Forget whatever revenge you have in mind and find your peace in the afterlife."

He sighed. "I would like to see her again. But he don't deserve to get off free. He's got a wife and four children, all younger than me. A big, happy family. I used to watch them going into the church in their Sunday best, talking and laughing. He wouldn't even look at me or Ma."

"Is that what you wanted? For him to look at you and know that he was your son?"

He nodded. "I used to think I wanted to punch him in the

245

nose." He looked skyward and his own nose twitched. "Now I want him to know that his eldest son knew him for the arse he was. Pardon me, miss."

"Forgiven."

"I want him to know that his happy life were built on a lie."

We both looked to the butcher as he wrapped up some bacon for a customer. She paid and made her exit, and he was left alone in the shop.

"What's your name?" I asked the lad.

"Teddy Bunker, miss."

I folded up my newspaper and marched inside. Teddy followed.

The butcher looked up and smiled. "Good morning, miss. Lovely day out. How can I help you?"

"You can listen." I steeled myself. I didn't usually confront strangers on behalf of spirits, but I'd promised Teddy. "You, sir, are a liar. Your life is based on a lie."

The butcher's nose twitched and his eyes winked in nervous habit, just like his son. "Eh?"

"Teddy Bunker was your child. You refused to acknowledge him and help his mother."

"How do you know?"

"Have you seen him?"

"Aye."

"Then you can't fail to know it too. He was your son, and now he's dead. You ought to be ashamed for never claiming him, or at least giving his mother financial assistance."

The butcher's twitching grew worse until his entire face seemed to be wracked with jumping nerves. "I...I don't know what to say."

"How about sorry."

"Sorry? Who to? They're both gone now. The lad died right out the front there. There was a right to-do, as it happens, thanks to him. There'd been rumors recently, as he grew to look more like me, but having him die right there was like a sign, so everyone said. Not to my face, mind, but I hear them whispering. My Jill does too, then she takes it out on me. Calls me a liar and adulterer, even though we weren't married then. She hates me now and I can't do nothing to win her back." He sniffed and occupied himself with reorganizing the trays of meats on display. "So if you think I ain't suffering, think again. I don't know why you'd bring this up again now, when the lad died a week ago, and I don't know why *you'd* care. It ain't fair."

I turned to Teddy and he gave me a broad smile with not a twitch in sight. "Thank you, miss," he said. "Now, I owe you."

I was about to tell him not to bother, but stopped myself. I was in no mood to reveal my power to the butcher and be forced to defend my sanity.

Teddy prattled on, oblivious to my discomfort. "They couldn't, or wouldn't, tell me much. Your Mr. St. Clair got into Purgatory for doing something bad in his life, but I don't know what. He died during the Third Crusade."

The crusades! Of course. He'd been a knight. It made sense that he'd fought in the Holy Wars. No able-bodied knight could avoid it at that time. That explained why he could speak Arabic. I wondered if that was also how he'd known the code used in the book we'd found in the society's library—perhaps it had been used in the crusades to pass messages in secret.

So I now had a narrower date for Quin's lifetime. I would need to look up the years of the Third Crusade.

I headed out the door and Teddy followed. "There's some more," he said. "He was the fifth son and he outlived all his brothers. Two died in infancy, another at the age of fifteen in a hunting accident, and the fourth youngest went to the crusade with your St. Clair. He died in the Holy Land too, but a little earlier. There were no sisters."

I kept walking and Teddy kept following and talking. It was strange hearing Quin's life laid out with no emotion, as if Teddy were reading an entry in *Debrett's*. It was like I was learning about a historical figure in the classroom, and not someone who'd kissed me with such tenderness that my heart still ached whenever I thought of it. I touched my fingers to my lips as I rounded the corner into an alley, and closed my stinging eyes before the tears spilled.

"His wife died a year before him."

"Wife!" I opened my eyes.

Teddy flattened himself against the wall at my outburst and nodded quickly. His mouth twitched and I apologized and backed away.

"Her name was Maria," he said. "There were no children."

No children. I tried to digest that, along with the fact that he'd been married. Of course, he must have been. A gentleman of his age would be in need of a wife. They married young back then, sometimes betrothed as children.

Quin hadn't needed to explain any of these things to me, yet it felt something of a betrayal nevertheless. He knew so much about me, and I would have told him anything if he'd asked, so why had he not told me these basic facts? Why the secrecy?

"I'm sorry it ain't much," Teddy said. "Can I go now, and see Ma?"

"Of course. Thank you for the information."

"Thank *you* for your help in there, miss. I think he's suffering a bit now, like me and Ma did."

It wasn't quite on the same scale but it seemed to satisfy Teddy. I smiled. "Go now. Be at peace and enjoy your afterlife."

He grinned and disappeared.

I slumped against the wall and sucked in deep breaths. Unfortunately the alley was filled with refuse from the butcher's shop and I got a hearty whiff of putrid meat. My stomach heaved and I threw up behind an empty crate.

Wiping my mouth, I hurried out of the alley and up High Street, quickly leaving Harborough behind altogether. The walk back to Freak House was reasonably long but I didn't care. I wanted to be alone with my thoughts and memories before I rejoined the household. No doubt Sylvia would be full of talk about the ball, now that Tommy was home safely. I looked forward to the distraction of her chatter, but not yet.

For now, I wanted to breathe in the scent of the flowers and remind myself that it was good to be alive, that the future might not be so grim without Quin in it.

It was hard to digest that idea, however. So very hard. I missed him so much. It was like an ache worse than anything I'd suffered with the supernatural fever. I wondered how long it would take to set aside my feelings for him and move on. I couldn't imagine it taking mere days or weeks, nor even months. The attachment was too strong to snap or fray.

I could perhaps take a ship back to Melbourne and leave England and the painful memories behind. The gentlemen weren't so dandy in the colonies and the way of life not so stifling. But that would mean leaving the portal, and the chance of seeing Quin again, and it certainly wouldn't help me forget him. Nothing could.

It began to drizzle with rain and I was not yet half way to Frakingham. I lifted my face and drew the scent of fresh, damp air into my lungs. Everything was so uncertain, but there was one thing I did know. I was alive and I had Quin to thank for that.

He was my warrior, my protector, and always would be.

NOW AVAILABLE

BANISHED

The second book in the THIRD FREAK HOUSE TRILOGY.

An infestation of evil spirits at Freak House keeps Cara busy, while a new enemy threatens her loved ones if she doesn't give him the book of spells. Is the danger enough to call Quin back into her life?

A MESSAGE FROM THE AUTHOR

I hope you enjoyed reading this book as much as I enjoyed writing it. As an independent author, getting the word out about my book is vital to its success, so if you liked this book please consider telling your friends and writing a review at the store where you purchased it. If you would like to be contacted when I release a new book, subscribe to my newsletter at http://cjarcher.com/contact-cj/newsletter/.

ALSO BY C.J. ARCHER

SERIES WITH 2 OR MORE BOOKS

The Glass Library

Cleopatra Fox Mysteries

After The Rift

Glass and Steele

The Ministry of Curiosities Series

The Emily Chambers Spirit Medium Trilogy

The 1st Freak House Trilogy

The 2nd Freak House Trilogy

The 3rd Freak House Trilogy

The Assassins Guild Series

Lord Hawkesbury's Players Series

Witch Born

SINGLE TITLES NOT IN A SERIES

Courting His Countess

Surrender

Redemption

The Mercenary's Price

ABOUT THE AUTHOR

C.J. Archer has loved history and books for as long as she can remember and feels fortunate that she found a way to combine the two. She spent her early childhood in the dramatic beauty of outback Queensland, Australia, but now lives in suburban Melbourne with her husband, two children and a mischievous black & white cat named Coco.

Subscribe to C.J.'s newsletter through her website to be notified when she releases a new book, as well as get access to exclusive content and subscriber-only giveaways. Her website also contains up to date details on all her books: http://cjarcher.com She loves to hear from readers. You can contact her through email cj@cjarcher.com or follow her on social media to get the latest updates on her books:

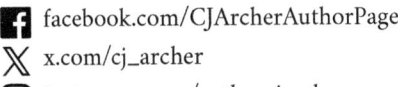

facebook.com/CJArcherAuthorPage
x.com/cj_archer
instagram.com/authorcjarcher